THE ASTONISHING LIFE OF AUGUST MARCH

The Astonishing Life of August March

A NOVEL

Aaron Jackson

NEW YORK • LONDON • TORONTO • SYDNEY • NEW DELHI • AUCKLAND

HARPER PERENNIAL

This is a work of fiction. Names, characters, places, and incidents are products of the author's imagination or are used fictitiously and are not to be construed as real. Any resemblance to actual events, locales, organizations, or persons, living or dead, is entirely coincidental.

A hardcover edition of this book was published in 2020 by HarperCollins Publishers.

FIRST HARPER PERENNIAL EDITION PUBLISHED 2021.

Designed by Fritz Metsch

Library of Congress Cataloging-in-Publication Data has been applied for.

ISBN 978-0-06-293937-1 (pbk.)

21 22 23 24 25 LSC 10 9 8 7 6 5 4 3 2 1

For Michael, always.

THE ASTONISHING LIFE OF AUGUST MARCH

PART ONE

The boy was born in the Scarsenguard Theater on West Forty-Third Street during the intermission of *These Dreams We Cherish*. His mother, Vivian Fair, had just flawlessly delivered the rousing speech that concluded act 1. As soon as the curtains touched the boards, thunderous applause still ringing in her ears, Vivian waddled backstage, closed the door to her dressing room, and delivered, not a stirring monologue, but her son. She plopped the screeching, slimy creature into a basketful of soiled blouses, severed the umbilical cord with an eyelash curler, and was back in the wings just in time for places, a consummate professional.

The play over, Miss Fair was removing her wig when the baby's cry startled her so that she nearly stabbed herself with a bobby pin.

A baby. She'd nearly forgotten. Vivian walked over to the basket and peered down at the newborn. Such a pathetic creature. Wrinkly and red and so very small, his tiny fists bunched, punching the air.

A sharp knock on her door caused Vivian to curse. She tossed a shawl over the newborn to hide it just as the knocker, a silly costar of Vivian's with less talent than a coffee mug, poked her head in.

"Oh, sorry. Didn't mean to startle you," said the costar.

"What do you want?" Vivian snapped.

"Didn't you hear? A producer was in the audience tonight. From Hollywood! He's at Carlisle's now!"

"Hollywood!" Vivian cried, clutching her neck. "Give me three minutes—I'll meet you outside."

With expertise, Vivian applied a becoming smear of lipstick, tousled her hair, and looked ready for even the most scrutinizing of closeups.

"You're a star," she whispered to her reflection.

The baby cried again.

Now here was a decision. She'd told no one about the pregnancy. *These Dreams We Cherish* was a period drama; hoop skirts had concealed her belly for months. And she certainly hadn't told the father, whoever he was. Vivian had been meaning to deal with the situation, to make arrangements, but life kept interfering: an opening, a party, a gala. Events like that were important to her career, she'd thought. She'd figure out what to do about the baby later.

But now that the child had officially arrived, she found she wasn't ready to be a mother. Not in the slightest. There was still so much she wanted to achieve.

Someone would find the boy and give him a marvelous home. Or that's what she told herself as she dashed off to Carlisle's with the rest of the cast for an evening of sidecars and schmoozing.

Much later that evening, as Vivian was kissing the bigwig Hollywood producer, he whispered to her what she'd told her reflection just a few hours prior.

"You're a star."

Vivian smiled, knowing she'd made the right decision.

Motherhood would be so horrible for her image.

* * *

Eugenia Butler was old. Ancient even. Brittle, bitter, and biting, she'd been employed as the Scarsenguard Theater's laundress longer than anyone could remember. Longer than even *she* could remember.

Eugenia liked her work. And even if she didn't, how else was she going to spend her evenings? Alone? Her mother had left her a quaint brownstone on East Twenty-Third Street, and though she loved it, Eugenia didn't need to wander through an empty house every night. She preferred to keep busy.

So the day after her mother passed, Eugenia went out and secured herself a job at the Scarsenguard. What year had that been? It was 1933 now. Or was it '34? Whatever year it was, her mother had most certainly died in 1865. Or somewhere right around there. Eugenia shrugged. Numbers had never been her strong suit. Common sense, good tailoring, and a solid work ethic were her gifts. The Scarsenguard was a perfect fit.

So though she enjoyed her job, Eugenia was dreading a certain aspect of it that particular evening: collecting Vivian Fair's wash. Though the actress was a smash onstage, behind the curtain she was chronically untidy.

"A goddamn slob is what she is," Miss Butler mumbled as she started to paw through the considerable mess. As she toed her way through the detritus, her foggy hearing suddenly registered a foreign, hiccuping squall. Pushing aside a bouquet of decaying roses, she stumbled on a basket of blouses and the baby that lay within.

It should be noted that Eugenia Butler, even at her wizened age, was a Miss Butler. Unmarried. A spinster. And it must be said that as a spinster, Eugenia Butler had never had a child. In fact, she had always prided herself on her lack of motherly instinct. Yet when Eugenia saw that babe in the basket, still slick with afterbirth, something in her ancient, unmarried heart fissured. She took the slippery foundling to her breast, plucked a wilting chrysanthemum from a half-drunk flute of champagne, and pressed the glass to the baby's lips. The boy sucked down the booze greedily while his wild eyes met those of Eugenia, and shortly thereafter he fell into a contented sleep.

Using a discarded brassiere, Eugenia Butler fashioned a papoose for the child and carried him about the rest of the evening, crooning half-forgotten snippets of lullabies and censored fragments of bawdy bar tunes.

The wash finished, Miss Butler wrapped the child in muslin and placed him in a crib she'd uncovered in the prop closet. After shutting off all the lights, she made her way out the stage door and caught a cab to her home at East Twenty-Third Street, a soft smile on her lips as she airily planned for the darling boy's future. She felt no guilt about leaving a newborn alone in a theater. After all, how the hell was she supposed to fall asleep with a baby crying all night?

* * *

That the boy survived his infancy was perhaps the greatest miracle in his miraculous life. Eugenia Butler, for all her good intentions, was a wretched mother, though she did manage to pick up enough formula that the boy's diet didn't consist solely of flat champagne.

In the beginning, Eugenia debated taking the baby to an orphanage so that he could find a proper family, but she kept putting it off. The boy was entertaining, and she found she liked lecturing a male who couldn't talk back. Eventually adoption was scrapped; Eugenia decided to keep him.

Justifying the sudden appearance of an infant in the Scarsenguard did pose a problem, but Eugenia resolved to simply hide the boy until she could think of a convincing explanation for his existence.

In those early years, keeping the boy undetected was a breeze. Actors are, in general, a self-absorbed lot. If performers ever heard the infant cry or squeal, Miss Butler would quickly ask them about their careers. Their meandering speeches concerning auditions and agents always outlasted any outburst from the baby.

The stage managers and the behind-the-scenes crew were more attuned to their surroundings than their onstage counterparts, but in hopes of avoiding the tyrannical demands of actors, the stagehands had long learned to keep their eyes on the ground and their thoughts to themselves. It was easier to ignore the fact that a baby was regularly heard screeching its way through act 2. Besides, it might be nothing but the wind or a randy tomcat.

And so the boy's presence remained unknown to anyone but the aging Eugenia Butler. It was nearly a year into the child's life before Eugenia realized she'd yet to christen the orphan; up to that point she'd called him "baby" or "the baby," or sometimes "little baby." Flipping through a calendar, she finally settled on a name: August March.

* * *

Soon August was mobile. Crawling, walking, running, climbing, falling; if it was dangerous, August was doing it. As a toddler, he excelled at all the toddling things toddlers are famous for. Try though she might, Eugenia Butler couldn't keep up with the boy. And by the time he was three and a half, she realized she could not keep August completely secret. Due to his increasing size, Miss Butler could no longer spirit him away whenever awkward questions were posed, or claim he was a rather lifelike prop.

Besides, he'd grown insatiably curious. Eugenia tried to keep August anxious about the human race as a whole with the occasional offhanded remark.

"It'd be such a shame if you were kidnapped like the last little one who lived here." Or, "Everyone in the world is a witch except for me and you, kid."

But despite these terrifying asides, August's inquisitive nature didn't seem to be a passing phase.

Still, Eugenia Butler had grown quite fond of August March; she found she actually enjoyed motherhood, except for all the parts of it that she didn't. One night, after everyone had left the Scarsenguard, Eugenia watched August carry on an animated one-sided conversation with a dress form and realized that she loved him. Loved him more dearly than she had ever loved anyone in her entire life. So, loath to have her companion taken away from her by child services or another ridiculous organization, Miss Butler put her wits to work.

After years of working in the theater, Eugenia Butler knew a thing or two about its inhabitants. Other than narcissism, actors are most famous for their superstition. Just whisper the word *Macbeth* inside a theater and watch as a group of grown adults crumble into delirium. It was this penchant for excess that Eugenia Butler planned to capitalize on.

A new play, *Father's Farthing*, had come to the theater, and after a few days' reconnaissance, Miss Butler had singled out the silliest, most impressionable ingenue from the cast, a girl by the name of Evelyn Rose.

The second preview performance had just concluded, and Evelyn Rose was the last out of costume. She was under the impression that to arrive at the bar simply fashionably late was gauche. One had to be *spectacularly* late, or why bother attending at all? Evelyn glided toward Eugenia, breezily dropping her soiled stockings into the bin at the old woman's feet.

"Good night, Miss Butler," Evelyn whispered, tears threatening to pool in her eyes as she soaked in this miserable old woman. God, how she longed for a mirror; these almost-tears probably looked fantastic.

"Good night, my dear," sighed Eugenia. Then, as Evelyn Rose was turning away, Eugenia gripped the young girl's wrist and drew in a great, rattling gasp. "He's here!" she cried.

Evelyn's wistful melancholy was quickly replaced by revulsion. While trying to win back her wrist, she surveyed the area. "Who's here?" she asked.

Eugenia adopted her most ominous voice. "He comes at night, or sometimes during the day. But if you see him before curtain or during intermission, that's him too!"

"Who? Who, you old bat?" screeched Evelyn, now violently tugging away her wrist.

"The Scarsenguard Spirit," Eugenia whispered, mustering all the raspy otherworldliness her vocal cords could provide.

Evelyn Rose felt the color drain from her face. Ah! Her kingdom for a mirror! In an almost unaffected stutter, she dared to whisper, "The S-S-Scarsenguard Spirit?"

"Years ago, a young boy died in this very theater. Some say a carelessly hung light crushed him. Others claim he fell into the orchestra pit and broke his leg, slowly bleeding out through a cold and lonely night. But me—I think he was murdered!"

An alley cat pawed at empty tuna cans Miss Butler had strategically placed by an open window. The sound they made as they crashed against the iron fire escape achieved the intended eerie effect.

"But who would murder a child?" Evelyn whispered in horror.

Miss Butler thought this a very good question, but seeing as how she had no answer, she plunged further into her tale. "At night he wanders the halls, but don't be surprised if he appears whenever, seeking revenge, or sometimes a ball that he's dropped."

Right on cue, the boy appeared; perhaps he would have a career in the theatre after all. Eugenia had been working on his costume for days. She'd commandeered a few pieces from the Civil War epic *Desire in Dixie*, and a few more from the British farce *Two Many Tuppence* (a travesty that had sprung from the same pen as *Father's Farthing*). With some creative stitching, Miss Butler had fashioned a convincing, if not entirely historically accurate, period costume for the boy. After slapping a cap on his head and covering him in flour, she had herself a ghost.

"August hungry," the child piped in his winsome soprano.

"He died in August!" Miss Butler cried, grateful at this stroke of luck; today was the third of August. "And now the month that claimed his life is hungry for another soul!"

The appearance of the boy ghost was too much for young Evelyn Rose. She shrieked in pure sincerity and fled, unconcerned with what a mirror might show her for perhaps the first time in her life.

At the bar, Evelyn flung open the door, let out a piercing scream, and then fainted dead away, spectacularly late at last. An elderly doctor who happened to be having a drink made several unsuccessful attempts to revive her, but she could only be brought to by the youngest, most handsome man in the cast.

After she had downed several gin fizzes to calm her nerves, the company and crew gathered around Evelyn as she breathlessly recounted her experience with the afterlife.

"What was it called again?" asked a fellow castmate, impressed by the delicate flutter of fear in his own voice.

"The Scarsenguard Spirit," Evelyn whispered, for what must have been the hundredth time. All in all, it was probably the best night of her life.

Meanwhile, the Scarsenguard Spirit was snuggled in his prop closet crib, being told a story about a terrible goblin by a clever laundress.

* * *

Eugenia's plan worked better than she'd imagined; legend of the Scarsenguard Spirit spread far and wide. She heard all sorts of different stories being whispered in the Scarsenguard's crooked hallways when other gossip was scarce. Whichever version people believed, Eugenia Butler didn't mind. They all meant that August could roam freely about the theater, and no bothersome questions would arise.

Except that, while August enjoyed parading about in his Sons of the Confederacy/chimney sweep costume, he found it disheartening that anyone who caught sight of him ran away screaming.

An additional demoralizing facet of August's life was the near constant hunger. Miss Butler provided square meals sporadically, and while the wranglers would often bring snacks, August learned early not to rely on outside sources for sustenance. He became an adept gatherer; chocolates sent to actresses by moony-eyed admirers became a key staple of August's diet, and he had the good sense not to develop an allergy to almond, coconut, or nougat. Other dietary fixtures were the half-eaten sack lunches of stagehands, bits of cheeses left to mold next to the celebratory bottle of champagne, and rose petals.

The happiest few months of August's young life were when *The Importance of Being Earnest* had a run at the Scarsenguard. During this enchanting time, August was able to gorge himself on all the muffins and cucumber sandwiches he could wish for, seeing as how they were integral to the play's plot. This did cause a bit of trouble one matinee, however. Onstage, the actor playing Lane offered a tray that was meant to hold cucumber sandwiches to the actor playing Algernon, a bit of business that takes place within the first five lines of the play. Upon seeing the very empty tray, relieved of its contents by none other than August March, the actor playing Algernon accidentally cried out, "Good heavens! Lane! Why are there no cucumber sandwiches?" This was not a clever bit of improvisation, but an actual line of dialogue that was supposed to occur halfway through the act. Fearing they'd missed their entrances, the actors playing Jack, Gwendolen, and Lady Bracknell stampeded onto the stage, and everyone had a horrible time covering all the exposition they'd inadvertently skipped. The audience left the play confused and crotchety, but then again, matinee audiences usually do. August was more careful with his pilfering after that.

Then there was the boy's lack of education. Miss Butler tried her best, but found she could hardly remember her own age, let alone basic arithmetic. Some days she would sit down with August, intending to impart some nugget of wisdom, but then there were always so many socks to be darned, and stage blood to be bleached out, and where on earth did she set her pincushion?

Physical education was taken care of despite Miss Butler's complete lack of interest in the subject. By hanging back in the wings or posing as a cast member, August was able to learn plenty of stage combat. He could tuck, roll, and wield a sword. Most children played tag; August played dead.

As for more bookish pursuits, August had many professors. Wilde, Shakespeare, Ibsen, Shaw, Chekhov—all left the lad with something. For example, he could recite King Richard II's mirror speech before he could the alphabet, and he had, if not a firm grasp of the language, then at the very least a fine understanding of patronymic and diminutive Russian names: all this before the age of five.

Though he lacked companionship, education, and for the most part food, August was a happy child, contented with the bizarre life that Miss Butler had carved out for him. There was always such fun to be had in a theater, so much to see. He loved watching the stagehands, their muscular arms straining as they created wild tempests or moved whole cities with the pull of a rope. He loved climbing up the catwalk and spying on audience members. But most of all, August loved to watch the plays. He had his own spot, a small crawl space once used for storage but now long forgotten, situated directly over the center spotlight. It was a cramped little cubby, but August drew comfort from its confines; it was his private place within the very public Scarsenguard.

August had already been in his hole for hours. To access his crawl space, he had to climb the ladder that led to the center spotlight and then, using some rather ingenious footholds, shimmy his way up to the abandoned cubby. Obviously, he couldn't do this in plain sight of the hundreds of theatergoers, Scarsenguard Spirit aside. So when August was in a mood to take in a play (which was nearly every night), he'd sneak into the theater hours before anyone was due to arrive and hunker down in what he considered to be the best seat in all the Scarsenguard.

When the house lights finally dimmed, August's heartbeat quickened as the audience hushed. He'd yet to develop a critical eye and believed all the plays at the Scarsenguard to be holy offerings, and he watched the play unfold, an ardent wide-eyed disciple.

* * *

The Scarsenguard and its productions kept August occupied those first few years of his life. There was so much to see, so much coming and going, that he never wanted for more.

But one evening as Miss Butler was packing up her handbag and preparing to leave, August stopped her with a question.

"Who is my mother?"

Miss Butler truthfully had no answer. She'd always guessed that the boy's birth mother was Vivian Fair, but in reality, he could've been born of anyone. Vivian had many enemies, and seeing her embroiled in a scandal involving an illegitimate child would have brought many of her adversaries great pleasure. Hell, even Eugenia would've had a laugh.

"I suppose I'm your mother," Miss Butler finally answered.

August eyed her skeptically. "No offense meant, my good woman, but I find it difficult to believe—"

"August. You're doing it again."

The boy had basically learned to talk from watching plays, so his style of speaking was often florid and long-winded. Eugenia was all for a lush vocabulary, but occasionally she just wanted to smack the child. Talk in sentences, not soliloquies!

"Sorry," August said before correcting himself with, "Aren't you too old to be my—"

"Careful, child," Eugenia interrupted. She scooped August up (god, he was getting heavy) into her lap and told him, "Your mother isn't necessarily the person who grew you in her belly. She's the person who's always there for you, even when she doesn't want to be. Blood isn't family. Families are the people, whoever they are, that are in your corner. And I'm in your corner, August. Understand?"

He was digesting her speech, and Eugenia thought the conversation over when he suddenly asked, "Where do you go at night?"

"Why, to my house," she replied.

"Can I come?"

Miss Butler sucked her teeth.

"But you live here. At the Scarsenguard."

August smiled. The Scarsenguard was his, and he was its proud owner. But though he undoubtedly had the best home in all the world, what was outside it?

Miss Butler dashed out before the boy could come up with any more awkward questions. She loved August dearly, but to share her apartment? With a child? Motherhood was fulfilling, but there were limits.

August didn't begrudge Eugenia her hasty retreat, for he had formulated a plan. Tonight, August was going to take a stroll. The first of his life.

The lobby doors were locked, as August knew they would be, but he wasn't deterred. Just as he expected, the women's room on the first floor had a cracked window. After climbing a toilet, it was a cinch to shimmy through.

And just like that, August March was outside. The drop was farther than he thought, but after dusting off his knees, he set to exploring. It was late, so the city had less than its usual bustle, but there were still quite a few citizens out and about. Excited to be himself and not his ghostly alter ego, August plucked up a pinch of courage and more than a dash of precociousness and introduced himself to a man leaning against a building.

"Good evening, kind sir," he said, extending his small hand. "August March is my name. What's yours?"

"You got any money?" was the gruff reply.

August thought responding to a question with a question was a bad bit of dialogue, but then he reminded himself that this was an actual person, not an actor, and their scene was entirely unscripted, and not a scene at all, in fact, but real life. Best to press on.

"No money on my person or any to my name, in fact," August cheerily informed him. "You might try a bank?" He'd just learned of the existence of moneylending from the character Shylock, and felt himself rather adult for suggesting it.

August's new acquaintance was less than charmed, however.

"You making fun of me, kid?"

Taken aback, August quickly replied, "I most certainly am not!"

"Seems to me like you got a silver spoon up your ass."

The man shoved August, and it was not a stage combat shove, where the victim was always in control. This shove was rough and meant to hurt.

August tumbled off the sidewalk and into the street, where a car had to swerve to avoid hitting him.

"Get the hell out of the road, dumb-ass!" the motorist shouted before driving off into the night.

August was shaken. His pleasurable stroll had not gone as intended. He scurried back to the Scarsenguard's bathroom window, but to his horror, he found that it was far too high to reach, even if he jumped. In desperation, he tried the lobby doors, but they were locked tight. Tears welled in his eyes. Never in his life had he spent a night outside the Scarsenguard. He was just a boy. What was he to do?

Rain started to fall, and August ducked under the Scarsenguard's awning, clinging to the theater's side as if it were his mother, shivering and terrified. The hours passed, and August eventually fell into a restless sleep.

The next morning, the box office clerk arrived at nine. August knew the man's routine: right after he unlocked the lobby, he set down his bag and then went to the bathroom. As soon as the man jiggled the handle of the bathroom door, August slinked in through the lobby doors, sprinted all the way up to the abandoned green room, fell onto the musty old couch, and wept with relief.

When Miss Butler arrived that evening, she was greeted by a viselike hug.

"What's gotten into you, child?" she said, laughing.

August released her before answering, "The outside world is a terrible place."

"Indeed it is," she replied, slipping August a piece of chocolate. "Full of hooligans, murderers, and tourists. You're much better off here, in the Scarsenguard."

August couldn't have agreed more.

* * *

A smash production of *King Lear* was playing at the Scarsenguard and had been extended for two more months. August adored the play. Storms, swordfights, betrayals, murder, secret identities, that part where the old guy gets his eyes squished out; it was all too wonderful!

Though August idolized all the actors in the production, he was especially enraptured by the old man playing Lear, a legendary star of the English stage by the name of Sir Reginald Percyfoot. August had been dying to meet the lead of his favorite play, but Miss Butler had strictly forbidden it.

"Old men hate young boys," she said, cutting an apple into slices for August. She found he was far more receptive to her demands when he was well fed. "They chop them up and hide them under floorboards!"

"That's not true," August protested through a mouthful of fruit.

"Yes it is! It's as true as anything I've ever said!"

"You told everyone I'm a ghost," August pointed out.

Miss Butler stared at August from behind her glasses. "You're getting far too clever for your own good. How old are you?"

"I don't know," August answered, truthfully. He was almost six.

"What year is it? We'll count from the year you were born until the year it is now and find out how old you are. That's called addition. You should know addition, love; write it down."

August had no pencil, and if he did, it wouldn't have done him any good; he had no idea how to write. Besides, even if he could write, he doubted scribbling down the word *addition* would help him comprehend the subject.

"I don't know what year it is," he said, again in complete honesty, "nor do I know what year I was born."

"For heaven's sake, child! How can you not know the year you were born?"

"What year were you born?" August asked.

Once again he received a pointed stare from Miss Butler. She soon realized, however, that her pointed stare was not going to win this argument. The boy was dead set on meeting Sir Reginald, though she could hardly understand why; at least the old windbag playing Gloucester had some of his looks left.

"Fine." She sighed, handing over the last of the apple. "You can meet him. But wear your ghost costume," she ordered over August's celebratory cries.

* * *

The curtain fell, and after what felt like a lifetime, the audience cleared. August could hardly restrain himself. He was bouncing on the balls of his feet and babbling so much nonsense that Eugenia was forced to dump an entire bag of flour on his head to shut him up.

"Now remember," she said, evening out the flour to make him appear more spectral, "if Sir Reginald threatens you or tries to strike you, swear that he'll be cursed with bad reviews until the end of his days. That ought to do the trick."

August couldn't say anything; he was too busy hacking, having inhaled a large amount of the flour in which he'd been doused. Eugenia Butler didn't seem to notice. She draped a length of chain across his shoulders and, with tears in her eyes, addressed the boy. "I suppose this day had to come," she whispered, mopping up her tears. "Look how big you've gotten, August!" she cried, fiddling with the boy's shirt-sleeves, which were indeed too short. She'd have to let them out. It seemed she'd done it only yesterday. "Now, go!"

Approaching Sir Reginald's dressing room, August was nervous. Perhaps he should just forgo this meeting altogether and instead admire Sir Reginald from afar, clinging to corners and curtains, a reverent shadow.

No. This couldn't go on any longer. How was he supposed to get on in the world if no one knew he existed? Though the boy thought Miss Butler bewitching, she couldn't remain his only acquaintance. Even the kidnapped changeling child in *Midsummer* led a more active social life. It was time for change.

With newfound conviction, August threw open the dressing room door, and cried out, "Sir Reginald Percyfoot, I have come to make your acquaintance!"

Sir Reginald was taken aback by such a forceful declaration, and when he saw the pale form of the Scarsenguard Spirit wreathed in the doorway, he knew his time had come. And just when his good-for-nothing agent had almost certainly gotten him a five-picture contract with Warner Brothers, too.

Reginald Percyfoot had played hundreds of death scenes in his career. He'd died bravely, nobly, pathetically, beautifully. He'd been shot, drowned, stabbed, strangled. He'd given speeches as he perished, or sometimes slipped away quietly, silent as a butterfly's wings.

Facing his actual death, he found there was a lot more screaming involved.

August tried to mollify his idol with nonthreatening gestures, but that only seemed to make matters worse. Sir Reginald was shrieking in a high-pitched whistle that was actually quite impressive, considering that he was known for his soothing baritone.

"I'm not a ghost!" August screamed over the commotion. "I'm not a ghost! I'm a boy, and I think your Lear is the most nuanced performance any actor has given in a generation!"

Without knowing it, August had uttered the only phrase that interested Sir Reginald more than his certain death.

"Really?" asked Percyfoot, screams completely forgotten. "You don't think I overdo act four? The scene with the flowers?"

"Oh no," answered August truthfully. "I find that to be one of the production's highlights."

Reginald was still unnerved by the presence of an apparition, but he couldn't refuse an opportunity to talk about himself. He offered August tea, and the two sat down for a lengthy chat, dissecting each and every moment of Percyfoot's performance. For August, it was the most stimulating conversation he'd ever had. Miss Butler's discussions of the theatre mostly centered on the merits of muslin and the fact that there was no such thing as a ruined stocking. To delve into the craft of acting, to examine Shakespeare's language—how the boy had longed to speak of such things! And to do so with an unparalleled champion of the stage? Nirvana!

For his part, Sir Reginald had never met a more charming child, or one with such a breadth of knowledge of the theatre. When they'd combed over the finer details of his performance for the third or fourth time, Sir Reginald suddenly remembered to whom he was speaking.

"But, my fine young lad, you're a ghost!"

August explained that he was not a ghost but an orphan, being raised in the Scarsenguard by the laundress.

This both fascinated and repulsed Sir Reginald. A boy growing up in the Scarsenguard was certainly a romantic idea. After all, a life in the theatre was the truest and noblest of all callings, and the boy certainly had a head start on his peers. But what of making chums in his age group? What of his education? What of life?

Percyfoot demanded to see Eugenia Butler, and August, unaware of the legal complexities surrounding his situation, led him to her, oblivious that the introduction he was about to make would very likely take him away from the Scarsenguard and life as he knew it.

The pair found Eugenia still in her chair, snoring lightly and drooling heavily. After August had shaken her awake and introduced his elders, Eugenia, completely aware of the legal complexities surrounding August's situation, instantly understood what Sir Reginald's stern expression entailed.

"Did you need some washing done, sir?" Eugenia asked, and, employing her keen knowledge of actors, added, "Such a marvelous performance tonight. I managed to catch all your really moving scenes, and believe me when I say I was . . . moved." It had been years since Eugenia Butler had seen *King Lear*, and she couldn't quite recall what it was about. She surmised that there was a king in it, but she'd been wrong before, so best to keep the details vague.

"Miss Butler," Percyfoot blustered, bravely ignoring her compliments, though desperate to get into specifics, "it has come to my attention that this delightful child is your ward, though if I understand it correctly, the arrangement is hardly . . . legitimate."

Eugenia paled but refused to be beaten. Quick as her bones could manage, she dashed off to the dressing room that belonged to the actress playing Cordelia, borrowed a bottle of champagne, and poured two glasses.

"I never discuss business without a spot of bubbly." She winked.

Two and a half bottles later, Sir Reginald had a new take on the very notion of custody. Could one really own a child? Are people properties to be bandied about? And the boy was happy here! He was looked after, and the American educational system was in shambles at any rate.

"Actually, I'd quite like to go to school," said the boy, bored senseless by all the dull adult talk.

"Have a glass of champagne, August," said Miss Butler, still nursing her first fluteful.

August, never one to turn down any form of nourishment, obliged. In two minutes he was drunk, and in two more, unconscious.

"A lovely lad," hiccuped Percyfoot, "though his theories on Ibsen are positively mad."

"Does this mean you won't inform the police about August?" asked Eugenia, tipping the last of the third bottle into his glass.

"My dear, the secret's safe with me," slurred the celebrated performer before joining August in unconsciousness.

Miss Butler finished up the wash and then caught a cab home, content in the knowledge that August and Sir Reginald were now fast friends and that she'd be nowhere nearby when they awoke to nurse their respective hangovers.

* * *

Lear had a limited engagement at the Scarsenguard, but while it played, Sir Reginald and August were inseparable. Because August's existence had to remain hidden, most of their meetings took place after the show ended each night. The boy had never kept a regular sleep schedule, and Sir Reginald operated on an actor's clock, so neither party minded the late evenings.

Due to the actor's deft portrayal of the senile Lear, August had always assumed Percyfoot to be ancient, older than Miss

Butler even. During their midnight meetings, however, August realized the man was somewhere closer to sixty. Though this made him considerably younger than Miss Butler, August still saw him as quite elderly. After all, to a person not yet ten, a thirty-year-old was helplessly old-fashioned; at sixty, Sir Reginald might as well have been Methuselah.

Long, rambling debates about the theatre, playwriting, directing, and acting could be heard from behind the doors of Sir Reginald's dressing room night after night. But art wasn't all they discussed. Sir Reginald, through subtle probing, was able to infer what lacked in August's admittedly slipshod education.

"What do you know of history, my boy?"

August was eager to prove himself. "Miss Butler started working at the Scarsenguard she can't remember when and has been here ever since, thank you very much."

Sir Reginald suppressed a shudder. "And tell me what you know of mathematics?"

"Most shirts have six buttons, but you can get away with five if the pants are high-waisted enough, though of course that all depends on when the play takes place. Also, you can stretch detergent for weeks if you splash in a bit of water."

At least that had some numbers in it. "Science?" Sir Reginald asked.

"What's science?"

Sir Reginald, initially aghast, realized that he didn't have a firm grasp on the subject himself. "It's when . . . people mix things together in beakers and use Bunsen burners."

"Like the witches in *Macbeth*?" August asked, excited.

Upon hearing that most accursed of names, Sir Reginald Percyfoot screeched, spit into his left hand, turned in a circle three times, and then said fourteen Hail Marys backward. Afterward, he was breathless and out of sorts.

"Tomorrow night we start your schooling, but it is imperative that you never utter that name so long as you are in a theater."

"What name? Macbeth?"

"Out!" screamed Sir Reginald, tossing the boy from his dressing room and slamming the door. In the hallway, August could hear the backward Hail Marys again, along with several other phrases that would give pause to even the most open-minded censorship board.

* * *

True to his word, Sir Reginald began the education of August March the very next evening. Though the boy was woefully behind his age group, he was nothing if not a quick study, and Sir Reginald was pleased to see that August took a keen interest in bettering himself. In less than a week, August could add together basic sums and write his name. A week later, he could recite all the kings and queens of England, though he had yet to hear of the Declaration of Independence; Sir Reginald's history lessons tended to skew British.

King Lear ended its run just a few weeks after August's schooling had commenced, but Sir Reginald refused to let his enchanting protégé's mind be neglected.

"You're to commit these books to memory, child," he ordered, handing over a heavy stack of freshly purchased tomes still wrapped in brown paper. Among the miniature library were mostly classic books for new readers, but also a few more advanced volumes, such as *Scotland Yard: A History*, and *Tutoring on Tudors*.

August, who rarely received gifts, was gracious to the point of deference. "Please don't go," he begged, his eyes shining with tears.

For all his pomp and, some critics said, self-indulgence onstage, Sir Reginald was uncomfortable when confronted with emotions in his actual life.

"There, there," he said, patting August on his back while hiding tears of his own. "As soon as I wrap this ridiculous picture in Hollywood, I'll try to get another play to come through the Scarsenguard." As soon as he'd spoken, Sir Reginald realized he truly meant what he said.

"Really?" August asked, clutching the books to his chest.

"Of course!" shouted Percyfoot with a bit too much bravado. "Why, you still know nothing of the Magna Carta, and I'd love to hear your theories on Sir Francis Drake and Elizabeth's rumored liaison."

August was used to adults speaking utter nonsense, and while it usually bored him, he couldn't help but be cheered by Sir Reginald's infectious tone. Dropping his books, he ran and threw a hug around the man's sturdy leg.

"Enough of this, child, I must be off!"

As soon as he was back in his hotel, Sir Reginald Percyfoot arranged a call with his no-good agent and told the nincompoop that he was no longer interested in the coveted five-picture deal with Jack Warner.

"Tell that greedy-pig stumblebum that I'll do one picture and one picture only! Then I want to be back at the Scarsenguard!"

Sir Reginald's no-good agent hung up the phone in complete confusion, and then, as agents are wont to do, forgot the conversation entirely.

* * *

The months after Percyfoot's departure were depressing ones for August. After all his stirring interchanges with his mentor, the boy found he no longer had the keen, dewy-eyed freshness of the amateur when watching plays. Now he was critical, snobbish, and bored, one of the churlish indoctrinated. Why on earth had the idiot director staged the scene in that fashion? And those cheap and tawdry sets hardly illuminated the playwright's intention, that is, if the lummox who wrote this dreck had any intentions to begin with. August's cherished cubbyhole above the center spotlight was no longer a harbor of divine theatrical transportation but the contaminated den of the most acidic critic in New York City.

To make up for the lack of artistic integrity in his life, August took to exploration. Not of the outside world. Miss Butler had been adamant that he never leave the theater and had spun many of her trademark tales to frighten him.

"Taxi drivers will steer straight for you, eager to run over anything in their paths. They scratch a tally on the side of their cabs each time they claim a new victim. And then there are the social workers. They hunt down little boys and throw them into orphanages. You know how terrible orphanages are, don't you, August?"

Indeed he did. The serialized account of the little orphan Annie was his favorite radio program. To him, an orphanage sounded like the worst place in the entire world.

"And don't even get me started on tourists," Miss Butler would sometimes add, barely daring to whisper the words. "Horrible creatures. Really, something ought to be done."

So it wasn't the city that August took to surveying, but the Scarsenguard itself. The theater held no secrets for him now. No corner went uncharted, no ladder unclimbed. He knew every inch of the place and could scale a rope or even a curtain with feline liquidity.

The heavy, musky scent of dust, tangible and oppressive, became August's constant companion. He could soon differentiate mouse droppings from those of a rat, and after only a few more weeks of applied research, could state with assurance the mood of any particular rodent by the quality of its squeaks. Such was his life, this boy in the rafters.

Still, he didn't forget his promise to Sir Reginald, and devoted plenty of time each day to his studies. He clung to books with the desperation that a drowning man might to driftwood, and as a result became even more precocious than he'd been just a few months prior. At times, Eugenia Butler found him downright cynical.

"Good gracious, child, what on earth are you reading?" she asked one evening, eyeing the opus August was leafing through. A worrisome (albeit impressive) eye-roll greeted her query. "Now see here, boy, I asked you a question. When you reach puberty, you're welcome to be as irksome or sarcastic as you'd like. I'll be dead and won't have to suffer through it. But while I'm alive, I aim to enjoy the charms of your youth. So please, pray tell, what are you reading?"

Sighing, August answered, "It's a collection of seventeenth-century Russian poetry."

Eugenia Butler was unable to stifle her boredom, even for the sake of the child's tender feelings. "Good god! What absolute rubbish! Boys your age should be reading comics!"

"What are comics?" he asked, unable to cork his curiosity.

Eugenia sighed. "Go talk to the rats, August."

Though rude and sullen, he was at his heart an obedient boy, and snapping the book closed, did as he was told.

Conversations of this ilk, of which there had been many, were distressing to Eugenia. For all her maternal faults, Miss Butler loved August, and even her cloudy eyes could detect that something was off in the boy. On her cab ride home that evening, she decided to throw the boy a party. After all, he'd never had a proper birthday. A party would be just the thing to lift his spirits and make him stop being such a horrible little bastard.

* * *

The next morning Eugenia went out shopping for August's surprise party. She intended for the day to be entirely marvelous, full of whimsy and maternal felicity. However, as she started her errands, she couldn't shake off a nagging paranoia that, due to today's efforts, August would be discovered and taken away. These suspicions somewhat soured her well-intentioned aspirations.

The tingle of bells above the door signaled her entrance to the cake shop.

"How can I help you today?" asked the baker, a smiling man with an overlarge nose.

"I don't see how that's any of your concern," Eugenia snapped, unfounded worry over August's discovery shattering her earlier fantasies.

The baker's eyes went dead.

"I'm so sorry," Eugenia said, embarrassed. "I've had a long morning. I'm here for a birthday cake."

At her apology, the baker visibly dropped the social armor he'd been donning. He smiled. "Will the cake be for a boy or a girl?"

Eugenia reached over the counter and slapped him across the face. "Keep your big nose out of my business, snake!"

Seven minutes later, she left the bakery with a stale spice cake.

She didn't fare much better at the toy shop, either. As soon as she arrived, a mob of children nearly knocked her over. Miss Butler looked for guardians to come discipline their charges, but all the parents present seemed to willfully ignore their unruly issue.

Since Miss Butler refused to offer any information about August's age or interests, the attendant had a difficult time helping her select a suitable gift. Exasperated, she finally gave up and purchased a jigsaw puzzle and an insipid picture book about a ball of yarn.

At the Scarsenguard, August was understandably confused when Miss Butler presented him with the rather pathetic spread meant to be his birthday party. The jigsaw puzzle was greeted with tepid enthusiasm and the picture book with unconcealed horror. As Miss Butler squawked her way through "Happy Birthday," August decided that birthday parties were on the whole disagreeable and was glad they happened only once every seven years or so.

Miss Butler tried to tell herself that she'd succeeded in lifting the boy's spirits, but when August nearly choked on the dry spice cake, she was forced to admit that the party had been a complete disaster. Conceding defeat, she was packing up her purse to beat a shamefaced retreat to her brownstone when she saw the corner of a postcard sticking from her handbag. The postcard! She'd nearly forgotten.

"Oh, August," she called. "Before I go, I have one more present for you."

The child's eyes widened in anticipation of the terrors he would be subjected to, but when Miss Butler handed him nothing but a postcard, his forehead wrinkled in confusion.

"Read it," she said.

The front showed the famed Hollywood sign, which, until that very moment, August had never seen. He flipped the card over. It was addressed to Miss Butler but intended for August.

"My dear boy," the card started, "Hollywood is even more deplorable than I expected. I said 'Sophocles' the other morning, and everyone thought I had sneezed. The people are wretched and the weather is worse! Constant sunlight? Can you imagine anything more harrowing? Good news, though: my scum-of-the-gutter agent managed to secure me a part in New York. In February, I'll be back at the Scarsenguard!"

August squealed in delight. The rest of the note was squeezed into the margins. "Must run. Keep up your studies and swear to never go west of the Hudson River!"

The signature —"Unabashedly, Sir Reginald Percyfoot"— took up half the postcard.

"What's today?" August asked.

"October ninth," answered Miss Butler, consulting a calendar.

"That means Sir Reginald will arrive in"—August's nose twitched as he calculated—"four months!"

August ran around the room, trumpeting his good fortune to the heavens, while Miss Butler looked on laughing. All her earlier failures were forgotten, and August leapt into the old woman's arms, planting a decidedly uncynical kiss on her cheek. From that time forward, though he was actually born sometime in April, August forever celebrated his birthday on October 9.

* * *

At first it seemed as though the four months leading up toward Sir Reginald's return would be nothing short of an eternity, but affairs outside the Scarsenguard seemed determined to finally introduce themselves to August March, whether he wanted them to or not.

The year was 1941, and nearly two months after August's birthday celebrations, an island called Japan bombed an island called Hawaii and apparently nearly every citizen of the globe seemed to harbor strong feelings on the subject. To August, the event was one of the many inconsequential idiosyncrasies of the world at large and had nothing to do with him or the Scarsenguard. Had the circumstances been different, he might've been correct, and would've continued about his life as he had before, giving current events about as much attention as a weary parent might to the incoherent babblings of a toddler.

However, just two short days after the attack, a large man with a larger mustache came trouncing through the theater, trailed by a bespectacled assistant.

"That's Mr. Barreth," Miss Butler whispered to August as Barreth stormed past. "He owns the place. Rich as chocolate. His father died a few years ago and left him property all over the city."

August's curiosity was piqued. The Scarsenguard had an owner? He'd never realized that anyone owned the Scarsenguard, let alone a man with a mustache so large it looked like a ferret suffering from heatstroke. But August wouldn't judge based on appearances. Instead, he'd get the measure of the man with a dose of harmless espionage.

Barreth and his assistant swept through the theater, August on their heels, undetected.

"Keep up," Barreth snapped to the smaller man as they descended staircase after staircase, finally ending up in the basement. August slipped into a vacant broom closet and kept watch.

Barreth paced the room, running his hands over the walls and looking it all over with a critical eye. Eventually, he seemed satisfied.

"I think this is the one, don't you?"

"I do, sir," the assistant agreed. "It's certainly a spacious venue. And may I just say, sir, I think it's so admirable, what you're doing for the country. I know that everyone's pitching in and looking to help where they can, but you're really going above and beyond."

August stifled a snicker at the assistant's pathetic attempt at flattery, but Barreth was not amused.

"Get this through your thick skull, you little nancy," Barreth spat, "I'm letting Uncle Sam borrow my theater to get the IRS off my ass. I'd donate my wife to the government to avoid an audit. Understand?"

"Of course, sir."

"Good. Now let's get out of here, this place gives me the creeps."

"They say it's haunted, sir," the assistant whispered.

"I know what they say! I own it!"

"Of course, so sorry, sir."

Barreth sighed. "I need a scotch."

Later, when August related the conversation to Miss Butler, she didn't seem at all concerned.

"Don't try to understand the rich, August. They're a different species. Best to avoid them altogether, I always say."

As it turned out, Barreth was only the first of many intruders the Scarsenguard was forced to suffer. The day after Barreth's arrival, a whole brood of strangers descended on the Scarsenguard, bringing with them a menagerie of wood and paint cans and all the wretched accoutrements of the fix-'em-up.

"What is going on here?" a flabbergasted August asked Eugenia after being nearly decapitated by a passing ladder.

"I've only just heard," she answered, wringing her hands in delight, "but it seems Mr. Barreth has lent the Scarsenguard to the war effort. They're converting all the backstage into a sort of recreational center for the soldiers when they're on leave. There's already a space like it in Hollywood. Scads of celebrities show up and dance with the boys—everyone who's anyone has been there. And now all those sorts of people will be at the Scarsenguard! Can you imagine it, August? It's a big to-do!"

Recreational center? Soldiers? But surely that sort of commotion would be distracting during performances? August voiced his concerns.

"But, darling, there won't be any performances. The soldiers won't be admitted until the sun goes down, and the ruckus those kids make will drown out anything the windbags upstairs would be saying."

August had read of a person's jaw dropping in some of the more plebian novels he'd devoured, but never until that moment had he experienced the sensation. "No plays?" he finally managed.

"Just not at the Scarsenguard," she added, realizing the drastic effect her words were having on the boy. "Broadway wouldn't shut itself down for a silly old thing like a war."

"How long do wars usually last?" August asked, grasping for even the faintest of silver linings.

"That depends. The Great War was around four years, if I remember correctly, but some drag for much longer. Years and years and years . . ."

August heard no more, for like the heroines in those banal best-sellers, he retired to his chambers to weep.

* * *

The date was March 2, 1942, and work on what was now called the Backstage Bistro (a horrible name, in August's opinion) was completed, the grand opening scheduled for that very evening. August ambled in a daze as volunteers strung gay lanterns from this pole to that or dashed through the doors with another armful of bouquets. To think that less than five months ago this had been a respectable theater. Now, August thought as he watched giggling women of all ages add finishing touches to the garish decor, this grand cathedral of art had been transformed into a brothel.

Just after Christmas, when August had come to a tenuous peace with his new lot, he was dealt another dire blow, this one in postcard form. It was from Sir Reginald:

Dear August,

Looks like the play's been canceled due to the war. Dreadful luck, but it was a ghastly piece of slop in any case. Picture wrapped, headed straight to London to appear in a benefit for the boys over there. Sorry, old chap, but keep that chin up, I'll be in New York as soon as the gods allow!

The gloom the boy felt upon receiving this bit of news was so palpable that Miss Butler took to avoiding him altogether lest she get swept up in the whirlpool of his melancholy. Besides, now that there was no laundry to attend to, she'd become a rather important figure in the Backstage Bistro's construction. She'd worked at the Scarsenguard for myriad years, and the volunteers, most of whom had never seen the inside of a theater, peppered her with questions ranging from "Where's the bathroom?" to "Is this beam weight-bearing?" Few had time to even notice the desolate child gliding about the place, and when they did, Miss Butler would quickly improvise that his mother had just dashed out the door. She was never refuted.

And so the weeks passed, for Eugenia in a state of bustling negligence, for August in malaise, until finally the inaugural evening was at hand. It was the least excited August had ever been for an opening night at the Scarsenguard, but he did have to admit he was looking forward to any distraction from his sour reverie.

August had avoided going downstairs as much as possible during the bistro's development, so when he entered, he was surprised by the swankiness. When the women had dragged in roll after roll of colored canvas a few weeks back, August imagined the place would look like a tatty fortune-teller's tent, but the bistro was anything but tasteless. The canvas, draped artfully from the ceiling and down the walls, transformed the Scarsenguard's rather utilitarian basement into a place of enchantment. Huge paper lanterns, delicate as soap bubbles, hung from the ceiling so effortlessly that they appeared to be floating. Elegant circular tables filled the room, though plenty of space was left near the stage for dancing. And the stage! The only other one August had ever seen was upstairs in the proper Scarsenguard Theater. But this one was rounded, smaller, and much closer to the audience. It would be a far more intimate evening, August concluded as he watched the band members, already in place, tuning their instruments. Everyone would feel part of the performance rather than a mere spectator.

Running the length of the right wall of the room was a long buffet covered in billowing white fabric. Behind the table stood a score of female volunteers, each in matching uniforms: light blue button-down shirts, black skirts that were perhaps a hair too short, and rather flirty paper hats. The first three-quarters of the table was devoted to serving sandwiches, while the last quarter of the table held the bar. The

Backstage Bistro was a strictly nonalcoholic establishment, so bowls of brightly colored punch sat atop the buffet while the strictly illegal bottles of unmarked booze stood underneath, a finger's reach away from the deft hands of the bartenders. Though it was a bit pedestrian, August had to admit it had a certain quaint charm. Amiably American.

The air was electric with nerves as it always was at an opening, the difference being that the staff of the Backstage Bistro were uninitiated to the theatrical life and were therefore even more atwitter than a company of seasoned vets would be on such an occasion. Shrill, nervous giggles sounded every half minute or so, while the more level-headed volunteers paced and barked and generally made things worse as they tried to brace for every conceivable mishap.

Finally, when their nerves were frayed to the breaking point, the doors opened, and just before the uniforms started pouring in, the band ripped into a tune so lively that even August had to tap his foot.

As soon as the soldiers entered, the girls swooped in, hooking their arms into uniformed ones and flirting mercilessly. August, who'd only ever encountered strictly scripted seduction, found this off-the-cuff coquetry quite shocking. The boys, however, starved as they were for feminine interaction, lit up like firecrackers, and what with the band blasting away like it was doomsday, the whole shindig was already in full swing before the first batch of guests had filed in.

The evening's formal entertainment began at nine, and August felt his heart rate rising as a hush settled over the rowdy crowd. What delights would this cozy little stage present? The first performer entered, a dancer with severe black hair and a plunging red gown, and August was already spellbound. When she raised her sharp, angular eyebrow to signal the start of her routine, August barely heard the chorus of whistles or the lusty wailings of the band's brass section. She dipped and kicked, bending gravity to her will, the diaphanous fabric of her dress trailing behind her, an enchantress, a witch.

The spell was broken by a roar of applause; August even saw one soldier pretending to cough to mask his wistful tears.

Next to the stage came a comedian August had never heard of, though, judging by the thundering cheers he received upon his entrance, August assumed that he was rather famous. His set was no longer than twenty minutes, and though August didn't understand much of it, as it had an awful lot to do with Germans, Italians, and the Japanese, his sides hurt from laughing.

"Thank you all, that's my time," the man said to a chorus of hoots and applause. "I've been told I have the honor of introducing your next guests. I've also been told to keep my hands off that dancer, but my short-term memory's been off lately." He gave a hammy wink. "So please get on your feet while that lovely lady and I get off of ours, and welcome to the stage some of Hollywood's brightest stars!"

In through the wings came a line of seven of the most elegant people August had ever seen. The women, of whom there were four, were dressed in flawless gowns, cut so exquisitely that August couldn't imagine them in anything else. The three men wore tuxedos, living testaments to the sartorial arts; August could almost hear Miss Butler clucking with approval.

From the excited murmurs and the flurry of flashbulbs, August gathered that the comedian hadn't oversold the movie stars, but the boy couldn't have cared less about the celebrities, because waddling out after these young and glamorous performers came an older man dressed in a tuxedo that was bravely attempting to mask a protrusion of gut.

"Sir Reginald!" August cried over the crowd. He rushed the stage, hurtled over the lip in one bound, and crashed into Percyfoot, throwing his arms around the man's ample waist as tightly as Othello had gripped fair Desdemona's neck.

Though August was oblivious, the energy of the room had shifted. Who was this boy? the masses seemed to be asking themselves. Where did he come from? Would it be possible to neck with one of those actresses later? And so forth.

Sir Reginald, reading the room with deft thespian assurance, cleared his throat. "See?" he bellowed to the young woman on his left, an actress named Vivian Fair, a woman so famous that even August recognized her from the covers of magazines Miss Butler left lying about. "I told you I was the bigger star."

The audience roared, all awkwardness forgiven, and the comedian rushed the band back onstage, where they immediately tore into a frenzied dance tune. The stars glided down into the bistro to mingle, all but Sir Reginald, who hiked August higher up so that he could speak into the child's ear.

"My god, boy, what an entrance! We'll make a proper actor out of you yet!"

The two friends shuffled off to a corner table where they could hear each other speak. Sir Reginald nursed an illegal bottle of whiskey and even gave August his first nip. He'd had loads of champagne, of course, and had even sampled gin on two past occasions, but this was his first foray into dark liquor, and though he found the taste deplorable, he did feel rather grown-up about the whole thing.

Percyfoot regaled August with deprecating tales from his time in Hollywood and explained that once he'd heard that the bistro was to open in the Scarsenguard, he bullied and threatened until he was finally invited to join the star-studded lineup of opening-night guests. "None of them had the faintest idea who I was, of course, but I just kept shouting, 'Jack Warner will have your head,' or 'When Mayer discovers how I've been treated!' Laid it on a bit thick, but most people are shockingly daft, don't you agree?"

The last of the uniforms finally staggered out, and August, Sir Reginald, and Miss Butler retired upstairs to the green room, which had remained unaffected by the Backstage Bistro's construction. Eugenia was patching up a few volunteer uniforms that had ripped during strenuous dancing, and kindly turning a blind eye whenever Sir Reginald poured August another nip of whiskey.

For his part, August was madly curious about the inner workings of Hollywood. After all, he'd never truly left the Scarsenguard, and his only introduction to the world of cinema had been through Miss Butler's discarded tabloids. He peppered Sir Reginald with questions about the contents of the magazine he was drunkenly waving about. The war was in full swing, but was sable really all the rage? And that tender young virgin by the name of Vivian Fair taking Hollywood by storm, the one Percyfoot had quipped with earlier that eve, was she really as marvelous as everyone said? Exasperated, the old man snatched the magazine out of August's hands.

"Bah! Don't be reading this filth, my boy!" he spat, nearly tearing the pages out of the rag as he venomously flipped through them. "Hollywood! All sex, no substance. And Vivian Fair a virgin? Why, she's seduced every man in New York, and half of Hollywood, too. My god!" he cried, expressive eyes bugging from his skull. "Did she really sign with Paramount? That vixen? Impossible!"

Try as he might, August could not get another word from Sir Reginald, who was now engrossed in the magazine he so clearly despised. But August didn't mind. He watched contentedly as Sir Reginald read the magazine and Miss Butler stitched up a shirt, basking in the comfort of being surrounded by his makeshift family. His eyes heavy, August fought sleep for as long as possible, but the exhaustion brought on by the excitement of the evening and the irresponsible amount of whiskey eventually overtook the boy, and he slipped into a drunken slumber, content.

* * *

The party raged every night at the Backstage Bistro for the next three years. Sir Reginald popped in when he could, but he'd become quite in demand playing secondary characters in war pictures, which were, of course, all anyone was making. He played the salty British general, the salty British POW, or the salty British prime minister.

August, who'd resisted the bistro with arched-back defiance, came to be its biggest proponent. It was there that he learned about popular music, celebrity culture, how to dance, how to swear. He traded conversation with the world's greatest thinkers and artists, gossiped with the volunteers, and shot the shit with sailors.

And how was August able to maintain his anonymity? Through the snares and sink traps laid by Miss Butler. Though soldiers were, as a rule, even more superstitious than actors, get them away from the terror of battle and they became far more practical. The Scarsenguard Spirit, therefore, finally fulfilled his unfinished business and passed on into the spectral plane. August was now a displaced child—usually French or British, though sometimes a Soviet, depending on Miss Butler's mood—whom the American government had taken into custody. When asked for specifics about his heritage or lack of accent or any other bit of bothersome minutia, Eugenia would wink and indicate through long-winded monologues that the boy's parents needed to keep their identities a secret.

Though his horizons were broadening, August did occasionally desire to escape the delirium of the Backstage Bistro. A year or so earlier, when the blasted war showed no sign of relenting, he had taken it upon himself to convert one of the cozier dressing rooms into a space all his own. Why not? There hadn't been a proper production at the Scarsenguard for ages, and no one else was using it. Books were crammed into every plausible nook, though the rest of the decor leaned more macabre. Several different versions of poor Yorick's skull had been abandoned in the Scarsenguard's prop closet throughout the years, and August commandeered all of them, hanging them from the overhead pipes with sturdy twine, while stuffed ravens and garish candelabras left over from a lurid revival of

Dracula added their own panache. Eugenia championed the boy's unorthodox approach to interior design and, to show her support, sewed him a blood-red quilt to throw over the equity cot they'd dragged up the Scarsenguard's narrow stairwells.

Yet even with his own morbid hideaway, August still felt that something was missing from his life. He needed a new stimulus, a new adventure. Perhaps coming into contact with so many brave young men risking their lives had rubbed off on him, or maybe, now that he'd reached the ripe age of somewhere around eleven, it was simply time for a change. Whatever it was, one night in September, when the bustle of the bistro seemed too much to bear, August sat alone in his room, finding no escape in his books. He missed the sensation of watching live theatre. He longed to see a scorned wife poison her husband or some wealthy family squabble over the contents of a will. Or better still, a swordfight.

Sitting on his bed, knees curled up to his chest, August pondered the small window, the only one in his room. He knew that next door to the Scarsenguard was another theater called the Walsh. Could he somehow make his way over in time for curtain?

The thought was at once dismissed as entirely ludicrous, yet seemingly independent of this conclusion, he found his trembling hands gripping for purchase on his window frame. With a yelp and a hearty tug, August lifted the ancient thing, and a September breeze, the kind that carried more than a hint of autumn on it, poured over his face like cool water.

What on earth am I doing? he thought as he contorted his body to crawl through the opening. His last sojourn into the city had been catastrophic. *But that was down at ground level.* The loopy iron trellises of the fire escape were now firmly under his palms, and as he gave them a steadying grip, wine-red rust flaked off the railings, floating lazily to the street below. He was outside! Outside! Once his eyes adjusted to the sheer brightness of Forty-Third Street, August saw that the Walsh wasn't the only other theater on the block. There was a second, and good god, a third! Their names, the Lockwood and the Graff, were lit up in bright bulbs, and hordes of people were making their way into all of them, waving and smiling at the soldiers who were loitering outside the Scarsenguard, waiting for the bistro to start swinging.

There was so much to take in, but buildings blocked most of August's sight line.

"Imagine the view from the roof," he whispered, and flew up the treacherous metal stairs. To his dismay, the fire escape ended at the fifth floor; there was no access to the roof. August employed some of the more colorful verbiage he'd learned at the bistro before noticing that the bright sign of the Scarsenguard protruded from the mortar ever so slightly. Slipping his dexterous fingers into the crevices that surrounded the blazing brilliance of the lit-up letter *C*, August was able to gain purchase and start his ascent. The boy had no fear of heights; he'd been scaling curtains barehanded since he was five years old, and found the meager footholds entirely satisfactory, now leaving the *C* behind and moving up to the *S*. In less time than it would take Eugenia Butler to stitch a button to a shirt, August had hauled himself onto the roof, wiping brick grit off his trousers.

When he finally did take in the view he'd risked his life to see, August gasped. Never would he have guessed what existed just outside the walls of the Scarsenguard. So many lights! And people! And sounds! Crowds of crooked chimneys burst from rooftops like the pipes of a haunted organ. Taxicabs painted the streets a vivid yellow, honking their horns seemingly just for the pleasure of it. Buildings were so tall that August had to crane his neck to see their tops. And a half-moon hung orange over the entire scene as if debating with itself whether or not it should turn away from all this captivating madness.

The play he'd snuck out to see was completely forgotten. August stayed on the roof all night, his oddly cloistered way of life forever altered. Here was a boy who'd met Mayor La Guardia, Bette Davis, even the vice president of the United States, but who had never seen a sunrise. When the sun did start peeking over the tops of the buildings, bringing with it the ringing bells of bleary-eyed cyclists already delivering packages, August, more than a bit blurry himself, scuttled down the roof and back into the ghoulish comfort of his room. He slipped into bed, exhausted, but too giddy to fall asleep just yet.

New York City. One look, and August had fallen in love.

* * *

The allures of the world outside the Scarsenguard kept August occupied for the better part of a month. Leaping from rooftop to rooftop and startling flocks of pigeons into flight, he realized Miss Butler's warnings had been more than slightly hyperbolic. He didn't hold it against her, however. She was just trying to keep him safe, and honestly, she embroidered reality so often, August wasn't sure that she knew when she was telling the truth.

After a stretch of time, however, the novelty of fresh air and sunsets wore off, and he remembered why he'd climbed out his window in the first place: to take in a play. August discovered an unlocked window at the theater next to the Scarsenguard, the Walsh. So one fine evening he waited until a few minutes before curtain, climbed out his own window, and with a few gravity-defying leaps, slipped inside the Walsh.

Now to secure a seat. August was creeping past guests, trying to locate an empty chair he might borrow for the performance. The trouble was, how could he be sure the seat would remain vacant? People arrived at the theater woefully late.

August noticed an unoccupied box seat that had been roped off. A large column ran through the center of the box that made it impossible to see the stage, obviously a botched remodel from when the place had been converted from a vaudeville house to a proper Broadway theater. No one in their right mind would pay good money for a view so obstructed. His lucky stars thanked, August snuck by a blessedly irresponsible usher who was dozing in the hallway and squeezed himself past the column into the box, heart aflutter not from nerves but at the prospect of a play.

The curtain finally opened, and August was treated to his first bit of live drama in nearly three years. The play was entitled *A Wardrobe Full of Miracles or an Armoire Stuffed with Dreams*. At first he watched with relish, but soon he was forced to swallow the bitterest of pills. The play was bad. Terrible, even.

"Perhaps my expectations were too high," he said to himself as he passed the sleeping usher he'd snuck by earlier, hindsight revealing that the usher's slumber was not negligence but a defense mechanism against theatrical dreck. "After all, every play can't be written by Lillian Hellman." Though wouldn't it be divine if they all could?

The next night he decided to see what the Graff, another theater on the block, had to offer, but alack, the staff at this establishment seemed to have a far tighter protocol regarding security; August couldn't find even a mouse hole to crawl through.

Depressed that he would never wipe the stain of *A Wardrobe Full of Miracles or an Armoire Stuffed with Dreams* from his memory, he moped into the bistro, where he crashed into a rather oily man who couldn't have been taller than five feet.

"Watch where you're going, brat," the weasel man snarled at August.

"You watch where you're going!" August retorted, his frustration at the last two eves robbing him of his usual originality.

"What the hell is your problem?" the seedy little man shot back.

"My problem," said August, rage boiling his insides red as lobsters, "is that if what I saw last night is any indication, the state of our theatre is in such a decline that we would do better to return to the Dark Ages and swallow the sermonizing drivel of the passion plays rather than accept that tripe playing next door. Furthermore, I can't deduce whether or not *A Wardrobe Full of Miracles or an Armoire Stuffed with Dreams* is but a rarefied blemish on the face of American theatre or, as I fear, merely an example of the chronic decay of the art at large, because all the blasted windows at the Graff are locked, and I have no money of my own with which to secure a ticket!"

August's small chest was heaving after his diatribe, and several onlookers' concerns as to his well-being were only assuaged by the palatable lies of Miss Butler. "Displaced after the London bombings, the poor dear. Come, have some bourbon."

The crowd was waylaid by Miss Butler's tale, all except the dodgy gentleman to whom August had spit out his tirade in the first place.

"You need to open a window?" the man asked, barely opening his mouth.

For the first time, August took a moment to consider the soldier he'd been arguing with. There was something off about him. The man's haircut was hardly the military standard; his dark locks weren't shorn to a tight buzz but instead hung like a limp mop, exuding a certain greasiness. Then there were the medals pinned to his chest. Somehow August distrusted that this man had accumulated quite so much merit. His puny frame looked like it could hardly withstand the weight of all the acclaim he'd apparently received. And speaking of puny, the man was short. August was no giant, in fact he was small for his age, yet the boy was inching perilously close to this man's neck. Weren't there height requirements in the army?

"You're not in the army," August stated.

"And what the hell are you? CID?" said the shifty-eyed stranger as he grabbed August by the arm and pulled him into a more secluded corner of the bistro. "Now look here, I didn't understand more than half of what you just said, but it seems like you need to case this guy Graff's joint, am I right?"

August, connoisseur of cheap detective pulp, knew very well what "to case a joint" meant. He gave a reluctant nod.

"Swell. I myself need a reference of character. See that bird over there with the huge . . . personality? I try to be . . . uh . . . generous with my affections, but for some reason, she won't give me the time of day. So whaddaya say? You jerk my . . . chain . . . I'll jerk yours? Goddamn it, I can't talk to a fucking toddler!"

August gave the man a shrewd stare. "Fine," he agreed. "But you have to teach me to pick a lock, not just do it for me."

"Sure, sure," said the man, rubbing his hands together in a cartoon parody of lust. "Now let's get over there before some other charlie gets her first."

"Hold on a minute," August protested as the man literally dragged him across the bistro. "You have to teach me how to pick locks before I subject that poor woman to you."

"What the hell, kid? I can tell from all your fancy talk that you're no dumb-ass, but it's usually the wordy kind that don't got the *aptitude* for my kind of work." He stressed the word *aptitude* so hard that August was sure it was the most polysyllabic one he'd ever uttered.

"If I give you a character reference first," August countered, "you'll just go ravage her in some sordid motel without teaching me anything!"

The "soldier" stared down at August. "What's your name, kid?"

"Iago Montague," August lied. "What's yours?"

"Sergeant Sycamore," said the man, also obviously lying. "You're sharp, Iago, I'll give you that. Bring me a bobby pin. Takes you longer than two minutes, can't promise I'll still be here." And with that, Sergeant Sycamore folded into the dance floor.

Pumping his legs as fast as they could stand, August made his way to the sandwich counter and singled out the volunteer with the most elaborately desperate hairstyle.

"Please, miss!" he cried when he'd finally reached her. "I need one of your bobby pins."

"What for?" she asked, nonchalantly popping gum.

"For the war effort!" August screamed.

The girl and her friends exploded into a titter of condescending giggles. "Scram, kid," she said. "You're scaring away the big boys."

Under normal circumstances, August would never debase himself publicly. In fact, it was a point of personal pride that he'd never done so. But the art of theatre needed defending, and if there was one thing he'd learned from his acquaintances in the armed forces (other than the existence of fellatio), it was that sometimes sacrifices had to be made for the greater good.

August started crying. Not a light smattering of delicate teardrops, but a crimson-faced, snot-discharging detonation of sobs that caused even the blaring band to falter.

"Here, take one," said the gum-smacker, casting furtive glances about the room as she shoved bobby pins into August's hand. "Take them all."

August's onslaught of tears instantly ceased, his face now determined as he dashed off to find Sergeant Sycamore, the calming falsehoods of Miss Butler fading into the background as he ran. "Poor child, they had it the hardest in Leningrad. Vodka, anyone?"

The dance floor was sardine-tin-packed as always, full of burly military frames and the swirling skirts of off-duty volunteers. Owing to the crowd, August couldn't find the so-called sergeant anywhere. Securing the bobby pins had taken more time than he'd anticipated, but surely Sycamore hadn't already left. August doubted there was a living woman who would willingly go home with the man, but perhaps there were some women of the night here. Oh, how dreadful if a prostitute were to shatter August's plans of learning to break and enter!

At the height of his panic, August caught sight of Sergeant Sycamore relieving an air force commander of his wallet.

"I've got the pins," August said, the sound of his voice causing the pilot to swing around and catch Sycamore in his act of theft.

"What's going on here?" he asked, noticing his wallet in another man's hands.

Sycamore offered August a withering curl of his lip before saying, "Just caught this little brat trying to lift your billfold, sir. Be careful, New York is full of these unsavory sorts." As he handed back the wallet to the officer, August watched Sycamore peel away a twenty with a magician's finesse. Before this misdemeanor was noted, Sycamore grabbed August and dragged him out of the bistro.

"This bit of skirt better be worth the trouble you're putting me through, kid." Sycamore slipped and ducked through the halls and stairwells of the Scarsenguard until he came upon the door that led to the safe where the evening's ticket sales were kept. He jiggled the doorknob, smiled when it didn't catch, held out an open palm to August, who quickly supplied a bobby pin, and set to work.

"Window's too advanced for a greenhorn like you," he explained, straightening out the bobby pin and inserting it into the keyhole. "Most of them won't open even if they are unlocked, things are so damn rusted, and if they are high quality, you need a crowbar or some glass cutters, but then you're leaving a trail. For your purposes, you're gonna want to find a door."

"They teach you all this in the army?" August questioned with a skeptical arch of his eyebrow.

"Sure, kid. In basic, right after a pair of redheads play 'The Star-Spangled Banner' on your kazoo."

The door clicked open.

"Now watch closely, 'cause next time, you're on your own."

Sycamore went slower, breaking down the purpose of each jostle. "Locks are like ladies," he disclosed. "Each one is different, but if you turn 'em the right way, they open up every time." Though August was sickened by the casual misogyny, he had to admit Sycamore had some showmanship; as if on cue, the door unfastened as soon as he'd finished his crude analogy.

"Okay," said Sycamore, "I'm gonna lock the room from the inside and wait for you to open it up. Shout out any questions." He disappeared behind the door, latching it behind him.

As he'd been shown, August straightened out the bobby pin and stuck it into the lock. After a twist or two, nothing happened. He shimmied the pin violently in frustration.

"You trying to break the door down?" Sycamore admonished from behind it. "Take it nice and slow, or you'll snap the damn pin in the lock."

August let out a steadying sigh and then tried to apply the advice. Nothing was happening, though. It felt like he wasn't doing anything but twiddling a stick through a puddle of mud, not that he'd had much experience with such bucolic pastimes, but he'd read his fair share of Twain and felt the simile apt.

Just as he was about to recommence his shake-with-reckless-abandon strategy, he met the slightest resistance against the pin. Careful not to lose his tenuous advantage, August pressed the pin a little farther and was sure he felt the tumbler shifting, almost as if he were balancing a repelling magnet atop another. Ever so gently, he continued to apply pressure until he heard the telltale click, and the door swung open. Beaming, August was greeted with the sight of an equally ecstatic Sycamore, who, the boy just now realized, had been unsupervised in a locked room that contained the Scarsenguard's safe. There wasn't much to take; the theater hadn't had a play running in years, so there was no money from ticket sales. Still, Sycamore's pockets looked somehow heavier than they had before he entered.

"Way to go, kid. You'll be a felon in no time. Now let's go find that broad."

"I want to give it another shot," said August, bending another pin into shape.

"No way. I said I'd teach you to pick a lock, not give you a master class. I upheld my part of the bargain." The sergeant was filled with such righteous indignation that August suspected this may have been the first time he'd ever seen a promise through and intended to capitalize on being sanctimonious while he could.

"Fine." August sighed. "Lead me to the unfortunate soul. Though her womanhood will be stained forevermore after tonight, I am nothing if not true to my word."

"Jesus, Montague, you really are something."

As they wound their way back down to the bistro, Sergeant Sycamore kept trying to coach August on what to say.

"Maybe tell her I adopted you from a real run-down orphanage. Or cry a little and tell her I saved your kitty cat from a tree."

"You have already tried your hand at impressing the lady and have failed most miserably. Please, leave the seduction to me."

Back in the bistro, Sycamore scanned the room before finding his intended. "There she is! The one with jugs for days! Er . . . bosoms. Bosoms for days."

August spotted her. She did indeed have impressive bosoms, though that may have been her only commendable attribute. Her hair was the tackiest shade of bottled blond, her cheeks painted a most garish pink. Her skirt was too short, her heels too high. August was not one to judge on appearances, but he was only human.

"She's an angel," whispered Sycamore.

"Quite," said August.

"Now remember, she doesn't like it when you come on too strong . . ."

But August had already left his comrade behind, transforming into character as he crossed the room.

The woman was honking loudly to some poor private about the specific qualities of her perfume. The private nodded vaguely, eyes glued to her cleavage. August feared he might be too late but pressed ahead, charging headlong into the woman.

"Son of a bitch!" she cried.

"Sacrebleu!" August shouted in tandem.

"Huh?" said the woman, most eloquently.

August had decided that a blind French child would be the best way to win this woman over. The blindness would gain her sympathy, while being French would lend him a seductive air of mystery. So he opened his eyes as wide as they would go, determined not to blink, and stared at the space just to the right of her face. "I am so sorry, madame," he began in an impeccable French dialect he had perfected when *Henry V* ran at the Scarsenguard, "I didn't see you there. Alas, I have not seen anything in years, not since the damned Germans invaded fair Paris." Here he let out a sigh.

"Whadda ya mean, ya can't see nothing?" she asked, massaging the shin that had taken the brunt of August's blow.

He'd thought that his skill at appearing blind would be enough, but he hadn't counted on the fact that this poor woman was unaccustomed to men making eye contact with her. August would have to be blunt. "I am blind, madame. Blinded by the Germans."

She gasped, then clapped loudly near the boy's face—to test his blindness, August supposed. "Geez, I guess you are blind. But what are you doing in a place like this?"

"Ah, you have come to the heart of the matter, madame. I am lost! Très lost!"

"Oh no," she cried, hands gripping her cheeks. Then she sneezed and stared vacantly into space, all memory of her current conversation seemingly obliterated.

"Madame," August continued, snapping in her ears to regain her attention, "you must help me."

"Excuse me," she said, "but I'm a mademoiselle, not a madame." She waggled her left hand at August, displaying the lack of a wedding ring.

August sighed. "I am blind and cannot see what you are doing."

"I'm unmarried!" she shouted, employing the tactic of volume.

August decided to apply some of the sensuality the French were known for. "Ah, madame, a mademoiselle is simply a maid unschooled in the ways of love. You have clearly been studying the art of love for quite some time."

What was meant to be a modest giggle but in all actuality was closer to a donkey's bray burst from her mouth. "How can you tell?" she asked.

August decided a lie was, in this case, kinder than the obvious truth. "Madame, a Frenchman, he always knows." He gave her a sly wink. Do blind people wink? Too late; he would own his choices! "You must help me, my fair coquette! I have become lost from the man who saved me from the evil beady-eyed Germans!"

"You mean, the man who saved you is here?" she cried, breathless with excitement.

"Oui! His name is Sergeant Sycamore, and a braver man has never lived."

"What's going on over here, anyways?" said Sycamore as he sidled into the conversation, dripping with lust.

"Scram, creep," the blonde said. "We're looking for a Sergeant Sycamore. Saved this here kid's life."

"But, madame," August interjected, "this is Sergeant Sycamore himself!"

"This guy?" she asked, her disappointment on full display.

"Be not so quick to judge. War is never fair, and it has been particularly unkind to Sergeant Sycamore's appearance."

"Come on, kid!"

"But when he rescued me, killing a roomful of Germans in the process, he was the very picture of swarthy shapeliness."

"What, you could see then?" she asked.

"Er . . . yes, but I was blinded right afterward by a fire set by the Germans to smoke us out. Sycamore saved me from that fire, too."

"Yeah, sure, and I killed forty Germans that time!"

August stared at Sycamore straight in his eyes. "Forty? Really?"

"Yeah, forty. With only a grenade and three bullets. It's how I got all these here medals," he said, indicating his bronze-laden chest.

"Those sure are shiny," said the blonde in complete and utter seriousness.

"Not as shiny as my heart felt after saving this here kid."

August had to remove himself from the conversation at this point.

The next night, however, he was blessing Sergeant Sycamore as he unlocked the rooftop door to the Graff. After only a few minutes of loitering, August was able to sneak past the usher.

While the interiors of the Scarsenguard and the Walsh were both lovely, the Graff was breathtaking. As he waited for the play to start, August flipped through a pilfered *Playbill*. Tonight's offering was entitled *Red, White and True*. Though he generally deplored puns as a rule, over the past few years August had become highly patriotic, and he was willing to overlook a saccharine title in the name of camaraderie and good, clean American fun.

After eons, the lights dimmed and the curtains opened. Two scenes in, and August would've sold Roosevelt himself to the first passing German if only this abortion of a play would cease. The playwright was hawking sentimental drivel, determined to wring the audience dry of its every tear. There was such a thing as restraint. In the final act, when the soldier returned home one-legged to his adoring wife, only to be shot by a vengeful Italian as soon as the reunited couple embraced, August stood, took off his shoes, loudly clicked the heels together, and announced, "I am done with this place."

He crawled back along the drainpipes and crooked chimneys to his bedroom, where he tried to clear his head by rereading *King Lear*, but alas, the stench of the substandard still befouled his senses. The boy tossed the play aside with a frustrated howl, punched his pillow, and then fell into a troubled sleep. It was that night that August was forced to accept the sad fact that someday all humanity must: sometimes art is just a great big pile of shit.

* * *

Nineteen forty-four died, and 1945 rose from its ashes. August had given up sneaking into nearby theaters; he didn't think his constitution could withstand one more fiasco. Instead, he set his mind to becoming the most proficient lockpick under the age of twenty. Deadbolts, padlocks, wall mounts, and doorknobs all trembled when August approached, pin extended, the tip of his tongue curling over his upper lip in concentration. He did exhaustive research on Houdini and had Miss Butler bring him some, in her opinion, dismally dull literature on security manufacture from the New York Public Library. By late February, not a single lock in the

Scarsenguard could best August save for the safe, and he was reading up on that.

Germany surrendered in May, and the Backstage Bistro threw its most riotous party yet wherein August, smashingly drunk, kissed a well-known actress onstage to the tumultuous cheers of the gathered military personnel. A photo of the kiss became quite famous, even appearing in *Harper's Bazaar*. The actress was none other than Vivian Fair, and had the public, which devoured the picture so greedily, known that the subjects of the photograph were actually mother and son, the photo would probably have caused an even greater stir, albeit for different, more taboo, reasons.

Summer melted into August (the month, not the boy) and eventually, two catastrophically persuasive bombs were dropped on Japan.

"It's over!" cried Miss Butler as she burst into August's room, upsetting a fern in her elation.

"What is?" August asked, not looking up from his novel.

"The war, you insufferable child! Japan's surrendered. Now get dressed! We're going out!"

For all his prepubescent ennui, the fact that the war had ended did cause August to jump on his bed and let out more than a few hoots and huzzahs. He was in the midst of a fist-pumping leap when the rest of Miss Butler's announcement finally registered.

Going out? As in outside? He'd left the Scarsenguard before, but aside from his disastrous first attempt, his escapades had been strictly rooftop affairs, private wanderings that belonged to no one but the city and himself. But Miss Butler slipped August into an altered suit, splashed some water on his face, and led him out the front door of the theater into a world he'd never known, as if it were nothing.

"Stop gaping, dear, you look like a tourist," Miss Butler chastised, gripping his hand in her gloved one, pulling him through Times Square. She was positively beaming, dressed in a festive yellow frock that made her look ten years younger.

Didn't she understand that he'd never been outside in daylight before? Never seen an operating storefront? Upon further consideration, August realized that Miss Butler probably wasn't aware of these facts. Her memory had been faulty for decades, and seeing as how she had surpassed the hundred-year milestone a year or two before, it would be unfair to expect her to remember such a trivial thing as keeping a boy inside a theater for the entirety of his life.

But August couldn't help but gawk. Everyone was smiling, laughing, talking; there were so many people! A girl with dark curly hair right around his age ran up and hugged him. August was dumbfounded. He'd hardly ever interacted with anyone in his peer group, let alone had a girl embrace him.

He was fishing for something to say to this wonderful person when the girl's mother appeared and grabbed her hand. "Sorry, she's just excited. I guess we all are!"

He watched the pair walk away, feeling a pang of loss when the girl's dark hair finally disappeared into the crowd.

His melancholy hardly lasted a minute; Miss Butler led August all over that day, chattering so ceaselessly that August feared she might asphyxiate. She bought him every sort of treat: cotton candy, ice cream, roasted almonds, hot dogs; the world, it seemed, was chock-full of sugar and simmering meats. Due to the sandwiches available at the bistro, August hadn't gone hungry for years, but he'd never lost the scavenger's mentality bred into him during his youth. He devoured whole each culinary delight he was offered.

When Miss Butler finally led him home at dusk, August collapsed in his bed, overstimulated, overfed, and exhausted, vowing to return to the outside world as soon as possible.

* * *

August was unable to fulfill his pledge as quickly as he would have liked, however, for the very day after the bombings, Mr. Barreth, the Scarsenguard's mustachioed owner, came plowing through the building, shouting demands. Though August had intended to sneak out into New York's streets, he felt it his duty to oversee the overseer lest the latter make a muck of things.

The Backstage Bistro, home to a thousand glittering parties, was already being disassembled. The decadent canvas, the gossamer glass lanterns, and the perfectly intimate stage were all being unromantically and, in August's opinion, rather disrespectfully removed or repurposed. A few years back, nothing would have delighted the boy more than the bistro's demise, but against his will, he'd come to love it.

"Get it all out of here," Barreth yelled, a smile distorting his face. "Isn't this wonderful?" he said to a nearby secretary. "The Scarsenguard can start making me money again! And no more darkies in my theater!"

So the decision to make the bistro unsegregated, a decision that had received heaps of mostly positive press, had obviously not been Barreth's. August was anything but surprised.

"I've got plans for this place," Barreth mumbled to himself, the grotesque smile growing ever wider.

Despite the sting of mourning he felt at seeing the bistro being so coarsely dismantled, August couldn't help but feel excited. Continuing to eavesdrop on Barreth, he overheard that a play, already rehearsing, was scheduled to start previews at the Scarsenguard in September. What bliss!

It turned out that the new play was a light, silly thing called *Flirty Bertie*. Seemingly after their sons and daughters had been killed overseas, people didn't have the stomach for tragedy. Still, *Flirty Bertie* was less loathsome than the offerings of the other theaters on the block, and August, in his reclaimed cubby above the spotlight, had watched every rehearsal and preview performance to date.

The young actor who played Bertie was named Avery Guy. Mr. Guy was currently locked in a terrible struggle with reality: he believed his waist to be a few inches smaller and his chest a few inches larger, while facts kept insisting otherwise. Miss Butler, back in the saddle as the Scarsenguard's stalwart laundress, was forced to listen to Avery's every complaint, and though she would wave a tape measure in the actor's face, indicating exactly what his measurements were, the young man was nothing if not persistent.

"Be a pal," he'd say, flashing his smile, flicking his eyes over her shoulder to see if he could beam his gorgeous teeth at anyone else.

And so she sewed, getting her revenge by taking in the pants several inches more than Avery Guy had requested.

"Let's see him squeeze his way into these," she murmured to herself.

It was a stupid thing to do. Eugenia knew she'd just have to let them out again the next day, but it was these quiet mutinies that kept a person sane, and so she threaded the needle, in and out, each new stitch an act of revolution.

Pulling the needle, Eugenia carelessly pricked her finger, a hazard of her profession, but a mistake she generally avoided. Worse yet, a tiny globule of blood fell from her finger and landed on the pants, which were of course white. The splatter was too noticeable to be left alone. Normally a little spit would take a blood stain right out, but her mouth was too dry to muster even a tendril of saliva, so she'd need to run the pants under cold water before she could continue her war against the waistline.

"Son of a bitch," she said.

Last words are a funny thing. They can't be planned or rehearsed and are more often than not unintelligible babble. But a person's final thoughts are even stranger. What should one think about at the end of their life? Miss Butler, who'd lived more than a century, had witnessed many world-changing events that might constitute one last moment of reflection. The Civil War. Prohibition. The crash. The Chrysler Building, and then the Empire State. She'd been buying stockings when a teller told her that the *Titanic* had sunk.

But none of these affairs were personal. True, they'd shaped the country, but they hadn't necessarily shaped Eugenia. So as her life neared its final moments, should she consider contemplating one of the smaller incidents of her existence, something uniquely hers, that still stuck out after all the years, red as a wagon after a rain? Perhaps the time her teacher, Mrs. Wilson, had called her foolish in front of the rest of her class, a flashback that could still bring a blush to her face, was a memory of merit. Or there was the terrier mutt she'd grown up with, so bored by fetch. What about Alan Conrad, who died in Virginia? Eugenia still wondered if he'd gotten that last letter she'd written.

And then of course, there was the night she found a baby in a basket of dirty blouses. Surely August, the greatest joy of her long life, deserved one final fleeting recollection, a misty reminiscence before death claimed her.

Alas, life is cruel, and Eugenia Butler's final thought was not of her beloved August, but of cold water and spit. She fell to the ground, dead at the overripe age of one hundred and three.

August, already squatting in his secret cubby, never saw the body. At intermission, he decided to stretch his legs and skip the second act, having seen it many times already. Careful to avoid contact with anyone, a habit he was having trouble readjusting to, August only accidentally discovered that his surrogate mother was dead through the hushed, excitable whispers of two cast members hurrying up a stairwell.

At first, he wouldn't believe it. After all, every death he'd ever witnessed had been played by an actor. The grief ended at curtain call when the performers came back and took their bows. And hadn't Miss Butler yelled at him earlier that day for being a precocious smart aleck? That woman, so full of punch and vigor, couldn't be gone. This was just her brief exit. Soon he'd hear her throaty laugh again, or she'd come rushing round a corner to demand he help her find a pincushion. She wasn't gone, though. She wasn't dead.

He wandered without knowing where his feet took him. Where should he go now? Who should he tell? What was he going to do? August felt tight and hot, like the walls were pressing in. This couldn't be happening. He couldn't think about this.

In a snap, August decided he would watch the rest of the play after all and rushed back to his cubby, determined to forget the whole thing. But as Avery Guy struggled through the play in his not-quite-finished, too-tight trousers, the weight of what he'd heard pressed down on August heavy as a curtain.

A memory came unbidden. August was younger, five perhaps, and sat curled under the crook of Miss Butler's arm, his little torso resting against her thigh and hip. She was reading aloud to him—what exactly, he couldn't remember, but that didn't matter. Something about Miss Butler's voice soothed him. It was rich and thick with sweet flavor, like taffy left too long in a pocket.

August hadn't been fully listening to the story, enjoying the comfort of the ritual more than the intricacies of the plot. Instead, his mind wandering, he was pinching at the couch they sat on. It was brown with a tiny white pattern printed across the fabric. The shapeless white designs that speckled the couch had always looked to August like little peanuts, and he loved to pretend to pluck them off the cushions and eat them.

Lost in his game, it took him a moment to realize that Miss Butler had fallen asleep, her mouth wide open and her neck bent painfully backward. August jabbed his bony child's elbow into her side.

"What? What is it?" Eugenia asked as she came awake.

"You fell asleep."

"Did I? Oh, I'm so sorry, dear. Now where were we?"

She picked up reading, and August went back to picking his peanuts.

A perfect memory.

Grief assaulted him. Still hidden in his cubby, August wept, and his unrestrained, naked agony was heard throughout the theater.

Mythology surrounding the Scarsenguard Spirit had all but died, what with the bustle of war. The legend was reborn that night, however. Attending the play that evening had been joyless theatre critic Margaret Clarke. Her scathing reviews were not known for their sentimentality, but the next day, an abnormally atypical article appeared in the *Times*.

> I know not what to say. Never in my life have I been so affected by a play as I have by "Flirty Bertie." Act 1 was an unintentional tragedy, brimming with farcical tropes that would make even a troglodyte check his watch. However, as the curtain lifted on the second act, something . . . otherworldly occurred. Even as I write it I feel foolish, but know this, dear reader: I was chilled to my very core.

Needless to say, Clarke's review was the talk of the town, and *Flirty Bertie* was an overnight smash. August, who usually followed the ups and downs of the Scarsenguard's productions with the solemnity of a priest at last rites, took no notice. Instead, he wandered the Scarsenguard, listless and empty, embodying the ghost he'd portrayed for so long without the aid of costume, flour, or chains.

Miss Butler was dead, and he was a boy, lost.

* * *

"My dear boy," said Sir Reginald, shoving a pastrami sandwich in his mouth, "you cannot live in the Scarsenguard forever."

August and Percyfoot were in a pragmatic deli on Ninth Avenue, autumnal sunlight streaking in through the large glass windows, casting shadows of backward letters on the deli's linoleum floor.

It was October 9, August's adopted birthday, and Percyfoot had come in from Los Angeles for the occasion, though the train cross-country hadn't been cheap. A month had passed since Miss Butler's death. When Percyfoot asked how the funeral was, he received the heartbreaking reply that August didn't know; he hadn't been invited, because no one knew he existed.

August surprised Percyfoot yet again by agreeing that he should leave the Scarsenguard. "But where am I to go?" he asked.

Truthfully, Sir Reginald could think of no better location for the boy. To send him into the care of the government would be criminal. There was no doubt that August's upbringing had been unconventional, but it had been genteel and pampered in its way. Throw him into a state-owned orphanage with boys who'd been shuttled in and out of foster care for the entirety of their lives, and the poor lad would get eaten alive.

August mumbled something.

"What was that, child? Speak up. We didn't spend hours on your vocal exercises to have you stammering like a simpleton."

"I said, could I come live with you?"

Sir Reginald inhaled sharply. Here was a dilemma. Financially speaking, he could take the boy in. But then he'd need to legally adopt August, and truthfully, Percyfoot was worried about the contractual quagmire that would entail. The authorities might look into his personal life and uncover things better left private. Not to mention the fact that Percyfoot enjoyed his unencumbered lifestyle. To suddenly have full custody of a child would certainly change the way he operated. Best to leave August safely tucked into the Scarsenguard for now; as soon as his next picture wrapped, he would find a suitable home for the child.

"My dear boy, I just don't think it would work."

August finished off his egg salad sandwich, the sour bite of pumpernickel he usually savored given nothing but a perfunctory swallow. Percyfoot sighed, the last few bits of his pastrami uneaten as well. What a mess this boy was in. They walked back to the Scarsenguard, chatted joylessly for an hour or so, before Percyfoot returned to his hotel and grabbed a cab to the train station.

"It will work itself out," he said to himself over and over again during the long first leg to Chicago, a mantra, a prayer.

It did indeed work itself out, though not as anyone had expected. Due to Margaret Clarke's controversial review, everyone in the entire entertainment industry had seen *Flirty Bertie*. Almost everyone agreed it was nothing but pointless fluff, and because of this, almost everyone agreed it should be made into a movie. The film rights for *Bertie* were secured, and Avery Guy was set to star. August was relieved. Perhaps if Mr. Guy's toothsome sorcery was absent, the play would have no legs to stand on and be forced to close, leaving room for another, more respectable offering to take its place.

August's predictions turned out to be only half true. After the departure of Avery Guy, the play quickly folded. What happened next, however, was a surprise.

The dreadful owner of the Scarsenguard, Mr. Barreth, came pounding through the theater. Would it really be so difficult to, even slightly, censor his footfalls?

Through corner ducking and a masterful usage of staircase banisters, August was able to spy out the reason for his nemesis's visit.

"We'll clear all this out," Barreth said in his blasphemous baritone, nearly swatting one of his underlings in the face as he waved at the Scarsenguard's impressive prop closet. "Do some sort of auction. Some idiot's bound to buy this shit. In any case, we won't need any of it in the hotel."

Hotel? Surely August had misheard. Later, hidden inside a wooden sarcophagus left over from a production called *Lust in Luxor*, he was able to piece out a bit more. The worst was confirmed.

"This will all be kitchens," came the muffled boom of Mr. Barreth, "and staff quarters and all that rubbish. We can make those small, cut corners where we can. We'll repurpose some of the chandeliers to save a buck. I'm going to make a mint on this place. Don't know what the hell my father ever got into the theater racket for in the first place. Art's for old biddies and queers. Give me a hotel! A big beautiful hotel!"

Unbelievable. Mr. Barreth planned on turning the Scarsenguard into a hotel? A hotel, of all things! Imagine, tourists befouling the air that was the rightful property of actors and directors and stagehands and playwrights! August's slight chest heaved in righteous indignation. Barreth, as the owner of the theater, was supposed to be a champion of the arts! Was the Scarsenguard nothing to him but a purblind cow to be milked for cash? A swollen sow slaughtered for coinage? This was profane, an atrocity. It could not be.

"For shame, Barreth!" August cried, bursting from the sarcophagus in his anger. "Leave this place and never return!"

"The spirit!" Mr. Barreth screamed. He sprinted to the nearest exit, his tribe of flunkies right behind.

After his divine fury cooled, August was rather pleased with himself. He'd defended his territory, villains be damned! He went to bed that night feeling happy for the first time since Miss Butler had died.

Dawn, however, brought grave tidings. August thought his outburst had frightened Barreth off for good, but alas, as the timid new day streaked light across August's bedroom, the boy stretched and went to the window. What he saw astounded him. Outside, standing at the ready, was a team of wrecking balls and a crew of thirty men. It seemed Barreth was determined to build his hotel, and the faster he could bury the Scarsenguard and its spirit, the better.

August rubbed sleep from his eyes, willing the demolition crew to be nothing but a horrid nightmare, but when the muck from his eyes had cleared, the crew remained. My god! Could this really be happening?

As if in answer to his unvoiced question, August heard a familiar bellow from an open window. "Hurry, boys!" screeched Mr. Barreth. "She won't tear herself down!"

If the hired crew was confused by Barreth's ferocious vendetta against a building, they put up a good show of hiding it. Most were former soldiers grateful for a job, so they followed orders.

The wrecking ball was being readied, pulled back as far as the narrowness of Forty-Third Street would allow, and still August refused to believe. Surely there would be some last-minute reprieve? August would've even welcomed a perfectly timed deus ex machina, a plot device he'd been known to lambaste at length. But the giant steel ball continued its unhurried backward climb, and all the boy could do was watch in openmouthed horror.

Its rise complete, the ball hung malevolently in the air for half a minute, an ominous god of ruin surveying the landscape. August thought to offer it a prayer or sacrifice, anything to stop its course, but before he could lay an offering at the base of the crane, the ball was released, surging through the air with hateful relish. Only when it finally hit, the sound of the impact so loud it nearly deafened the boy, did it occur to August that he needed to leave the building. If he didn't, he would be killed.

The crash had thrown him to the ground and scrambled his orientation. When he finally regained his footing, the wrecking ball had already rounded back for another collision, and August was hurled to the floor again, skidding forward on his stomach and crashing his head into the frame of the equity cot.

He was still on the ground when another blow hit the theater. They were already using two wrecking balls? This was happening too fast!

"Tear it down!" came the maddened cries of Barreth through the open window.

August forced himself to gather his senses. Should he take anything? What did he need? Another heavy thrust of the ball knocked the wind out of him as he was sent veering across the room. Desperately, he remembered the rats and mice, his first childhood friends. Where would they go?

Where will YOU go, you fool?

Valid point.

Dust rained from the ceiling. He could hear the walls creaking and moaning in protest. Another jarring wallop shook the building.

"That's it, boys! Bring the fucker down!"

Almost by accident, his frantic eyes settled on an old pincushion. Miss Butler's. Reality hit him, hard as the wrecking balls smashing the Scarsenguard. His home, his life. The Backstage Bistro, the countless plays. Was it really all turning to dust?

Before his emotions could overwhelm him, August dashed out the window to the fire escape. Here, clutching the brick walls of the Scarsenguard, he had no time to think. True, August was a confident climber, skilled as a monkey, but one false move, one errant crumb of sentimentality, would send him plummeting down to Forty-Third Street. It was time to turn off his mind and let his body take over. Hand over hand. Foot on brick. Instinct and reflex were all he allowed himself.

He was making good progress when a particularly crushing smash from the wrecking ball nearly knocked August from the building. He clutched a protruding brick with one sweaty hand, the rest of his body dangling freely. Calling upon all the dormant strength in his stringy muscles, he heaved his weight back at the Scarsenguard, clutching at the bricks. A desperate grab with his free hand, and August was able to secure himself on the building's wall. Momentarily safe, he was still for a second, eyes wide, breath wild, like a squirrel halfway up a tree, grateful to have escaped the jaws of the Labrador.

He gladly would've stayed there all day, the rest of his life even, but he knew he had to keep moving. Swallowing his terror, he scurried up the facade before the crew could launch another strike. He hauled himself onto the roof just as one of the balls hit again and knocked him to his knees. Still there was no time for pause; the weight of the Scarsenguard was shifting beneath him. There was no telling how long the roof would hold; it might collapse at any second, plunging August back into the unstable innards of the theater, from which he might never escape. Picking himself up, August leapt the short distance to the neighboring building, then the next, then the next. As he skipped across the skyline, a wrecking ball slammed, and though he felt the impact, he wasn't thrown to the ground. Nearly collapsing with relief, August stopped, knowing he was out of immediate danger.

Only then did he allow himself to turn around and watch, but the sight brought him no comfort. From his new viewpoint, August could see that several chunks of the Scarsenguard were already missing, exposing the interior of his home to the elements. All day long he watched as Barreth pummeled the beautiful Scarsenguard, every crash of the wrecking balls taking away another piece of his life. Then, just before dusk, she finally fell.

He'd never even said goodbye.

PART TWO

The first night, it rained. Of course it rained. Still, August couldn't leave the rooftop. After the Scarsenguard fell, he watched the downpour pelt her rubble.

Blow, winds, and crack your cheeks! Rage! Blow!
You cataracts and hurricanoes, spout
Till you have drench'd our steeples, drown'd the cocks!

Had he just said that? Or had he simply thought it? Or had he screamed it?

Hours passed. It was time to leave. Before he could lose his courage, August turned his back to the corpse of the Scarsenguard and walked away, stepping across the slick rooftops. He needed distance. He needed space. He needed to forget his reality, which with the swing of a wrecking ball had gone through an inalterable seismic shift.

Who is it that can tell me who I am?

"Don't think of that. Don't think of anything," August whispered.

But his head was so clouded, and there was so much to consider. Where would he go? How would he eat? Where would he sleep? Where was Sir Reginald? Would he ever find him?

Who is it that can tell me who I am?

It was no use. He couldn't quiet his racing mind. August decided he might as well get out of the rain, and curled his soaking body up against a chimney. As he pressed into this makeshift shelter, avoiding the worst of the storm, tears came unbidden, mixing with the rainwater streaking down his face. He surrendered to his fears and sobbed, a little boy lost on a rooftop.

This cold night will turn us all to fools and madmen.

Where would he go?

Nothing will come of nothing.

Miss Butler was gone.

The grief hath crazed my wits.

Where was Sir Reginald?

Who is it that can tell me who I am?

Would he ever find him?

Never, never, never, never, never.

Who is it that can tell me who I am?
Who is it that can tell me who I am?
Who is it that can tell me who I am?

* * *

When August woke, he felt hollow yet lucid. A night of weeping had emptied him out, but with the emptiness came a certain clarity: Sir Reginald would find him. If August could just scrape by until then, he'd be fine. This shred of hope settled him, and now that the issue of his homelessness was, if not resolved, momentarily put on hold, he could attend to the next most pressing point. Food.

He shuffled off the building, weak from his crying jag, but safely landed squarely in the heart of Times Square. Say what you will about that wretched hive of bustle; it always had plenty of food. But how to get it?

A fruit stand on the corner of Forty-Fourth caught August's eye, particularly the basket full of plump peaches.

"Excuse me," August said to the vendor, "how much for a peach?"

"Just one? It'll run you a dime."

August hardly knew why he'd asked; he didn't have a cent to his name. Still, he went through the pantomime of patting his pockets, checking for loose change.

"Oh," he finally sighed.

The fruit seller was no softhearted saint, but August did look particularly waifish and pathetic. He cracked.

"How 'bout a nickel? You got a nickel?"

August shook his head.

"Look, I can't just start giving away peaches, or else every bum on the block—"

"I understand," August interjected, salvaging a bit of his dignity.

"Come back when you've got a nickel."

So he'd need a job. August was savvy enough to know that he didn't have many practical skills, but surely he could sell his labor somewhere and earn a small sum of money?

August walked into a locksmith's.

"I'd like to earn a nickel," he announced.

"And I'd like to retire," the locksmith countered.

"Then perhaps we can both help the other achieve—"

"Get the hell out of here."

A pharmacy and shoeshine yielded similarly unsatisfactory results. August remained unnickeled.

Panic was mounting, which wouldn't do. Panic might open up the torrent of emotions just barely being held at bay. The simple, straightforward task of earning a nickel was anchoring August, but if he couldn't even do that, then what? Would he starve? What was he going to do?

August snapped out of his dismay when he found that he'd aimlessly wandered into the midst of a small crowd. Hungry though he might be, the familiarity of a large group assembled to spectate kindled some primal comfort in August, and he couldn't resist trying to make out what all the fuss was about.

Snaking through legs and under arms, August was able to secure a more advantageous position within the mob. A street magician was the object of all the attention, and August, having been spoiled by masters of sleight of hand at the Backstage Bistro, watched the proceedings with a condescending air. The magician, a tiny man with oily hair, wasn't half bad, certainly good enough for the likes of these tourists, but his tricks were quite pedestrian, and his unctuous manner, brash and uncouth, albeit strangely familiar, rubbed August the wrong way. After a few minutes, August dismissed the whole thing as far too plebian and started shouldering his way out of the audience.

Find food.

He'd only moved a few feet when he caught the scent of roasted nuts wafting from a nearby blazer pocket. A brief interior moral debate fluttered within his breast, but as is often the case, survival trumped scruples. With one fluid flick of his wrist, August stole the almonds and snuck out of the crowd, popping a few into his mouth as he did so, nearly fainting from pleasure.

The magician's show was over, but August hardly noticed as the onlookers dispersed. He had set to licking the paper bag that held the almonds, musing that the nickel hadn't been necessary after all, when a rough hand grabbed his shoulder.

"Just what the hell do you think you're doing?"

August, who'd fully expected to see the man from whom he'd stolen, was surprised to find he was being battered by none other than the street magician. He was even more surprised when he recognized him.

"Sergeant Sycamore?" August cried.

"Who?" replied the magician, genuinely befuddled.

"You're Sergeant Sycamore! I met you a few years ago at the Backstage Bistro! You were trying to have sex with a blond woman and taught me how to pick locks!"

People were staring.

"What is this, a tell-all?" the magician said as he manhandled August down the street to a less crowded area. August didn't mind the rough treatment he was receiving. Here was a familiar face! Here was the Scarsenguard made flesh!

Who is it that can tell me who I am?

Free from the stares of his all-too-curious former audience, the magician backed August into the wall of a building. "Talk," he said, "and you better start making sense."

August delved into the tale of their former acquaintance. No joy lit in the magician's eyes at the recollection. Instead, he lifted August by his shoulders so that the boy's toes were dangling several feet off the ground.

"Sure, I remember you," the magician said. "You're the little rat bastard who introduced me to my wife!"

August gasped. "You married that . . . nice lady?"

The magician didn't let August down, but some of the anger left his eyes, replaced with a deep sorrow.

"She's dumber than the chewing gum stuck to my shoe." He sighed, near tears.

"But she has jugs for days!" August offered, trying to lift his captor's spirits by reminding him of the woman in question's best attribute.

"Sure, but so does a turkey, and at least those things never learned to talk. Hand to Christ, she makes a salamander look like Thomas Einstein."

"I think you mean Albert or Edison, depending."

"You're in no position to get fresh."

But it seemed Sergeant Sycamore, or whatever sobriquet he was currently adopting, had lost the last of his bite along with his bark. He released his hold on August.

"All this is beside the point," he said, shrugging back into his usual tone of flip arrogance. "What the hell were you doing moving in on my con?"

August, brushing brick dust off his shoulders, answered truthfully. "I'm afraid I have no idea what you're talking about."

"And I thought my wife was dumb. That magician thing is a front. You think I live on the money those marks put in my top hat? I got guys out in the crowd picking pockets for me. Now why don't you give me whatever it is you took, and I'll give you some change to buy a lollipop?"

Though his street smarts were admittedly low, August was nothing if not a quick study. Turning out all his pockets to prove he wasn't hiding anything, he made his move. "All I took was a bag of almonds. I need . . ." And here August struggled. What did he need? He had nothing, so he needed everything. But how could he say that? "Can you help me?" he finally managed.

The magician-sergeant scowled; generosity was clearly not his area of expertise. However, he seemed to be considering something, making cold calculations in his head. August waited him out.

"You were pretty slick lifting those almonds. Especially for a greenhorn." Here the older man took August by the chin and examined the boy, like he was a horse or a cut of meat. "And you're cute. I can use cute, even if you are sort of a freak." Here he sighed and ran a hand through his hair. "Truth be told, I'm getting sick of this magic shit anyways. How many times can you pull a quarter from behind a fat boy's ear, ya know?"

Again, August had no idea what he was talking about, but sometimes adults just liked to speak.

Finally the man offered an oily shrug. "Why not? You got the job."

"What do you mean?" August replied.

"I mean you can join the gang. Kids are good for cons."

"Are you asking me to be a professional felon?"

"What do you want, an engraved plaque?"

August didn't know what he had expected. A dollar, perhaps? Some advice? Certainly not a job offer. Should he actually join this ruffian's crime syndicate? Play Oliver Twist to his unsavory Fagin? Unimaginable as it might have been the day before, August didn't have any better options at present.

It's just until Sir Reginald comes back, he thought. A few days perhaps. Maybe a week.

"I'll do it," August stated, more confidently than he felt.

"Congrats. I'm sure your mother would be proud. I'll find you tomorrow. Start teaching you the ropes."

August fired off a stringent salute at the man he'd decided to continue calling Sycamore. "Tomorrow it is."

"I need to get my fucking head examined." Sycamore sighed as he walked away.

* * *

August spent the next week shadowing Sycamore and learning his new trade. Mostly he just annoyed his tutor with constant questions. "Where's Central Park?" "What are cross streets?" "Is being an asshole a prerequisite for driving a taxicab, or is it merely preferred?"

Sycamore usually dismissed him before noon.

So August would spend the rest of his time exploring. New York City is, for the most part, laid out in a neat little grid. The street numbers ascend as one goes north, while the avenue numbers descend as one moves east. People with a logical frame of mind find this design to be most satisfactory, as one can quickly discern which direction one's headed with a simple glance at a street sign. People who were raised in the higgledy-piggledy maze that is a theater, on the other hand, find such rationale absurd, disorienting, and more than a bit offensive. August was lost more often than not. When asking for directions, he quickly learned to profile his targets to make sure they were proper residents of the city and not tourists, who couldn't tell him where the Brooklyn Bridge was if they were standing on it. People walking dogs were usually locals, as were those carrying briefcases, but someone who looked angry at the person walking in front of them was always a guaranteed New Yorker.

When he wasn't charting the city, August filled his days loitering in Times Square, hoping to find Percyfoot. He'd mostly been camped around the ruins of the Scarsenguard until a construction team started to clear away the rubble. The sight of his precious home being loaded into dumpsters with indifferent haste was too much to bear. August vowed never to return to West Forty-Third Street lest his heart break.

The nights were harder to occupy. He'd given up stoops and began sleeping on park benches, but some of the more dedicated homeless (August still considered himself temporarily homeless) were quite territorial. After being screamed at by a man with a rat perched on his shoulder, August gave up benches as well. It was all for the best; a child sleeping on a bench generally attracted pity, and August still had a deep-seated fear of the police and social workers thanks to Miss Butler. Instead he started scaling walls and sleeping on fire escapes and rooftops.

Though he'd obtained more desirable sleeping arrangements, the nights still troubled August. It was in the night that the enormity of his situation threatened to devour him. The first few evenings he'd kept fear at bay by thinking of Percyfoot. *He'll come soon. He'll come soon.* It had been his mantra against the dark. But now nearly a week had passed with no sign of his mentor. Not an hour went by without August cursing Barreth. If it weren't for that unholy miser, he'd be sleeping on a cozy equity cot instead of massaging a stubborn cramp out of his neck while trying to fashion a blanket out of newspaper. He couldn't go on like this; hope was stretching thin.

Tears were coming, and that wouldn't do. August had been constantly terrified this entire week. He didn't want to become a man with a rat on his shoulder. He wouldn't.

August forced himself to take a deep, restorative breath. Percyfoot would rescue him, August was sure of it. But for whatever reason, Percyfoot wasn't back yet. Perhaps he'd gone on a bender and hadn't read the news. Or more likely, he was wrapped up in some film and had forgotten about everything outside his character's motivations. Whatever the reason, he wasn't here yet, and the sooner August faced that fact, the better. He needed to find a home. Sleeping on rooftops was already losing its charm, and it wasn't even winter yet. He couldn't sit around waiting for Percyfoot to find him.

When the solution came to him, he shuddered, but it was his best option, his only option. He needed to impress Sycamore so that the man would let August stay with him, just until Percyfoot returned. It was impermanent, a transitory fix, but it was what had to be done. However, there was no way Sycamore would deign to live with a delicate moppet like August. The man was too hard.

"I'll toughen up until I'm as callused as any ruffian," August promised, wiping away some tears he hadn't quite admitted were there. "Then he'll have to take me in."

For practice, August cursed at a pigeon he was sharing the roof with. "Damn you, you winged wretch! A hex on all your eggs!"

It was a start.

* * *

When August next met up with Sycamore, the magician act was back in full swing.

"There's a cop that's been trailing us around town for a while," Sycamore explained. "Wears a gray coat and hat. Haven't seen him in a week or two, but just in case, you're going to play lookout today, got it? If you see that cop, or anybody else who looks suspicious, give a whistle. The guys'll know to lay off when they hear your signal."

"I can't whistle," August admitted.

"Jesus. Well, what can you do?"

"I know all of Shakespeare's major soliloquies, and more than a few of his minor ones," August offered.

"We can't have some toddler spouting off poetry in the middle of the act. You'll steal focus."

August started to explain the difference between poems and soliloquies but then remembered his pledge to be rougher and interrupted himself by spitting.

Sycamore eyed the attempted loogie, perplexed, then pretended nothing had happened. "It shouldn't be a problem. Like I said, we haven't done the act for half a week and we keep a random route. I'm sure the heat won't turn up, but if they do, get our attention somehow. Got it?"

August gave his best approximation of a serious, thuggish nod.

Sycamore sighed. "God help me."

Within a few minutes, the show was under way. August watched from across Broadway, trying to look casual as he scanned the area for any sign of the police, but it seemed that suspending the act for a few days had done the trick; there wasn't a single cop in sight.

Ten minutes in, August stopped standing sentry and instead watched the pickpockets at work, trying to acquire some of their techniques. He was about to applaud a particular thief's deft handiwork when he spotted him: the cop in the gray coat, sucking down a cigarette. Blast and double damnation! He'd failed at the simplest of tasks! August needed to warn his compatriots lest the entire outfit be incarcerated due to his negligence.

He moistened his lips and attempted a whistle, knowing the exercise would prove to be fruitless, but determined to follow orders nonetheless. Alas, though he expelled copious amounts of both breath and will, August could create no sound, and as he blew in vain, he saw the cop rather pointedly stamp out his cigarette. This was to be the bust! All would be lost if he failed to act!

August hurled himself across Broadway, darting through traffic, and tumbled into the crowd. A few confused murmurs and swear words were tossed his way, and then the circle parted, all eyes on the boy.

The limelight. August had seen countless performers rise to its call, but he had never been forced to do so himself. His mouth was dry. His nerves were raw and sharp. What to do?

August opened his mouth and was surprised as anyone when he started singing.

Hey there, boys, I'm mighty lonely.
Hey there, boys, I want you only,
For my own. Let's have some fun tonight.
Hey there, boys, I'm awful frightened,
Hey there, boys, turn off the light and
Be my friend. Let's have some fun tonight.

It's been said that even someone suffering from the most terrible case of dementia can recall every word of a song supposedly long forgotten. August was having such an experience now.

He'd heard the tune only once, a late-night act at the Backstage Bistro. Now, slightly older and slightly wiser, August understood some of the implications of the lyrics and found, as they sank further and further into depravity with each passing verse, that he was now in danger of being arrested for inadvertently soliciting sodomy. However, for the sake of the gang, the show had to go on. He undid the top two buttons of his shirt and exposed his bony shoulder, as he'd seen the singer do those many years ago, adding a lurid wink as a bit of punctuation.

The reactions of the crowd varied. A few were red in the face from laughter, others from embarrassment. Needless to say, August created quite a stir, and as he belted out the last few notes, he saw that all the members of Sycamore's gang had slinked off to safety.

The applause was scattered at best, but August didn't take this half-heartedness personally; good art was polarizing. Besides, now that the deed was done, he had to make his escape before the plainclothesman, bewildered as Caesar on that fateful March afternoon, decided to haul him off for prostitution.

* * *

After his burlesque fiasco, August was taken off lookout duty. Abject failure notwithstanding, Sycamore could see that August had a certain utilizable panache. The trick was diluting the boy's natural excitability and his tendency toward logorrhea.

"What am I to do, descend into a state of aphasic muteness?" August moaned after being chastised yet again for an overabundance of vocabulary.

Sycamore was exhausted; he'd taken to carrying around a pocket dictionary so he could understand August. "Even now you're doing it," he said, locating the word *aphasic* with frazzled fingers. "Kids don't talk like this."

"Of course they do! Haven't you read *Great Expectations*?"

"No. And you shouldn't have read it either! That's my point!"

Both parties were at their wit's end. Sycamore had ordered his band of pickpockets to lay low for the time being. With the dissolution of his syndicate, however, he'd lost the most sizable portion of his income. He was depending on August to haul in a big score.

The boy, on the other hand, was near starving, but what was really rattling August was his lack of shelter. He needed Sycamore to take him in, and for that to happen, August had to prove his worth.

So the pair commenced with what seemed like hundreds of tense rehearsals, where the quoting of Shakespeare was explicitly banned, until Sycamore finally decided that August was ready to pull off a con.

That morning they set up camp at Grand Central Station beside one of the larger ticketing booths, just outside the footpath of bustling commuters. Some unseen sign seemed to assuage Sycamore, and he gave August an imperceptible nudge on his shoulder: their signal.

August started trickling tears while Sycamore rubbed his back, parodying a comforting parent. The intended victims, an elderly couple, passed them by without sparing them so much as a glance. August didn't worry; perhaps he'd been mistaken, and their mark was still in line. But after a couple minutes, Sycamore knelt down and whispered to August, "All right, save some of that salt water for later."

August used his sleeves to dry his moistened cheeks. "I don't understand. Why isn't it working? Perhaps I should play it bigger."

"No! God, no! It's New York, kid. You stop for every person sobbing on the street, it would take you half an hour to move a block. I thought that couple might've been coming from Toledo or something, but they're probably just a pair of Park Avenue prigs. We'll wait for the rubes."

A drought seemed to be sweeping through Grand Central Station, however, for though Sycamore had promised a plentiful crop of marks, the landscape was an arid badland of hardened New Yorkers. The morning perished, and most of the afternoon with it.

A nudge from Sycamore roused August from his vegetative trance of boredom.

"What?" he asked.

In response, Sycamore raised his eyebrows and tilted his head toward the ticket line. This was the signal! Tears leaked from August with Pavlovian speed, and he felt the warm touch of faux assurance from Sycamore.

"What seems to be the problem here?" came the question, languid but sharp somehow, like honey cut with arsenic.

While Sycamore dove into the well-rehearsed sob story about a dying woman in Boston, August commenced a lidded study of the mark. He could see why Sycamore had picked her. She was old. Not elderly, but well over sixty, and to a boy of elevenish she might as well have been a reanimated corpse. It wasn't her age that had caught Sycamore's eye, however, but her wealth. Genuine jewels dripped from her neck, dark and rich as molasses. A manservant stood a breath behind her, dragging an elaborate set of alligator-skin luggage. Impressed as he was by all this finery, August was most taken aback by her clothes. Though Miss Butler had failed in most ways as an educator, the boy could sew like the dickens and appreciated a good piece of stitchwork better than most. The woman's travel wear was all drama, clearly custom, with none of the popular do-it-yourself rayon technique sweeping the postwar nation. August was dazzled. So dazzled, in fact, he hardly heard the question barked in his direction.

"Why aren't you in school, boy?"

Immersed as he was in the woman's attire, August hadn't noticed the actual woman. Though she was finely bedecked, she clearly possessed a hardened cunning that put August in mind of a gruesome stone gargoyle.

Caught off guard, the boy was temporarily struck dumb, but Sycamore had a hardened cunning all his own, though his variety of guile was decidedly more ferretesque. "His absence is excused, dear lady," Sycamore explained. "After all, what administration could be so coldhearted as to keep a boy from his mother's deathbed?"

"What school does he attend?" asked the woman, unfazed by Sycamore's attempts at sympathy. August, still weeping, could easily see that the scam was doomed. Though she was from out of town, her dialect distinctly southern, she was no rube.

"P.S. Thirty-Nine," Sycamore lied.

"A public school?" gasped the woman. "He should be in a private institution!"

Sycamore, finally seeing the lost cause for what it was, barked out, "If you ain't gonna help us, lady, why don't you scram?"

The southerner huffed. "I'm trying to decide whether to report this case to the authorities. A child's well-being is no laughing matter!"

Mention of the police threw Sycamore, and he was struggling to extricate himself unscathed. It seemed the gargoyle would soon devour the ferret if August didn't intercede. He knew they'd get no money from Lady Antebellum, but he had no wish to involve the authorities. Despite his homelessness and all-around destitution, he'd rather be dead than in an orphanage. Honestly, how dreadful to beg a second ladleful of gruel off a man with a name like Bumble?

"My good lady," August whispered, "please, I implore you, let me and my poor father alone so that we may wallow together in our miserable grief. My mother, bless that darling woman, is dying a most wretched death. Before we put her on a train toward Boston to stay with my sainted aunt, Father and I were her sole caregivers. You can't imagine the strain. She could hardly walk. She couldn't keep food down. Father lost his position as a high-powered prosecuting lawyer, not daring to leave the side of his beloved for even the briefest of instants."

"What is her sickness?" asked the woman, with none of her former ferocity.

"Consumption," said August, while Sycamore at the same moment replied with, "Cholera."

"Choleric consumption," August corrected, without missing a beat. "The doctors were baffled. When a bout of explosive diarrhea quite literally lifted her off the bed, Father and I knew we could do no more. She had to be sent up to Boston where, as I'm sure you know, specialists from around the globe deal with these sorts of diseases. Alas, even these men of superior learning were at a loss, my mother's case being the worst the world has ever known. We do not ask for your money. Perhaps by denying it, you are in fact doling out a blessing, for surely my sweet mother's condition has worsened, and it might be better to remember her as she was, a gaunt and hollow specter desperately clinging to life, than as what she has almost certainly become: a corpse. But give us not your pity, either, for as of this morning she was still alive, and after all, the weariest and most loathed worldly life that age, ache, penury, and imprisonment can lay on nature is a paradise to what we fear of death." The Shakespeare was blatant mutiny, but August was on a roll. "Perhaps, when Mother surrenders and leaves behind this earthly plane, Father and I will be able to pick up our lives where they left off, or better yet, relocate to our country's celebrated Dixieland, which I hear is quite lovely," he added, not above a bit of flattery.

The woman grasped at the clasp of her necklace and deposited the blood-red gems in August's hands.

"Madame," August began, "we couldn't—"

"Silence!" she cried. She shoved a sizable wad of money against Sycamore's chest. "Take this," she whispered, "and may God have mercy on her soul."

August had apparently learned more from Miss Butler than needlework; he could spin a lie with nearly as much aplomb as the old laundress could.

* * *

"I got you something," Sycamore teased as he led August through the Lower East Side.

August had been worried that Sycamore would be angry with him for going so far off script, but his anxiety proved baseless; Sycamore was elated. August was now his cash cow, and Sycamore frequently said things like "Good job" and "Incredible!" It was borderline affectionate.

"Gosh, what could it be?" August said, feigning innocence. He'd already guessed what Sycamore's surprise was: a room all his own in Sycamore's apartment. But even though he had it all figured out, he wasn't going to spoil Sycamore's fun. He played dumb.

Just as August suspected, Sycamore stopped in front of a run-down building, produced a set of keys, and unlocked the front door.

"Right this way, sir," Sycamore said with mock formality, holding the door for August.

They walked up five floors, the keys came out again, and Sycamore unlocked the apartment door with a flourish. "Ta-da!" he cried, just as he did in his street magician act.

It was a studio. One room that contained a half-stove, an old mattress on the floor, a single window that faced an alley, and a wooden chair.

"Where are the other rooms?" August asked.

"Bathroom's down the hall," Sycamore replied, mistaking August's question. "You share it with the rest of the floor."

"That's not what I meant."

Sycamore got defensive. "Look, I know it's not the Plaza, but it's a good place. We made a lot of cash off that lady, but believe me, money doesn't last forever, especially when—"

"No, it's not that," August interjected. "I guess I just thought that I was going to live with you."

Sycamore's eyes bulged with stupefaction before he burst into laughter. "What? Live with me? Are you joking?"

August shuffled his feet in awkward shame. But why was he embarrassed? He'd gotten shelter. That had been the goal.

But there was more to it than that, August realized, his face flushed with humiliation. He hadn't just wanted a roof with walls. He wanted someone to be there, someone who noticed if he came home at night. August didn't even like Sycamore, not really. But Sycamore had been inside the Scarsenguard. He remembered it too, and his remembering made it more real. Made Miss Butler still alive, and made it so that Sir Reginald would come and get him and—

"Oh, Jesus, kid, don't cry," said Sycamore, kneeling down to August's level. "Listen. If you lived with me, I would kill you. I wouldn't want to, but I would. It just wouldn't work. I'm not the fatherly type. But here you got a place all to yourself. You can have your friends over and stay up all night, whatever you want! No parents! Right?"

August steeled himself, something he was getting good at. "Right," he replied.

"Good," Sycamore said, shaking off the guilt. "Here's your keys, and I paid rent for the first three months, but after that you're on your own. Got it?"

"Got it," said August. "See you tomorrow?"

"Actually, I'm off to Atlantic City with the missus for a holiday. Let's meet on Monday." Sycamore stood in the doorway, about to leave. "You okay?"

"I'm okay," August lied.

Sycamore smiled, shut the door, and left August.

Alone.

* * *

Months later, August was kicking around on the outskirts of Times Square waiting for Sycamore. They were going to run a few surefire cons before lunch, then call it an early day.

But of course Sycamore was late. Probably nursing a nasty hangover, August thought, now aimlessly strolling through the crowded avenues.

He was considering nicking a couple of wallets for himself, Sycamore be damned, when his chest hitched and he stopped dead.

Without realizing it, August had wandered onto West Forty-Third Street and was standing directly in front of the Scarsenguard. Or more accurately, he was standing directly in front of where the Scarsenguard used to be. What stood there now was a colossal hotel with the tackiest giant gold letters emblazoned across the front entrance spelling out the most accursed of names: THE BARRETH.

Once August recovered from his initial shock, he was furious. First with himself. He always took such special care to avoid this block. In fact, he hadn't been back in so long, he'd missed the entire hotel being built.

But mostly his fury was directed at Barreth. How dare that feckless man build such a horrid thing atop his childhood. Damn him! Damn that bastard. That cuckold. That brainless, bottom-dwelling, trough-mongrel.

This could not stand. Did Barreth just get to win without contest? Something had to be done.

Inspiration struck. From across the street, August bided his time until the doorman, laden with luggage, ushered a couple inside. The entrance now unguarded, August dashed across the street, ascended the entry steps, undid his button fly, and let loose a torrent of hot piss that flowed steadily down the stairs. His stream was still gushing when the doorman returned.

"Hey! What the hell are you doing?"

August turned, his spray unceasing.

"Tell that craven half-wit Barreth that the Scarsenguard remembers his folly!"

The doorman, too busy avoiding urine to snatch August, was understandably confused. Rather than explain it to him, August spit on the ground, tucked himself away, and then slipped into the bustling anonymity of Times Square.

A minor revolt, but August did feel better for it.

* * *

August had taken to throwing dinner parties in his apartment. The guest list varied. There was usually a famous actor or actress in attendance, of course, but August had entertained notorious radicals, artists, even royalty. The evenings were raucous affairs full of lively discussion, but sadly they often ended in scandal, even murder.

Tonight he was hosting a rail-thin debutante (a lead pipe), her stocky admirer (a brick), and a well-respected duke (a terra-cotta pot holding a dead fern).

"We're honored you traveled so far to join our little dinner party, Your Grace," August said to the duke, though he knew the duke harbored a secret desire for the eligible young lead pipe. The brick was obviously seething that the duke was receiving special treatment, but what could August do? Social niceties must be observed. Besides, if August's suspicions were correct, then Duke Terra-Cotta and Miss Lead Pipe were already secretly engaged!

"And how is your father, dear? Healthy, I hope?"

Conversation positively wallowed in the first course, but after August got the ball rolling, communication began to flow freely. However, tragedy struck at dessert. While August was cutting an apple into slices, Terra-Cotta fell off his perch and shattered on the ground. August rushed to the pot and cradled it in his arms, distraught. The poor duke! How could this happen?

The faux sorrow August was pretending to feel abruptly became authentic, but before he started crying, it switched just as quickly to rage. August stood up and hurled the shard of terra-cotta against the wall, where it shattered.

"Damn it!" he screamed to no one. "Goddammit!"

What kind of life is this? he thought, snatching his coat off the ground and storming outside. Why was he eating alone with trash as his company? August started walking to clear his head, furious at his circumstances. It just wasn't fair. It was outrageous.

The walk cooled his anger but didn't leave him feeling any better. He found himself standing outside the gates of Gramercy Park, a private space forbidden to anyone who didn't have a key. How strange to lock a park, he thought, holding the bars and looking inside. What was so special about this little patch of green that it had to be sectioned off and guarded? August could climb the fence easily and find out, of course, but he didn't feel like it. He didn't feel like doing much of anything.

August walked southeast, heading home, with nothing but an evening of sweeping up terra-cotta to look forward to. He was in a daze for several blocks, not really seeing anything, until a particular brownstone on Eighteenth Street caught his eye. The windows were lit up, and through them he could see a family sitting down to dinner: a mother, a father, and a young girl about August's age, with dark curly hair. Something about her stopped August, and he paused to take in the tableau. The father was giving a long-winded speech while the mother nodded, and the girl was trying not to look bored. August stared through the window and ached.

This, inside the brownstone—this was a family. Families had dinner. They talked too much. They were boring. But they were there. August had thought he'd had a family, but he'd been wrong.

Percyfoot wasn't coming. August just suddenly knew, deep and fully. The Scarsenguard had fallen ages ago, and a hotel stood on its grave. You didn't leave a child alone for that long if you intended to save him or adopt him or whatever August had hoped Percyfoot would do. It wasn't that Percyfoot hadn't read about the Scarsenguard or was too busy. He knew August was lost; he just wasn't coming. In fact, he was probably glad to be rid of the child.

So August was no longer the boy in the theater. Every part of that life was gone. But now what? Was he really just a thief who lived alone in a squalid tenement on the Lower East Side? How sordid. How had this happened?

August was still staring into the window when the girl turned and noticed him. Strangely, however, she didn't look away. August continued staring, confused. So did she. Then she waved. August waved back. With a sly look, she checked that her father was still babbling on. Then she snuck away from the table, opened a window, and leaned out.

"Hello!" she called.

More than a little dumbfounded, August yelled back, "Hello!"

Her uprising, harmless though it was, had finally been discovered, and the garrulous father rushed to the window, pulling her inside.

"I say," the older man shouted, leaning out the window, "who the hell are you?"

August considered telling him everything. Why not? But instead he ended up shouting "I'm no one," before running all the way back home.

* * *

The years passed, thirteenthish to fourteenthish, until somewhere around his fifteenthish year, August's formerly fecund association with Sycamore went fallow. Of the many contributing factors to their eventual parting, both could agree that the worst offender was the relentlessness of time. August, smooth cherub of boyhood, had finally entered the first harrowing stages of puberty. His features were currently arranged in that awkward mask of in-between all adolescents are forced to don.

August's inevitable predicament seriously hampered most of their cons. A young lad weeping for his mother is heart-wrenching, a sobbing teenager unsightly. Winsome precocity in a beardless youth is viewed as unearned bitterness in an adolescent. Then there was the fact that boys of a certain age simply inspire suspicion. August could no longer enter a department store without being marked as a potential shoplifter. Matronly women who would have once pinched his cheeks now flared their nostrils at him in disgust. Policemen constantly asked him where he was headed, and members of the oldest profession teased him mercilessly, cackling when he scurried away, hunched and scarlet.

As a result, Sycamore and August met more sporadically. August had taken to picking pockets to supplement his income; it had been well over a week since their last joint con. However, they were scheduled to meet at the Plaza Hotel around noon.

"It's over," Sycamore said, chomping street nuts.

"What is?" August asked, his newly changed voice still unfamiliar to his own ears.

"You and me. We're through. You're slowing me down."

Ingesting this announcement, August examined his feelings and couldn't say he was particularly surprised; they'd been drifting apart for some time. Nor could he admit to any heavyheartedness. Truthfully, his tolerance for Sycamore's singular brand of humor had worn thin. How many veiled references to fellatio, no matter how original, could one person stand?

Still, August was human, and at the end of any era there is a certain feeling of melancholy. Crass and crude though he was, Sycamore had taken August under his wing and given him the chance he'd so desperately needed. Sycamore could never be viewed as a father figure, no matter how dim the light, but perhaps it wouldn't be too far a stretch to think of him as an irascible older brother, one who came through when it really counted.

August's reminiscences were cut short by a trumpeting fart from Sycamore, who then added, "Christ, will you look at the set on that broad?"

Just two months prior, August would've rolled his eyes at Sycamore's lecherous comment, but as has been previously mentioned, the incessant beat of testosterone had started thrumming through his veins, and the boy was ashamed to agree, albeit inwardly, that the broad was quite well stacked.

"Thank you for the opportunity," August said, offering Sycamore an outstretched hand.

"Jesus, kid, who are you, J. P. Morgan?"

August sighed without malice and turned to walk away. A few steps later, Sycamore called after him. "You're all right, August. But if I ever hear you ratted on me, just remember, I know where you live."

An apt farewell, August thought, strolling downtown.

* * *

August's early teenage years passed in a recalcitrant streak of petty crime. To put it candidly, he became a punk. His chronic quoting of Shakespeare abated, the mellifluous language of the bard replaced by strings of obscenities so profane that even Sycamore might've blanched. This was done partly to blend in with the loose collective of similarly aged boys he ran with, but mostly as a rejection of his former life. The moment he finally understood that Percyfoot had abandoned him, August turned away from all things theatrical with a relish that was nearly feral.

Sex was a watershed event of the era. Some of his older, more experienced companions practically dragged August into a whorehouse with savage delight. He was terrified, but the woman he was paired with took pity on him, probably because when naked, August resembled a skinny fledgling stork that had fallen from its nest. The woman told August to put his clothes back on, sat him down, and explained the mechanics of intercourse more clearly than the soldiers at the Backstage Bistro ever had.

"Come back when you're ready," she'd said.

As it turned out, August was ready the very next night.

"Guess you're a quick study," the woman said, laughing, when August came in.

It was a short-lived, pants-around-the-ankles experience (as were most of the encounters that followed), but it was also incredible. August, in a moment of erudite relapse, found himself contemplating Helen of Troy, a tale he'd hitherto found ridiculous. Now he understood. Why did Romeo drink the poison? Why did Lancelot betray Arthur? Why did Edward abdicate the throne? Because sex was a legitimately compelling pastime.

It was around this time of carnal awakening that August noticed that the police force as a whole held a particular fondness for him. True, all his set received skeptical glances or pointed threats when passing an officer, but it seemed to August that the gazes of the NYPD lingered a little longer on him than on the others. For months he brushed this off as unfounded paranoia, but even his comrades eventually took notice.

"Got yourself a boyfriend, March?" they'd tease when an officer gave August a double take.

Years spent in the company of Sergeant Sycamore can teach even the dullest student the art of the crass rejoinder, and August was no half-wit.

"Must've seen how the girls walk when I get through with them." Afterward, he'd grab his crotch, for emphasis. Good god, what a scoundrel he'd become. Sometimes he shocked himself.

Uproarious laughter would follow these comments. August would laugh right along with them, and quiet his nagging worry with a burning pull off a bottle of cheap liquor, but sometimes he would lie awake, staring at the multitude of cracks in his ceiling. Why was he being watched?

Any doubt he still harbored about the police interest in him was brought to a halt when one afternoon, enjoying the spoils of a wallet he'd stolen, August was addressed by an officer.

"August March?" the lawman ventured, his voice colored with uncertainty.

Hearing his name escape the lips of a bona fide keeper of the peace sent a profound jolt of terror straight to August's jaw. He took off at a mad sprint, making full use of every shortcut he knew.

When he was certain he'd escaped the cop's clutches, August pressed his back against a building, breathing heavily. So the police were watching him. Not only watching, but actively seeking him out. They knew his name! But that wasn't particularly unusual, was it? The NYPD were well aware of August's gang and knew the names of more than one of its members. But those were the idiots, the ones always getting caught. August had never spent one night behind bars. Yet he'd just been singled out by name. By name!

Had his reputation as New York's most notorious pickpocket become legend among the city's police force? August doubted it. True, he was a successful thief, but not a notably greedy one. He took enough to make his rent and see a movie every now and then. It's not like he was Al Capone. What did they want from him?

Once the adrenaline of his one-sided chase had fully abated and his mental facilities were restored, August determined that this was simply routine. He'd become a well-known face, an entry in the criminal lexicon. He vowed to keep his eyes open and to stay vigilant, but he walked home with more than a bit of swagger in his step. August March was a wanted man.

* * *

In a rare fit of normalcy, August went to dinner with a girl his age and brought her over to his apartment afterward.

When they'd finished, August didn't fall asleep. Instead he watched the girl doze. Her shoulders were exposed, goose pimples trickling down her arm, his ratty blanket not big enough to fully cover her. The hard look she wore while she was awake was gone, replaced by the vulnerable mask of sleep.

Her clothes lay piled beside his too-thin mattress. August picked up her bra and examined it, this delicate piece of armor foreign to his sex. Toying with the underwear, lacing it through his fingers, he realized he would never fully understand what it was like to be a woman. He would never fully understand this person.

A line from his past suddenly surfaced:

Who is it that can tell me who I am?

He hadn't thought of that in years. What was it? Shakespeare? Not Molière, surely.

Don't think about that.

Sleep was pointless. Naked, August stood up, went to the window, and stared out. He was a night owl who hated the night. The nights were too long, too empty, made it too easy to remember.

Who was this girl? Why was she here? And why had he begged her to stay? Practically cried when she put on her stockings?

"Please," August had said, trying to control the waver in his voice. "We can steal some sweet cakes in the morning. I know a stand."

"I'm leaving," she stated, putting on a shoe. "I mean, Jesus, I'm not your girlfriend."

"I know you're not." August was nearly shouting, and he hated that he was nearly shouting, so he grabbed her arm, harder than he'd meant to. "Just stay. Stay."

He started kissing her collarbone, worked his way up her neck, found her lips.

"Stay," August whispered, inside her mouth.

And she had.

But who was she?

August needed to pace. He needed to move. He dressed too quickly and went out.

As was often the case, his midnight wanderings led him to East Eighteenth Street, to the brownstone with the family inside. After that first encounter, August took better care not to be spotted, but on occasion, the girl with the dark curly hair would still notice him and tease him through the window. But as the years went by, she appeared less and less, sometimes vanishing for months at a time.

August wanted her to be there tonight. He didn't have many constants in his life, but this willful girl with the boring family was a tether.

He stood on Eighteenth Street for hours, but the lights never came on.

* * *

August, somewhere around sixteen, sat on a rooftop and smoked a hand-rolled cigarette, weighing his options. Should he meet up with the boys and get drunk? Or share the companionship of an elegant young woman?

He slipped down the fire escapes, an urban ape, still deciding. The purse he'd nicked at a concert in Central Park contained a hefty amount of cash and an unimpressive necklace that nevertheless would still pull in some money at one of the shadier pawnshops August frequented. So rent was made. Booze, then? Or a girl? Both?

But what about the police, his consistent constabulary shadow? Underage drinking and prostitution weren't exactly the hallmarks of an upstanding citizen.

August's feet hit the ground of Eighty-Fifth Street, and he started the trek downtown, banishing thoughts of the NYPD to the far recesses of his mind. What's the worst that could happen?

* * *

"Fuck you, you goddamned pig!" August screamed, throwing himself against the bars of the holding cell in which his person currently resided.

What a whirlwind of an evening he'd had. Honestly, a madcap succession of hours.

After he'd left the Upper West Side, August decided a brothel would be a perfect end to a perfect day. However, experience had taught him that a whorehouse could be a rather depressing place. August didn't judge the women employed there, nor did he have any shame about the act of sex itself; it was generally the men haunting these erotic institutions that were so embarrassing. Husbands would dart furtive eyes this way and that, terrified of being spotted by a friend or coworker. And then there was always the giggling, sweating type, cartoon parodies of naughty indulgence. All in all, it was best to be drunk at a brothel, even some of the nicer ones, so August made a pit stop or six on his route to carnal bliss.

After offering a few windowless pubs his patronage (including the adored Beggars Can't Be Boozers, the most reputable Beer Hole, and the aptly titled Drinks), August eventually entered a whorehouse.

The deed done, August quite literally tripped down the stairs and out the door. He was attempting to whistle as he made his way home, and there his night might have ended but for the sultry interruption of a voice.

"Hey there, handsome," came the call, full of innuendo.

At this stage of his life, August had few positive attributes, so when an attractive woman catcalled him, though he was freshly postcoitus and logged with drink, the virile youth felt nature stirring him to answer, which he did with the imaginative quip "Let's go upstairs, baby."

Who'd ever heard of the so-called vice department? August was leery of the whole operation and kept demanding to speak to a representative from internal affairs. All he received, however, was a cursory explanation that ever since climbing off the roof earlier that evening, he'd been tailed by two cops who'd thought it suspicious that a teenage boy was shimmying down the wall of an apartment building.

Though August was officially charged with soliciting prostitution, he was at the time guilty of several other offenses, including but not limited to intoxication in public, underage drinking, resisting arrest, carrying a concealed weapon, larceny, and throwing a ball at someone's head for pleasure (a favorite pastime of August, who'd mastered the game after years of development). Still under the powerful influence of drink, August railed and scorned each indictment, employed the use of every swear word he knew, and tossed off more than eight death threats.

This is standard behavior for an incarcerated drunk, as is that blessed state they all succumb to eventually, commonly known as "sleeping it off." August seemed unfamiliar with protocol, however, and shrieked throughout the night, not even stopping when he'd shouted himself hoarse.

Finally, well past midnight, a gentleman came in and paid August's bail, demanding to take the boy out of the station immediately. He needn't have commanded with such bluster; the police were more than glad to be rid of him. They led the man to the boy's cell.

At seeing August, the gentleman cried out, "Good lord!" He was British and more than a bit overblown. "Absolutely wretched! Makes Caliban look like the Duke of Cornwall."

"Who are you?" August intended to say. What he actually said was, "Ruuggah borscht?"

After much prodding, the meaning of the question was eventually discerned, and the gentleman answered. "You don't remember me? Or perhaps you're simply too befouled by drink to make a proper identification. A horrid habit, my friend; don't make a custom of it." A flask from the man's coat pocket tinkled as he squared his shoulders. "It is I, child, Sir Reginald Percyfoot, beloved star of stage and screen, knighted by the King of England and recipient of one Academy Award nomination, though I wouldn't have accepted such rubbish even had I won, not with the cinema being the morass it is these days. Do you know they're filming yet another remake of *Little Women*? Honestly, how much progress must those poor pilgrims attain before we're granted amnesty?"

August, not understanding a word of this, vomited a spew of rank bile onto the cell floor.

"My sentiments precisely," Percyfoot said. "Now come along. We're leaving."

"Hey! You gonna clean that up?" asked the attending officer, gesturing toward August's sick.

"Of course not," Percyfoot snapped. "It was no doubt nothing but a response to the police brutality the child underwent through the course of his hellish evening. In fact, I have three-quarters of a mind to press charges."

August, stirring from the lull vomiting had caused, caught sight of the officer. "You fucker!" he screamed, regaining some of his former flair. "I'll string you up by your dick and piss in your eyes! May the devil rape your soul for all of time!"

"My heavens what a disgusting mouth you've grown into," said Reginald, hurrying August out of the building and into a cab. "Though that last bit about the devil was rousing, I'll grant you that."

August was plastered and hadn't fully registered Percyfoot's presence. "Where we going?" he asked.

"Home," came the reply.

"I live downtown."

"We're not going to whatever den of depravity in which you currently dwell, my boy. We're going to your home. The home bequeathed to you."

August got so confused, he puked again.

"No need to fret, dear lad," said Percyfoot, heartily slapping August on the back. "Everything will make sense in the morning. Or most likely it won't, but at least you won't be gushing putrescence with such frequency."

* * *

As it turned out, Percyfoot had been searching for August ever since the boy had disappeared.

"Came running as soon as I heard they planned to demolish the Scarsenguard, and a damned ordeal it was, too. Had to storm off the set and break my contract, a true calamity. They replaced me with a drunken old character actor, the ghastliest sort of creature. You know the type, still pining for vaudeville and juggling pins. Mucked up the whole picture."

August sat in an ornate wooden armchair, drinking tea and feeling enormously awkward about where to place the porcelain saucer the teacup had been served on. Balance it on his knee? Place it gingerly on the floor? Tuck it into the crook of his armpit with measured nonchalance? A dilemma to be sure.

Percyfoot, indifferent to August's struggle, continued. "Haven't left New York since. Been playing the most sickening material. All anyone wants to do after a war is laugh. I've no aversion to comedies, but these rip-roaring slamming-door farces do tend to grate on the nerves after a time."

For all his pomp and circumstance onstage, Percyfoot was not very demonstrative in his civilian life. Yet he was trying to relate to August how much the child's disappearance had affected him. How he'd tossed for hours each night before succumbing to fitful sleep, how he'd walked the streets of New York canvassing strangers about a young boy with an unusually prolific vocabulary. He was trying to describe the quagmire of maintaining proper American citizenship. Demanding that his agent find him another part, *any* part, as long as it was in New York. And how could he divulge to August, now a total stranger, the agony of his mornings? How he would steel himself before flipping to the obituaries. How he had learned to hate hope. What were the odds that August could possibly still be alive? Percyfoot would think as he leafed through the paper, ignoring the hammering of his heart as he scanned the ages of the dead.

82.

Good.

64.

Probably drank too much.

11.

Fuck. Fuck. Fuck. Fuck. Fuck.

Peter Summers, 11, survived by his father, Grant Summers . . .

Oh, thank God. Thank Christ. Just some foolish boy who was struck by a car. Thank you, God. Thank you, you abhorrent evil God, just let him be dead, let him be dead so this can stop, all this unknowing, this chasm of ambiguity, this endless, ceaseless—oh shit, I've ruined the eggs.

Instead of revealing these feelings, all Sir Reginald could seem to do was moan about the state of Hollywood, complain about the tripe he'd suffered through. But what to say? What on earth to say to this lost boy, or was he a man now? Neither. He was so terribly betwixt. What to say?

Reginald had stalled as long as possible before getting the police involved. Too long? Most definitely. So much time had passed, in fact, that he'd had to pretend to be a distant sort of uncle who'd only just realized, through years of miscommunication due to his busy schedule, that the boy had been misplaced. Didn't help that he was a semi-famous actor.

"Weren't you in *Night for the Reich*?" they'd asked, eyes aglow.

"Of course I was in *Night for the Reich*. The most important film made that year, if you can call any film important. These composers overdo it so. I don't need my death scene underscored by scads of sentimental violins. Just point the goddamn camera at my eyes. I've played Shaw, you fools. You think I can't manage this drivel, penned by a screenwriter who only just started wearing long pants?"

Of course he'd never say that. He'd simply smile graciously, sign an autograph or two, and then gently steer the interview back to the fact that a child had been missing for over three years, and Percyfoot thought it would be such jolly good fun if he were found.

Though it had taken them years, the police actually did locate August, and were able to successfully confiscate him at a whorehouse, of all places. Percyfoot, whose bosom had ballooned with cancerous hope when he was awakened by the phone call, was certain that a mistake had been made, but went down to the station at any rate, trying with all his soul to kill the longing optimism that quickened his step, to run it through with a serrated knife.

Miracle of miracles, however, it was August! The police weren't entirely incompetent! The prodigal son had returned! But he was more than just prodigal. Skinny, drunk, swearing, mean. Still, he was alive. Alive! Breathing! Tangible! Percyfoot popped him in a cab straight to East Twenty-Third Street, where he was now attempting to explain everything.

"This brownstone is yours, my good boy. Left to you by none other than Miss Butler. You do remember Miss Butler, of course?"

August nodded in the affirmative, causing him to drop his saucer, where it promptly shattered on the wood floor, which was apparently *his* wood floor. Feeling stupid, inelegant, and at a loss for words, August spit to fill the horrible silence.

Percyfoot reddened. How does one respond to spit?

It turned out that he would say nothing at all, for after shattering the saucer and spitting, August stood and said, "I need to take a piss."

Percyfoot blubbered out directions to the facilities, utterly scandalized.

For his part, August was unused to the softened likes of Sir Reginald. The streets, as they are wont to do, had hardened him. Not wanting to offend his benefactor, but unused to the complexities of polite conversation, he had asked about the bathroom simply to escape.

Once free, he found the nearest open window and climbed out, seeking refuge on a rooftop.

Percyfoot waited a full half hour for August to return. When it finally became clear that boy didn't intend to, Sir Reginald attempted to dust off his bruised feelings and busy himself about the brownstone. But he wasn't one for housework—he'd never held a mop—and cooking was as foreign as Finland, so he ended up pretending to read until it was time for bed.

Tucked into a cozy guest room, Percyfoot extinguished the lamp and sighed. He'd finally found August, but now that he had, just what in the hell was he going to do with him?

* * *

Late that night, Percyfoot awoke with a start. He smelled smoke. Was there a fire? Good god: August!

He rushed through the house, following the smoke to the sitting room, where August stood emptying a vase of water into a flaming trash bin. This did the trick, the fire immediately extinguished.

Percyfoot, however, stamping on a dying ember, was still inflamed. "What in damnation happened here?"

"I was having a cigarette," August mumbled.

"And why, might I ask, was the rubbish bin aflame?"

August stared at the floor. "I couldn't find an ashtray, so—"

"So you thought you'd toss your lit cigarette into a bin filled with dry paper? Good lord! Why not pour in some kerosene while you're at it?" Percyfoot was aghast. They both could've been killed because August had no more sense than a Neanderthal, and even less manners! "Now see here, young man, I'm happy to have found you safe and sound, living the carefree life of a street rat, but setting fire to rubbish bins? And spitting? I assumed I'd have to play a bit of Higgins to your Doolittle—I remember all the key speeches, of course—but this is absurd!"

This reference to *Pygmalion*, a play he hadn't thought about in years, shamed August to his core. He was able to see himself for what he'd become, and Percyfoot was right. He was as foul and uncouth as Eliza Doolittle, the flower peddler.

"Sorry," he muttered.

"Sorry?" Percyfoot shouted, sounding rather impressive as he employed his years of theatrical training. "I've been looking for you every day for five years, and all I receive is the mumbled apology of a simpleton? And to commit yourself to that most torrid cliché: a life of crime. Really, my boy, with a mind like yours, you could've applied yourself to so many other things!"

A heavy silence followed Percyfoot's speech.

"You weren't there," August finally said.

"What was that?"

"You weren't there," August snapped, scarlet from rage. From embarrassment at his rage. "No one was."

And there it was. The truth. Percyfoot hadn't been there when the boy actually needed him. But that was the whole arrangement, wasn't it? Miss Butler was the untraditional mother, and he, Sir Reginald, the offbeat father. Who needed convention? Who needed society? August was their experiment, and together they'd show the world how to create the perfect boy through an intentionally unorthodox upbringing. But only when they wanted to, of course. Only when convenient. The child was cute when he was cute, and unnecessary when anything else. On to the next project. A movie, perhaps, where he'd play an avuncular old bachelor while some talentless ingenue walked away with the picture. That had seemed far more preferable, far more *important*, than raising a child at the moment.

Percyfoot was mortified. They'd done wrong by August, he and Miss Butler, and standing before him, a hangdog child, was the proof.

"I tried, my boy," Sir Reginald sputtered. "Please know that I tried. I thought that you wouldn't be able to keep away from the theater, having been reared in one. I asked every usher, every ticket taker, every janitor, if they'd seen a boy. I thought perhaps that you'd . . . that you might've been crushed in the Scarsenguard. I thought—" Here he broke off, trying to conceal blustering sobs, but failing.

August watched the heaving shoulders and didn't know how to feel. His emotions were coiled into confusing knots. For years he'd nurtured the hope that Percyfoot might come and find him, rescue him, and take him away to a fabulous life of theatre and gaiety and security. And now he finally had come, but August found resentment and anger where he'd dreamed he'd find joy. He no longer knew this man. Sir Reginald, along with everyone from his former life, had been given up for dead. Even the boy that had been August March had perished. Now he was someone new. But who?

Sir Reginald eventually stopped his uncharacteristic display of emotion and looked up to see August flustered and uncomfortable. "Please forgive me," Reginald begged, his eyes red.

"I'll try," August replied with perfect honesty.

* * *

Their relationship on tenuous footing, Percyfoot set out to shape August into a proper young gentleman, though he took careful steps to ensure he wouldn't offend him. In turn, August tried to be receptive to his tutor's lessons, but found Percyfoot to be a ridiculous old codger. Still, in the name of peace, he was trying his best to please.

Sir Reginald never rose before noon, so August took to exploring the brownstone he'd been bestowed in the morning hours. Though a five-story building can never be conceivably called humble, due to the decorating style of Miss Butler, the whole place did have a quaint and cozy feel. Lace and frills and rugs dominated the landscape, and any surface that could facilitate the display of bric-a-brac did the work of Atlas, shuddering under the weight of saccharine glass figurines. August knew his tastes ran to the spartan (he'd decorated his apartment with nothing but a mattress on the floor), but still, this was all so very . . . *close.* However, he had to admit it was comfortable; there was many a nook in which to share some private companionship with a book.

Reading was what he'd missed most. It was hard to justify spending what little money he'd stolen on books, and when he did splurge, his peers, most of whom were illiterate, subjected him to vicious torment. One can only be called Poindexter so long before the habit of reading is dropped. The fading of the pastime had been lamented, despite the jeers, and August sank back into books with the desperate joy of the relapsing addict.

August read often. Percyfoot noticed, and let the boy be. He also let the boy be when he stumbled home past two in the morning, reeking of gin. He also let the boy be when he swore, pissed in inappropriate places, or unexpectedly shattered one of the knickknacks that cluttered up the house. (Reginald had shattered a knickknack or two of his own. There were thousands!) In short, Percyfoot found he was letting the boy be most of the time, for when he faced facts, Reginald realized he didn't know how to deal with his new charge. He was good with young boys and adults; this intermediate stage was not his forte.

That was always abundantly clear during their scheduled lessons. Sir Reginald was already in a foul mood, as a solicitor had the audacity to ring for him at the ungodly hour of eleven in the morning. "Don't these people have any decency?" he grumbled as he aggressively smeared his toast with butter. "Learn this, if nothing else, my boy," he said, gesticulating with the knife. "Morning people are detestable villains. Condescending, sanctimonious bastards. I guarantee I accomplish more in a day than they do during their precious sunrises. I've no objection to *mornings*, mind you, but morning *people*? Was there ever a more self-satisfied, holier-than-thou race of man? Goddamn Pecksniffian hypocrites! Pardon my French, lad. Oh, but don't get me started on the French."

But it seemed he had started, and there was no obvious way of damming the flood of his tirade. After a millennium of French disparagement, August was able to force in an interjection during a rare breath from Percyfoot. "Are we done?" he asked, as politely as he could.

"Done?" Percyfoot blustered. "Done? Why we haven't even begun! We were going to cover the Crusades today, my lad. Rousing stuff!"

August tried to look interested, but Sir Reginald wasn't deceived. The boy was slumped in his chair as if his spine had committed suicide. What to do? Sir Reginald was no teacher; he was one of the world's finest actors. Still, he'd made a vow to finally give August the life he deserved. But the boy was so goddamned annoying. Sit up straight, for the love of god! Piss in the toilet! Don't set fire to the sitting room!

Mirroring the boy's slouch in dejected self-pity, Percyfoot was suddenly struck with an ingenious idea. Why not make use of that hallowed device that rich and unskilled parents had been relying on for generations? The boarding school! Such an obvious solution! August would meet well-bred peers his own age, be taught by men who knew how to navigate the awful labyrinth of youth, and best of all, he would be gone, so Percyfoot wouldn't have to deal with him!

But, alas, the boy was a special case. He'd never attended school, and even if he had, he had no identification. He was so nonexistent. What facility of higher learning would ever accept such a foul-mouthed enigma like August?

The slouch of despair was resumed as Reginald resigned himself to an early death due to homeschooling-related causes.

After a few minutes, however, he broke his depressed silence with a roaring laugh. August jumped.

"What's the matter?" he asked.

"Nothing's the matter, my boy," Percyfoot boomed. "In fact, everything's been fixed. Go out and get rip-roaring drunk. You won't be able to much longer!"

August didn't like Percyfoot's ominous tone, but the suggestion did seem like a good one, so he slipped out the door and was off to a pub.

Percyfoot continued laughing. What an old fool he was! How could he have forgotten? As luck would have it, he was more than well acquainted with the headmaster of a very prestigious institution where August would receive the best education that his horrid homeland could offer.

Still chuckling, Percyfoot slathered another piece of toast with too much butter as he hashed out the finer details of his plan. Blackmail was going to be fun.

PART THREE

The Willington West Academy for Gifted Boys was situated on a sprawling apple orchard in eastern Massachusetts. The fact that the school's name, Willington West, and its location, eastern Massachusetts, didn't coincide in the slightest was never mentioned. Established in 1834, WWAFGB accepted only the most gifted of boys, as long as they were gifted with plenty of money.

The current headmaster was named Archibald Haven Ferdinand St. Christopher Richmond IX. He'd attended the Willington West Academy for Gifted Boys in his youth, as had every previous headmaster save the first, and had held his position for seven years. Breaking the stereotypical mold of the stodgy old academic, Archibald was in good health, had a full head of hair, kept a lean figure, boasted a confident smile with a handshake to match, and clocked in at the almost suspiciously young age of sixty-seven. He was adored by the boys, tolerated by the board's crotchety elders, and ignored by the students' parents, who generally had no time to waste on parenting.

Of course, Archibald Haven Ferdinand St. Christopher Richmond IX hadn't always been a headmaster. In fact, his distant past was about as far removed from dusty libraries and desk-drawer decanters as it could get. In his early twenties,

Archibald had taken it into his head to study abroad in England. His parents were delighted, not only that he showed such an interest in his education but that there would be an entire ocean between the couple and their lovely spawn. Perhaps due to the unfamiliar bucolic terrain, perhaps swept up in the romantic fantasy of a life on the road, but almost certainly in an act of flagrant postadolescent rebellion aimed toward his conservative parents, Archibald dropped out before the end of his first term at Cambridge to join a traveling troupe of actors. Needless to say, the Richmonds were outraged, and a delighted Archibald went on to have one of the most exciting chapters of his life. In the course of this year he collected experiences and friendships in abundance, but no one he encountered would have such a profound effect on him as Reginald Percyfoot.

The pair became fast friends, Percyfoot recognizing Archibald's sheer intellectual brilliance while the latter reveled in the former's enormous talent onstage. The entire company would stay up until all hours every night, a hallmark of traveling actors in their twenties, but long after the last of the lights had been shut off, Archibald and Reginald would still be extrapolating the finer points of Molière or Wilde.

The blatant fact that Archibald had little to no acting talent was obvious to both, and after a year on the road, the defiant rogue reentered the hallowed halls of academia where he belonged. However, the two had managed to maintain a steadfast friendship through the years, a friendship Percyfoot was planning to exploit.

Percyfoot sat behind the wheel of a Chrysler or Chevrolet (he could never tell the difference). Having lived the majority of his adult life in London, with the occasional sojourn to New York, he'd never learned to drive, nor had he felt the lack. That was until he'd been forced to inhabit the smoggy cesspool that is Los Angeles. The poor man was forced to learn the mechanics of the automobile, a skill he felt he was better off not knowing.

Alas, he now could operate a car, and he jammed his foot on the clutch, slamming the blasted contraption into gear as he headed toward the Willington West Academy for Gifted Boys, the vehicle shuddering in protest all the while, as ill at ease with its driver as the man was with the machine.

After getting lost more than twice and employing some acrobatic swearing, he finally pulled into the long drive that led to Willington. To say that the school was impressive would be an understatement most egregious. It sprawled, but in an ivy-choked, milk-and-honey sort of way.

Percyfoot parked his car near what he thought was the school's main building, though in all likelihood it was probably the servants' quarters, or perhaps the lost-and-found. Standing in the cavernous entryway, however, was Archibald Haven Ferdinand Et cetera, beaming his trademark smile.

My god, he's thin, thought Percyfoot, consciously sucking in his paunch. Hasn't aged a day.

"Reggie!" cried Archibald, jogging the remainder of the distance to his friend and wrapping him in a hug.

How American, thought Sir Reginald, smiling all the same at the generous greeting. This folksy charm was what had drawn him to Archibald in the first place, that and the man's splendid mind.

"Archie." Percyfoot laughed through the hug. "I see you're just as demonstrative as ever."

"Well, come on, let's have a tour!" Archie said, bouncing on the balls of his feet. At the moment, he looked far more like the schoolboys under his charge than a dignified man approaching old age. Percyfoot had to practically skip to keep up with him.

As the tour progressed, Archibald calmed, his voice settling into a stately tenor as he described the history of the school, the architect's intent, the style of the gardens. After the long and stressful drive, Percyfoot would've preferred a hot meal and a large chair to the echoing chambers of Willington, but he could see Archibald was having a good time showing off and he wanted his friend properly subdued before he sprang his ambush. One can only see so many archways, however, before the mind wearies. When Archibald led him toward yet another building, the school's oldest dormitory, the seasoned actor finally snapped.

"For the love of god, man! You needn't detail the history of every brick! Let's have a sit."

Archie, accustomed to the artist's capricious mood swings, was unoffended and took Percyfoot straight to his office, an oak-paneled paradise with all the trappings of scholarly masculinity. Brass busts, varying bottles filled with amber liquors, oil paintings so dark one could hardly make out what was depicted; a veritable utopia for a bespectacled bachelor. Percyfoot found the most impressive of the leather wingback chairs and sank into it gratefully.

"It really is lovely to see you," said the headmaster. "Care for some scotch?"

"Oh, just a drop, how kind of you to offer. A bit more, if you don't mind. Oh, for god's sakes, man, we aren't Protestants, fill the damn glass."

The two men clinked their libations together and each took a taste, savoring the liquor and one another's company.

"I admit, I was most intrigued as to the reason of your visit," Archibald eventually said, alluding to the phone call Percyfoot had placed regarding August's installation at the school. "Really, Percy, you needn't have gone through the hoopla of inventing an orphan child just to stop over. I'm more than happy to entertain an old friend." Again he flashed a winning smile, sparkling with mischief.

So the subject had been broached without him having to bring it up. Sir Reginald corrected his posture and prepared to pounce.

"I'm afraid the boy is no fib, Archie. His name is August March, and he's my ward. I intend to adopt him."

A furrowed brow of genuine puzzlement replaced the headmaster's sly grin. "You mean to say that you've really taken in a child of the streets? Forgive me, but you're hardly the model of paternal devotion. In fact, you're the most selfish narcissist I've ever met. Again, no offense intended."

"None taken," Percyfoot replied truthfully. He swilled the scotch gently in its tumbler before changing the subject. "Do you remember, in the year we traveled together, that little town we played all summer? It was close to Brighton."

"Of course," answered Archibald. "Quite fondly, in fact."

"What was the name of that town? It's escaped me."

"I can't recall."

"Such a quaint little place," said Percyfoot. "We had quite a summer there."

"We've enjoyed many summers together."

"Indeed," Percyfoot said, letting the weight of memory fill the room. "You're going to accept August March into your school."

The headmaster guffawed. "You're joking!" Archie saw by Reginald's face that there was no jest intended. "But you can't be serious? We have Rockefellers at Willington, boys who've grown up in the shadow of the White House. You can't expect their sort to mingle with a foundling just because you've taken a shine to him. Even if I were to accept the child, the board would have my head! I'm sorry, but it's ludicrous. It can't be done." Archibald was nearly winded by his friend's obstinacy. Nothing in the forty-some-odd years he'd known the man had prepared him for his sudden dive into the sugary waters of fairy-tale sentiment. Was this to be a rags-to-riches story Percyfoot planned to capitalize on? The waif transformed by the beneficent godfather? It made no sense. Percyfoot was a pompous, self-absorbed, egocentric, libidinous debaucher.

Percyfoot smiled, swishing some scotch about in his mouth before swallowing, savoring the burn. He continued as if Archie had said nothing. "You're going to accept August into your school, or I'll expose you. Imagine the controversy. A man of your particular . . . inclination running Willington? What would the board think? What would the parents say? You wouldn't last a minute once the story broke." Percyfoot finished his scotch with a triumphant swallow. "Good stuff," he said. "I think I'll have another glass."

Archibald, his hand not even inching toward the scotch, looked at Sir Reginald with cold contemplation. "What's the meaning of this?" he asked. "You mean to come in here and ruin me for the sake of some trash you've taken in off the street? After a lifetime of friendship? I can't understand you."

Percyfoot's smug air of victory vanished. "Archie, you must know I'd never do anything to seriously harm you."

"Then what in the name of god was—"

Percyfoot put a hand up to stop the onslaught. "A spot of fun that I, admittedly, took too far. But please believe me when I say that nothing in this world means more to me than the future of this boy, even your reputation. He's brilliant. Take him under your wing. I wouldn't trust him to anyone else."

The headmaster, tempered after Reginald's speech, remained unconvinced. "We only accept the best families here at Willington. A ruffian from the street hardly constitutes—"

"Damn your prejudice!" Percyfoot yelled, slamming his fist down on the end table. "He's a remarkable child who's had despicable luck, yet against all odds he's survived. We must do right by him!"

This was most peculiar. Reggie, huffing and moist-eyed? For some child? After a brief respite, Archibald stood and, with a generous pour, refilled Percyfoot's scotch. "I must admit your determination surprises me. I've never seen you take this much interest in a human being before, save for certain deceased European playwrights."

They sat for a few minutes in the comfortable silence of long acquaintance, sipping scotch and pondering.

"I'll take the boy on," Archie finally acquiesced. "On a limited trial, of course."

"Perfect!" Reginald exclaimed, bouncing to his feet, echoing Archibald's previous enthusiasm. "Everything's settled! Now kiss me, you old devil. You look positively ravishing!"

* * *

The transition from Scarsenguard orphan to street thief had hardly been a smooth passage, but that was nothing compared to the shift from street thief to proper boarding-school boy. Life at Willington was so foreign, August felt he might've adjusted sooner had he moved somewhere Asiatic; a new culture and alphabet would hardly present as many challenges as the gaping gulf of the class divide.

The boys were simply impossible to relate to. In New York, if August gave someone half an apple or helped a fellow pickpocket shake off the cops, an alliance was formed, simple as that. The lines were not so clear at Willington. Unaccustomed to the differences between old and new money, August committed so many graceless faux pas within his first week that he was quickly banished to the very outskirts of the community, a chronic social leper detested even more than Richie Simon, the boy whose father had made his fortune in the newspaper industry; tradesmen were tolerated, but a journalist? One's values can only stoop so low.

August didn't mind being a pariah; he was used to operating alone. The truth was, these persnickety virgins filled him with an amused pity. The height of rebellion was to sneak off and smoke a cigarette. For god's sakes, hadn't anyone stolen the tires off a car and then gotten blackout drunk to celebrate?

The boundaries between the Willington set and August came to a head one afternoon when the students were given a bit of time to loll about on one of the lawns and "just be boys," as the professors sometimes put it. August suspected this time was more for the professors to "just get drunk," but that was neither here nor there. Most of the boys lay about together in that affectionate chummy way that only exists at boarding school, while August sat separately, his back against a handsome oak, blatantly smoking and not giving a damn if he was caught, a habit the other students all loathed and respected him for.

He was enjoying his cigarette when a boy, kicking a ball around with some of his friends, shouted, "Think fast, March."

The ball whizzed through the air and hit August hard on the side of his head. He wasn't hurt; it was more shocking than painful. But that wasn't the point. This was clearly a power display, and the boy who'd kicked the ball, a bossy loathsome prick by the name of Prescott Alderly, was testing him for weakness. Well, if Prescott wanted an enemy, August was more than happy to give him one. After all, it was hard to be frightened of a Willington bully when just a few months prior, he'd seen one of his friends stab another boy in the leg.

August rose, crossed to Prescott, handed him back his ball, and in a flash, delivered three quick jabs to his stomach. Prescott, winded and clutching his midsection, fell to the ground, groaning.

"Bastard," Prescott moaned through his pain.

"I'd rather be a bastard than a priggish little fuck like you," August replied.

He strolled off back toward his dorm, tossing the still-lit butt of his cigarette on the lawn, while the Willington boys stared in wide-eyed wonder.

* * *

Rumors spread like good jam. Had August March really beat up Prescott Alderly? And was he really and truly a bastard?

None of the students had ever met a bastard before, and all felt a mixture of shock, disgust, and pride knowing that they'd consorted with one. August's dorm mates, two boys who were pale as milk with less than half the flavor, gave August such a wide berth that they inched along the wall when heading to bed, both practically wallpaper. Even the professors were impressed by the scandal.

"It seems this March boy is a right and proper bastard," Professor Firestone, head of history, said to Professor Sharp, head of mathematics.

"Can't be," Professor Sharp replied, balancing an ashtray on his protrusive gut as he smoked yet another bowl of tobacco from his resin-caked pipe. "Even old Richmond wouldn't stoop so low as to let a bastard into Willington, no matter how far left he leans."

"Still," said Firestone, pouring himself a third fingerful of gin though he'd sworn not to drink before nightfall, "it is odd, his joining midterm and all that. He's been less than exceptional in my class."

"Indeed," Sharp agreed. "I find him onerous at best."

A moment of silence as both men surrendered to their vices.

"Did you hear he made a fool of Prescott Alderly?" Professor Firestone eventually offered.

The ashtray shattered on the floor as Professor Sharp shot up, clapping his hands together like a biddy at the opera. "No! Oh, tell me everything! Tell me everything!"

For his part, August hardly noticed his evolving status. When he entered a room, he did perceive a certain hush, but he attributed it to his classmates' disgust rather than their interest. What truly troubled him were his studies, for though he played the part of the carefree rebel, August was actually quite concerned to discover just how far he lagged behind his peers.

English was a breeze; when given the syllabus, August was happy to see he'd already read every book on the list, most of them before he was ten. But the other subjects were baffling. Physics? Latin? And just what was a fraction? His primary tutors up to this point had been Miss Butler, Sir Reginald, and Sergeant Sycamore. None of them had prepared August for something so ridiculous as the periodic table of elements. All his life, August had counted himself among the cleverer half of humans, but to find that he was duller than the boy who chewed on the bottom of his necktie all through algebra was a revelation most cruel. Instead of rigorous application, August adopted the classic defense mechanism of withdrawing completely, his marks suffering for it.

The plain fact of the matter was, now that all his basic human needs were consistently met, August had time to think about what he wanted from his future. The trouble was, he had no idea. Should he study ferociously so that he might be accepted into some Ivy League university like the rest of his Willington peers? That life didn't interest him in the slightest. But now that he was off the streets, he no longer aspired to be a bookie, the coveted career of the boys he used to run with. He hated that he academically trailed these snobbish spoiled dandies. August liked being intelligent. He wanted to make a mark. To change things and to impact people.

But how?

* * *

Whenever he needed a respite from the overindulged boys of Willington, August would scale the eight-foot stone wall that bordered the grounds and take himself on a walk, reminiscent of his midnight mind-clearing strolls through Manhattan. On one of these expeditions, August happened upon another campus, Sainted Sisters of the Slaughtered Lamb, which believe it or not, was a Catholic school—but, more important, a Catholic school for girls.

It became August's favorite pastime to slip through the fence of Sainted Sisters well past curfew and make the acquaintance of one of her pupils. Not in a disreputable sort of way. The girls attending Sainted Sisters were all set to become the wives of senators, high-powered hostesses who secretly oversaw their husbands' careers. They weren't about to partake in a schoolgirl liaison and end up in the family way, least of all with someone like August. But that didn't mean they weren't above sneaking out of their rooms at night and flirting with a troubled rebel from New York City.

For his part, August appreciated that though the girls at Sainted Sisters were just as haughty and stuck-up as the boys at Willington, they had a second sight his male classmates lacked. Yes, they were born to wealth, but they were still women; the world wasn't handed to them on a platter in the same way. Even the wealthiest woman in the world still had to find an angle if she wanted to play the game. August liked that, respected it.

Plus they were prettier.

August's tactic was to stand outside the main dormitory, throw pebbles at windows, and when he got an answer, invite the girl down for a night of illicit flirtation. Not the most original method of courtship, but most of his peers were ignorant of Cyrano, so being wooed by an eloquent oddball still evoked a romantic thrill. Sometimes a particularly devout or conscientious student rejected him, but more often than not, his intended would smirk and then rush downstairs for a coquettish amble.

Unfortunately for August, tonight there were two nuns outside the dorms, deep in a serious conversation that didn't look like it was about to end anytime soon. Damn. He supposed he could try to wait them out, but crouching behind a bush all night watching two women in wimples chitchat wasn't why he'd snuck out of Willington and risked expulsion.

August would try again later. He had a flask of whiskey, filched from a professor's desk. Why not have a drink, enjoy the sights, and swing back in an hour or so?

"Splendid idea," August whispered to himself, setting off to explore the grounds.

* * *

The liquor filled August's stomach with a pleasant warmth, and he was humming lazily, approaching what he guessed to be some stables. It seemed every rich person knew how to ride a horse, but August couldn't imagine it. He'd seen the beasts pulling carriages through Central Park; they were massive. Who in their right mind would climb atop one and kick it in the ribs?

His equestrian reflections were interrupted by a voice behind him. "Who are you?"

August spun around, worried he'd be faced by a burly nun, but instead there stood a young woman near his age, clearly a student of the Sainted Sisters, eyeing him with just a hint of amusement beneath her suspicion. Something about her trace of playfulness comforted August; it was even familiar in an odd sort of way. Assured that there was no immediate danger, August turned on the charm. "Don't worry about me," he said with a wink. "I'm nobody. And you are?"

She smiled. "Me? I'm just a girl trying to assess your threat level and wondering whether I should call for the headmistress or go straight to the police."

This was unexpected. His sangfroid allure usually worked wonders on schoolgirls. This particular schoolgirl, however, was unimpressed.

"You could call for neither?" was August's feeble suggestion.

She sighed. "I suppose you're right. As much as I'd love to see you lashed for trespassing, I'd also be punished for breaking curfew. I'm afraid your squirming and yelps aren't worth that. Besides," she added, assessing him with a cold flick of her eyes, "you don't seem like much of a threat at all." With that, she walked off without another word, her long dark braid whipping behind her.

August was stupefied. Where were the giggles? The wide eyes full of veiled vanity? She'd gone nearly ten paces before he'd gathered his wits and started chasing after her.

"Excuse me," he whispered.

She ignored him.

"Excuse me," August tried again.

She stopped and turned, humorless. "What?"

Yes. Exactly. What? What precisely did he intend to say?

"I have whiskey," August offered, pulling out the flask.

Here she sighed again. "Follow me."

How divine!

The girl led August to the stables, and after peeking her head in with a furtive glance, pulled him inside.

"We should be fine in here," she said, grabbing the flask and taking a healthy swig. "They hardly ever check the grounds after lights out." She started absentmindedly stroking one of the drowsy horses' snouts while August tried to decide how to stand so that he might appear careless and dashing. He leaned against a gate, then nearly screamed when a horse gently nickered behind him.

"Not a horse person?" asked the girl with a cocked eyebrow.

"What? No! They're incredible creatures. Very . . . tall."

"I love them," she said, continuing to pet the mare behind her.

"Of course you do," August mumbled.

"What's that supposed to mean?"

Something about this girl put August on the wrong foot. He backpedaled. "It's just that you're wealthy. Wealthy people like horses."

"You go to Willington?" she guessed.

"Yes," August answered.

"Then you're wealthy, too."

"I am not," he snapped back.

The girl rolled her eyes. "Oh, I suppose you're there on a scholarship? The bigots who run that place are famous for their generosity."

It was too difficult to explain his rather confusing situation to this spoon-fed person who probably grew up on some palatial estate on the back of a horse.

"I didn't mean to offend you," August said. "It's hard for me to relate to the affluent at times. My circumstances are abnormal, to put it lightly."

The girl took another drink from the flask. "My mother died five years ago. Less than two months after her funeral, my father remarried. His new wife doesn't care for me much, so ever since the wedding, I've been attending private boarding schools. I hardly ever go home, my father rarely writes." She didn't say any of this with self-pity, just a sort of dull resignation. "You're not the only one with an interesting life."

August was sympathetic to her plight, but couldn't help adding, "My life is pretty interesting, though."

She laughed. August did, too. He'd made her laugh.

"Go on then, Mr. Interesting," she said, "fascinate me."

Obviously she'd known hardship, but August still feared she'd judge him if she learned he was nothing but an urchin. However, he didn't want to lie after she'd been so vulnerable. What could he tell her without giving too much away?

"I'm from New York City," he finally decided.

"Me too," she replied. "What part?"

"What?" August asked. A horse girl from the city? She must be very rich indeed.

"I said me too. I grew up on Eighteenth Street. What about you?"

"The Scarsengua—I mean the Lower East—I mean Twenty-Third Street."

"Did you move a lot?" she asked.

"I guess you could say—" But before August could finish his thought, a revelation overtook him. "Did you say Eighteenth Street?"

"Yes."

"It couldn't be," he whispered.

"What?"

"East Eighteenth Street? Between Irving and Third?"

"Yes," she answered, visibly disturbed.

August jumped into the air and hooted.

"You're the girl with the dark curly hair!"

"What?"

"I used to stand outside your window! You would wave at me!"

Realization dawned on her face. "That was you?"

"Yes!" August cried.

"Oh my god! You're the weirdo!"

Now it was August's turn to be disturbed. "What?"

"The weirdo! The kid who always hung around! My dad hated you!"

"Why are you the girl with the dark curly hair, and I'm the weirdo?"

But she was laughing too hard to answer. "This is crazy," was all she could manage. August started laughing, too. It was suddenly the most hilarious thing that had ever happened.

"What's going on here?" a sharp voice demanded, serious as a guillotine. A grim middle-aged nun stood in the entrance to the stables. When she saw August, her eyes widened. "Good heavens!" she gasped.

Instantly the girl started crying. August was surprised; he hadn't taken her to be the type to crack under pressure.

"Explain yourself immediately," the nun commanded, clutching her rosary so tight August pitied the beads.

"He tricked me, Sister," said the girl through a sheen of tears. "He told me he was a stable boy. Right before curfew he came up to me and said one of the horses was hurt. And then, when we got here, he wouldn't let me leave." She was sobbing now.

Incredible. Truly astounding. August had seen some fine actresses at the Scarsenguard, but this performance was the stuff of legend. He wanted to fling roses at her, weeping out her name, but realized he'd forgotten to ask what her name even was. Tragedy! He settled back in to watch her work.

The nun bought her act completely. Reaching for a heavy shovel mounted on the wall, she growled, "Sinner. Wretched boy."

Before she could dismember August, the girl rushed into the nun's arms and aggressively wept. "I was so scared, Sister. I couldn't run away."

August watched the proceedings with awe.

"I said, I couldn't *run away*," she cried again. Finally, she pulled herself off the nun's breast and turned to August. "Run away."

He finally understood. While the girl flailed about in the nun's arms, practically pinning the older woman to the wall, August dashed out the stable door and started sprinting back to Willington. He'd covered quite a bit of ground and thought he was in the clear when he heard a gunshot ring out.

Jesus Christ! Could nuns own guns?

Another gunshot sounded in answer.

"The fearful and the abominable and whoremongers," screamed the nun in the distance, "shall have their part in the lake that burneth with fire and brimstone, which is the second death!"

August decided not to return to the Sainted Sisters of the Slaughtered Lamb. Even the girl with dark curly hair wasn't worth dying for.

* * *

Archie,

How's the weather, old man? Bloody miserable in London, but it is nice to be back. Was fearing I'd have to appear in a musical if I stayed in New York. Honestly, what a desperate commercial ploy. They'll never last.

[Several paragraphs eviscerating American theatre, followed by several more on the fallacies of Hollywood.]

Speaking of August, how is he adjusting? Headstrong bastard won't answer a single one of my letters, though I write him at least twice a day. But that's teenagers, I suppose. Horrid people. Please respond with everything he's up to, no detail is too mundane.

I must off. Miss you most ferociously. Give the boy my love, but take care not to embarrass him in front of his friends.

Yours,
Reggie

FACULTY ANNOUNCEMENTS

Greetings, Gentlemen,

Another school year bustles along. Congratulations are in order to Professor Saunders, who led the crew team to a second place victory in the nationals this past weekend. Well done, Saunders! Drinks are in order.

Professor Roberts asks me to remind everyone that auditions for Romeo and Juliet *are fast approaching. Appearing in at least one production while at Willington is a graduation requirement for all students, so please encourage the boys to attend, especially if they might have a flair for the dramatic. See Professor Roberts for more details.*

That's all for this week. As always, don't hesitate to reach out with any questions or concerns. And please keep me abreast as to how the students are faring, particularly any new students that are just settling in here at Willington.

Until next week,
Headmaster Richmond

To: Headmaster Richmond
From: Professor Sharp

August March is a nuisance and, if I may be blunt, rather dull. His marks are teetering very close to failing in my Level 1 Algebra. When I told him this, he replied (in front of the entire class), "Polynomials? Inverse trigonometric functions? I understand it takes all types to make the world go round, but merciful god, there are limits."

Please expel him.

To: Headmaster Richmond
From: Professor Firestone

I have found August March to be a disruptive force on several occasions. For example, yesterday he was violently snoring during my lecture on the French and Indian War. When I roused him with a sharp application of my ruler, the boy said my lessons were so dull that not even those who'd been involved in the French and Indian War would be bothered to care.

He needs a firm hand, or perhaps a prison cell.

To: Headmaster Richmond
From: Professor Thompson

August March frightens me.

Dear Reggie,

August is acclimating well.

Must dash,
Archie

Dear August,

Now listen here, I understand you're very busy, but this is ridiculous! Is it so much to ask for one brief response? Have you made any friends? Are you enjoying your studies? Are you alive? I hate to beg, but bloody hell! Tell an old man what's happening!

Imploringly,
Sir Reginald

Sir Reginald,

I am alive. Thank you for your (belated) interest on the subject.

—August

FACULTY ANNOUNCEMENTS

Greetings, Gentlemen,

Nearly November already. My how the time does fly.

I suppose I should skip the pleasantries and get straight to the point. As I'm sure you're all aware, on Thursday afternoon, the south side of Willington's cathedral was defaced. We're all privy to the rumor mill's merciless hyperbole, so forgive my impropriety, but I feel it best to be clear: depicted in great detail is a gigantic mural of Professor Sharp and Professor Firestone engaging in a graphic act of simultaneous fellatio. We know the figures are meant to be Sharp and Firestone as their names are legibly printed on their robes, though the likeness is clear in any case.

The vandal remains at large. Some professors rightfully demanding justice have insisted that the culprit is August March, but his rooms have been searched and no evidence was found. Innocent until proven guilty, this is America after all. Rest assured we are doing everything we can to find the culprit.

The custodial staff is working tirelessly to remove the mural, but have informed me that the paint is proving to be rather stubborn. Please have patience and know that it remains a top priority.

In less lurid news, Romeo and Juliet *has been cast. Congratulations to all involved!*

Until next week,
Headmaster Richmond

Archie,

Any news on August? Sorry to pester, but I must admit to being dreadfully worried.

Yours,
Reggie

Reggie,

Boy is good.

Archie

To: Headmaster Richmond
From: Professor Kuhn

As you know, one of my duties in running the English department is to oversee the school newspaper. I rarely censor the boys, but I received a submission for this month's edition that I felt couldn't be printed (though it was quite spirited). I thought you might be interested to read it over.

Willington Monthly Opinion Column Submission:
STUDENT NAME: AUGUST MARCH

Willington West is supposedly one of the finest institutions of learning the Americas have to offer. But after my brief experience with Willington's theatre department (or lack thereof), it is my opinion that no school allowing such maladies to befoul its stage should be legally allowed to remain open.

I had been warned by peers and even a professor or two that the dramatics at Willington were a "touch weak," but after enduring a few rehearsals for *Romeo and Juliet*, I can safely say that a blistering, infected sore would be a more apt description.

After giving what I thought to be a rather good audition (for an amateur), I was cast in the role of Paris. Not one of Shakespeare's finest creations, but then again, they can't all be Falstaff. I intended to make the character as three-dimensional as possible (given my limited skills), and was excited for the challenge.

However, once rehearsals started, I saw I was the only person present who held even the slightest bit of enthusiasm for the project. The boys, a collection of clutched scripts and shuffling feet, inspected each other from the corners of their eyes with suspicion and delivered their lines with all the relish of particularly stale crackers. The bard's words fell from their mouths like lead: cold, empty, metallic.

In my naïveté, I thought our director, Professor Roberts, might be able to awaken something from his wooden players, but after getting us onstage and telling us what page to start from, Professor Roberts would, without fail, fall into a chronic sleep, loudly dreaming while we butchered our way through a masterpiece.

One afternoon, the students playing the titular characters announced that, even though it was integral to the plot, they refused to kiss one another (these Willington boys are the most prudish pack of virgins I've ever associated with. A brothel would do them a world of good). I understandably exploded. Using the support of an extended rib cage, an activated diaphragm, and the full range of my larynx, I cursed the production, the cast, and our director. Had the boys onstage cared to improve their talents, they might've taken note of my technique and learned a thing or two. Alas, they didn't care. They didn't care at all.

My shouting did manage to stir Roberts from his coma. I thought: Finally! Some direction! Instead, all we got was, "Well done, lads. Take five. Or ten. Actually, we're done for the day." Then he slipped back into slumber, obviously proud of his quick thinking. I stormed out.

Burning the theater down and salting the scorched earth would be far too lenient a solution. I fear for the souls of all involved.

To: Professor Roberts
From: Headmaster Richmond

As of today I'm removing you from your position as director of Romeo and Juliet. *Going forward, you will act as an academic supervisor. The production will now be overseen by a student, August March. I understand he suddenly quit the play, and I've decided to employ a rather unconventional disciplinary approach. Finish what you started, et cetera. To be honest, I'm looking for an activity that might occupy the boy and keep him out of trouble, and it seems he feels quite passionately about the arts.*

When I told August of his punishment, he accepted on one condition: that he be allowed to choose a new show. I told him he was in no position to make demands, but he insisted that the boys were too immature to play a romance, and something with a bit of blood and guts (his words) would excite them more. He suggested King Lear, *and though I think a piece whose central theme focuses on aging and senility might be a touch inappropriate for school-age boys, August seems enthusiastic. I trust you have no objections? As rehearsals have only just begun, I hardly think it will be an issue.*

Check in every now and again, but the extra time is now yours to do with as you please. Might I suggest a midafternoon nap? Several countries in the Mediterranean have apparently been employing the practice for years.

To: Headmaster Richmond
From: Professor Roberts

Sounds splendid!

INFIRMARY REPORT

PATIENT NAME: Gregory Ashford

INJURY: Gash on cheek

CAUSE OF INJURY: "Sword fighting"

PATIENT STATEMENT: March comes from backstage with a giant bag. Tells us that *King Lear* is not a lot of sentimental drivel but a play steeped in violence, storms, and swords. Then, right when he said the word *swords*, he emptied the bag and it was full of . . . swords. Swords! The blades were pretty harmless, they're meant for the stage, but I still got nicked when we were using them. Can I go now? I don't want to miss any more of rehearsal.

TREATMENT: Disinfectant and a small bandage

To: Headmaster Richmond
From: Alan Grange, Head of Custodial Staff

The leak in the Southern Dormitory has been fixed.

There are hundreds of cigarette butts in the theater every evening. Hundreds. I went in this afternoon to see who the hell was leaving them around, and all the kids doing the play were smoking. I yelled at them but they told me someone named March said it was okay. I gave them a bucket full of sand and told them to ash in there. I'm fine with the rules changing but a fire hazard is a fire hazard.

The mural still won't come off the church. Ordered some industrial bleach.

Archie,

"Boy is good"? "Boy is good"? Never in our many years of correspondence have you sent me such a letter. I feel as if I'm trying to decipher the guttural utterances of a cave dweller. Really, Archie, these boorish grammatical bastardizations are hardly in your vein. Give me some answers! Your monosyllabic replies bring far more discomfort than August's lack of response—after all, he is a teenager and can hardly be counted on to behave with even an iota of courtesy. I demand a thorough reply or I

will be forced to storm the gates of Willington shouting the Crispin's Day speech. And you know I'm far too old to play Hal! Don't make me do this!

Desperately,
Reggie

My dearest Reggie,

How are you, old chap? Things are well at Willington other than an unseasonable amount of rain, but as you're in London, I'm sure I've no cause to complain when it comes to overzealous precipitation.

I suppose I should cut to the chase, as we say here in the States, and let you know that August is directing a production of King Lear *here at Willington. I'm giving him rather a free hand with the whole thing, and though it seems to be going well, I admit I'm hesitant to see the outcome. As I'm sure you're no doubt aware, August tends to eschew all rules and regulations when they don't coincide with his unique worldview. But after all, it's Shakespeare. How much harm can he do? Actually, I shudder to think. Dear god, what have I done?*

With love,
Archie

Archie,

When is it opening? I'll book a ticket immediately.

Reggie

P.S.
Don't tell August I'm coming.

FACULTY ANNOUNCEMENTS

Greetings, Gentlemen,

The semester draws to a close. Please have all your marks in before the holiday break, though I'm sure the students would much prefer you didn't.

This year's play, King Lear, *is on Friday night. Attendance, as always, is mandatory. In a Willington first, the production is student-directed. Perhaps if you relay this fact to the boys, they might show a bit more mercy than they have in the past. Before entering the theater, please check the students' bags for any fruit or other projectiles. We cannot have a repeat of last year's* The Winter's Tale *fiasco. Those poor boys in the bear costume never stood a chance.*

See you all there (attendance, as always, is mandatory for the professors as well).

Until next week,
Headmaster Richmond

Dear August,

I'm sure you won't respond to this letter and you've every right not to, but I felt I had to write and let you know: I saw your production of Lear. *Headmaster Richmond told me you were directing and I simply couldn't miss it. Please don't be upset. Or rather, feel free to be upset, but do me a favor and read this through to the end before you toss it into a fire?*

First off, let me say that I thought the whole thing was utterly brilliant. Honestly! I haven't seen a production of

Lear *that lively in years. True, great chunks of integral text were slashed and the acting was unfocused at best, but better broad than banal, I always say. You really brought it to life!*

Right from the start, you showed a real eye for design. When Lear divided up the kingdom among his daughters, dragging a brush covered in red paint across the large map? So effective! The bleeding red lines raked across the map like gashes, a clever dab of foreshadowing.

Though you made judicious cuts (quite wisely, in my opinion. The poor chap playing Kent was in over his head, wasn't he?), I thought the swordfights you added were quite a good spot of showmanship. I lost count after twenty-two bladed altercations, but the thing had punch!

The plucking of the eyes was legitimately chilling. Sincerely: I was (and still am) disturbed.

You had the audience in the palm of your hand long before you got to the storm (Oh, the storm! Fabulous! Just how on earth did you achieve the effect of Lear being lifted off the ground? I didn't see any rigging), but the crowd was positively frothing by the final duel between Edgar and Edmund. This encounter was truly your pièce de résistance (pardon my French). Where was the actor playing Edmund concealing the false arm he hurled into the audience? (I also appreciated the gallons of stage blood he sprayed on the first few rows. Again, where was he hiding everything? False pockets?)

I know you're probably angry with me for coming. But I just had to see it. I had to. I didn't congratulate you afterward because I couldn't risk spoiling your triumphant night but please know that I've never been more proud in the entirety of my life, and that's coming from one of the most selfish bastards the world has ever known.

I hope to hear from you soon, August. Be well.

Love,

Reginald

* * *

August responded immediately. From that time forward, Sir Reginald and August March enjoyed much written correspondence, each piece of mail earning a prompt and thorough reply.

* * *

The next two years of August's education passed with many an outlandish instance, but most are anecdotal in nature. Needless to say, August never fully conformed as the ideal Willington student, though he did settle down enough to pass all his classes and managed to stifle the nature of his rebellions from felonious to misdemeanorish.

At the graduation ceremony, which Sir Reginald proudly attended, August was one of the few boys singled out afterward to receive a few words and personal handshake from Headmaster Archibald Haven Ferdinand St. Christopher Richmond IX.

"Well done, August," said Richmond, smiling.

"Thank you, Headmaster."

"Not the easiest of students, but certainly one of the most interesting. And your production of *Agamemnon* will haunt me until my dying day." After the success of *King Lear*, August had been given full rein over Willington's theatrical endeavors. Never had the drama department been so popular, or so drenched in spectacular displays of bloodshed. The grisly machinations of Titus Andronicus, Ajax slaughtering the sheep; August even managed to make Hedda Gabler's suicide, scripted to be played offstage, an elaborate show of gory carnage. Archibald was pleased with what the boy had done in regard to getting the student populace excited about theatre, but he often worried about the sanctity of the plays being butchered, and for the safety of the boys involved in the productions as well.

"Did you enjoy the ceremony?" the headmaster asked, gesturing politely at the lawn currently filled with chattering students and parents.

"I found it trite and overwrought. A tired ritual celebrating mediocrity and wealth."

The headmaster sighed. "Oh, for god's sakes, August, do lighten up. Such ostentatious idealism grows wearisome." He turned to Percyfoot. "Will you be in New York long?"

"Long enough to get August settled."

"I'm thinking of popping into the city for a week or so in July."

"Well, do please call on me."

"What was that about?" August asked as he and Percyfoot walked toward the car.

"What?" Percyfoot replied.

"Are you friends with the headmaster?" August actually quite liked Headmaster Richmond, but he honestly couldn't see him running in the same circles as the famous actor Sir Reginald Percyfoot. He was nothing but an old schoolteacher, after all.

Percyfoot laughed. "You may know more than most boys your age, but you don't know everything."

They settled into the Chrysler or Chevrolet or whatever the hell it was called and started puttering to New York. August was delighted as Willington disappeared behind them and felt not even the slightest tinge of nostalgic loss.

"So what's next?" Percyfoot asked after they'd been traveling for some time. "University?"

August laughed so hard at this that tears actually sprang from his eyes. Eventually he said, "No, I think I'm done with the educational system, thank you."

Percyfoot, who had no love for institutions of learning himself, was unoffended by the reply, but was still curious as to what August had in mind for his future. "All right, no school then. But what will you do?"

August watched the lush green landscape blur by through the window of the car, eager for it to be replaced by the muted gray terrain of the city he loved so dearly. "I don't know," he finally answered. "But I'm sure I'll figure it out."

PART FOUR

New York's Greenwich Village was a thrilling place in the 1960s, if you went in for that sort of thing. No matter what door one opened, it seemed, a rapturous bohemian diversion awaited. Poetry, cabarets, the off-off-Broadway movement, folk music, rock music, the beats, coffeehouses, drugs; the neighborhood was a veritable paradise for the nonconformist.

Simon Helmer, a mustachioed man with overlarge ears, was not taken with the enchantments of the Village. Though he was settled comfortably in his mid-thirties, he still considered himself young, yet whenever he was forced to slog downtown, he found that not only was he the oldest person in any given room, he was the oldest by nearly a decade. Insufferable.

Yet it wasn't just the neighborhood's youth that irked Simon so. Draped in ill-fitting tweeds, Village locals loped about like languid Irish wolfhounds, battered copies of Kerouac in their back pockets. Simon tittered in disapproval as he straightened his exquisitely cut jacket; long had he held an inherent distrust of anyone clothed in a slouchy blazer. As he dodged a passing man whose nose was buried in a predominately displayed Faulkner, Simon sighed; never had he known that it was possible to read with ostentation until the Village. Ah, well. Better this breed of showy scholar than the detestable strain so obsessed with shawls and constellations. One doubted if this type *could* read, let alone ostentatiously.

The Village wasn't all moony-eyed twentysomethings deluding themselves into believing they were changing the world for the better, however. Carefully hidden amid the pretentious poetry readings and shaggy-haired guitarists, a small sect of society that wanted nothing to do with all this affected bohemia could be located: the grotesquely rich. One of these families, the Kingsleys, had invited Simon to a dinner party, and as he hurried through the streets, worried that his suit might become besmirched by a well-meaning dropout offering him a wreath of flowers, Simon checked his reflection in every shop window he passed, preening and primping as he went, his robust mustache receiving particular attention.

After Simon rang the bell, a butler led him into the sitting room, where Mrs. Kingsley, a tall woman with a distracting feather headpiece in her hair, rushed to greet him.

"Mr. Helmer, so good of you to come. Honestly, it's so nice to have some young people in the house for a change." Simon thought that given her way, Mrs. Kingsley, who was rapidly approaching sixty, would gladly drown every young person alive with her own two hands, but of course that wouldn't be polite conversation. "Now you simply must meet Miss Bayer."

And thus the night began. It was the usual set that appears at these sorts of things, a mixture of young and old, male and female, rich and very rich. No one would be offended; no feelings would be provoked. It was the perfect cocktail for a joyless evening of social obligation. Though Simon would've normally gotten quite tight to face such a tedious affair, he sipped his martini thoughtfully, careful to avoid drunkenness. For Simon had his own personal reasons for attending the party, and inebriation would do nothing but encumber his agenda.

The dinner bell was finally sounded, and the guests were shuttled through the townhouse by the butler. Most continued their previous conversations, but Simon stayed back at the rear of the group, admiring the grand staircase that swept up to the second floor and the beautiful paned windows that climbed with the steps.

He must have been gaping most preposterously, because he was completely surprised when a voice interrupted his admiring stare.

"Keen on architecture?" The voice belonged to Mr. Kingsley, who had also hung back to secretly refill his tumbler of scotch.

"Not really." Simon blushed. "It's just a hobby of sorts."

"Rather peculiar hobby," said Kingsley, taking a swig. "How does one muddle about in architecture? Seems like a subject you have to go whole hog on."

"Not architecture, sir. Sketching. I draw. Just for leisure, of course, nothing serious."

Kingsley brightened. "Why, that's wonderful! The missus and I absolutely love art. Crazy for it. Do you write?"

"No, sir, just draw. And not well—"

But Kingsley interrupted, listing the artists and writers who'd been guests at a dinner he hosted just last week. Simon had heard that in Los Angeles, name-dropping was a sort of sport. In New York, however, one was supposed to pretend not to care about such things, *pretend* being the key word. If name-dropping was a sport in LA, then in New York, it was an art—delicate, refined, and far more pretentious. Simon had no idea what to add to this conversation. Luckily, Mr. Kingsley was of the class that could converse without the aid of a partner, and peppered his one-sided discourse with a few more celebrity names before he finally seemed to remember that Simon was present.

"But if you love to sketch, then you must have a tour of the place after dinner."

Simon stuttered like an engine that couldn't quite catch. "Sir—it would b-be—but I—I wouldn't dream of imposing—"

"Nonsense! Nonsense! It'll be nice to show the place off for once. Most of our friends think we're crazy for living down here, but Mrs. Kingsley's of the mindset that uptown is a bit country, and I must admit I agree. We have a place on Park, of course, though we're here most of the time. When we're not in Newport, obviously. Or Paris."

The babbling continued as they made their way to the dining room, but now that he'd been promised a tour, Simon was able to relax. After all, that was why he'd come to this awful party in the first place.

* * *

Dinner was full of the vapid gossip and uninspired colloquy that would normally send Simon deep into a bottle of gin. Armand Constance, a hideous short old man with a hoary nose, was so drunk that he more than once dropped a racial slur, while his wife, seated down the table, refused to remove her mink, though its presence was obviously giving the butler conniptions. A young woman, probably somewhere in her mid-twenties, bore a tumble of red curls and would've been quite beautiful if she weren't so stupid. Simon had never understood the kind of man who favored a dumb woman. It would be nice, he supposed, to have your every word treated as if it were a pronouncement of genius, but surely the gratification was counterbalanced when the woman in question began speaking passionately about how fun bubbles were. This was the current topic of the young redheaded lady's conversation, and Simon shoveled a forkful of fish into his mouth so that he would not be literally forced to bite his tongue.

Mercifully, dessert was served, a tart raspberry sorbet, and dinner concluded without any other major infraction. The ballet of folding napkins and scraping chairs took place as Mrs. Kingsley suggested the ladies sojourn with her in the sitting room, while the men went and smoked, a very old-fashioned custom, Simon thought, for a couple who forced themselves to live in the Village so that they might keep abreast of all things young.

Worried that Mr. Kingsley might have forgotten his promise of a tour, or even renege on it in favor of a cigar, Simon sidled over to the master of the house and gently reminded him of their prior agreement.

"Of course I remember," insisted Mr. Kingsley, although he clearly didn't. Apparently their interchange was louder than Simon had intended, for the empty redheaded girl so fond of bubbles found her way into the conversation.

"A tour," she squealed, "wouldn't that just be grand?"

Simon could hardly think of anything less grand than sharing the same air as this defective model of humanity, but he could hardly say so. Again, the truth, no matter how blatant, rarely made for polite conversation.

"You must come along," said Kingsley with tongue-lagging lust. He may have been drunk, but not drunk enough to forget that his wife was present, for he quickly added, "In fact, everyone should join us."

"Join what, darling?" Mrs. Kingsley asked. She'd witnessed the entire exchange, and the venom in her question was lost on no one, except perhaps the redhead, who wouldn't have registered the presence of venom if a cobra's fangs were buried in one of her calves.

"Mr. Helmer here is a budding artist and wanted to see the place so that he might be inspired to sketch." Kingsley appeared so natural, so at ease in brushing off his wife's suspicion, that Simon was sure that his interest in pretty, hollow-headed women was nothing new.

Simon's inferences were confirmed when Mrs. Kingsley, hard as flint, fixed a stare on her husband, entirely unconvinced by his nonchalance. "Would anyone care to join my husband, Mr. Helmer, and—I'm so sorry, what was your name, dear? It seems to have slipped my mind."

A normal person would've been mortified by the slight Mrs. Kingsley had just leveled. A hostess would never, under any circumstance, forget the name of one of her guests, especially if that person were an eligible unmarried young woman. It has been previously mentioned, however, that the redhead's intellect was similar to that of a moose, or even a particularly witty daffodil, so the insult went unregistered.

"Please don't apologize, Mrs. Kingsley. I'm Miss Ava Cardew, and my dear aunt sent you a letter of introduction. Do you need to be reminded of my aunt's name as well?"

Though it seemed like a well-pointed jab, anyone could see the sincerity and guilelessness in the girl's wide eyes; Miss Cardew simply thought she was being polite.

Mrs. Kingsley's cold stare had not abated, but she managed to add some warmth to her voice as she said, "No, of course not, dear. Just a temporary lapse of good sense." This last bit was directed at Mr. Kingsley, who had managed to find something very interesting in one of his fingernails. The mood was stiff, and Mrs. Kingsley, consummate hostess, decided against making a scene. "Would anyone else care for a tour?"

The guests feigned polite interest, but it was clear that the idea was revolting to all involved. They struggled to find a cordial way of saying they'd rather commit ritualistic suicide on a butter knife than be forced to tour the household when Mr. Constance, drunk as a scorpion in a tequila bottle, saved everyone by saying, "I'd rather commit ritualistic suicide on a butter knife than be forced to tour the household."

Everyone nodded in concordance, and left the three outliers to their tour, god help them.

"Well," said Mr. Kingsley with a conspiratorial air, "now that those old farts are out of our way, let's have some real fun!"

"Oh yes, let's!" Miss Cardew agreed.

Simon tried to join in the spirit of the thing, but the fact that Miss Cardew was hanging about put a definite wrench into his plans, as Simon cared nothing for sketching.

"After you," said Mr. Kingsley, gesturing grandly. Miss Cardew gave a silly little curtsy and then began to ascend the staircase, Mr. Kingsley watching her so closely one would have thought the secret to immortality lay within her buttocks. As he observed Mr. Kingsley's less-than-platonic interest in the young woman, Simon decided that his concern about Miss Cardew's presence might have been a bit premature.

* * *

"And this second door here leads to the music room," Kingsley said, ushering them inside.

The tour thus far had been comprehensive and tiresome, but Simon, keenly focused on his private motivations, forced himself to stay alert, cataloging information away for later use. However, he did allow himself a fleeting moment to appreciate what an enchanting space the music room was. A grand pianoforte, a harp, guitars, woodwinds, reeds, and brass were displayed most advantageously.

"Oh my," gasped Miss Cardew.

Seeing her alight with pleasure seemed to smolder the coals of Mr. Kingsley's lust.

"Do you like it?"

"I love it! Mr. Kingsley, do you play?"

He laughed. "Not well."

"Oh, please play us something. Please!"

"I couldn't, really," he said, already striding toward the piano. "Well, perhaps just one song."

Kingsley stroked the keys, and Simon had to admit, he wasn't halfway bad. Then he started to sing, and Simon had to admit that he wasn't halfway good. Still, Miss Cardew was a creature enraptured; it was as if Apollo himself had deigned to play for her. When Mr. Kingsley (finally) finished, she exploded into applause. "Please play another, Mr. Kingsley. You must! You must!"

"Perhaps a duet?" he offered, patting the seat on the bench next to him.

She placed a hand to her breast in shock. One would have thought she'd been offered a starring role in the Met's latest opera.

"I'd be honored," she whispered, marching toward the bench with such solemnity that Simon had to bite his cheek to refrain from laughing.

But this was no time to relish another's foolishness. Fate had dealt Simon a good hand, and he didn't mean to squander it. As the happy couple prepared to delight each other with song, Simon interjected. "I'm so sorry, sir, but might I use a restroom?"

"Yes, yes, of course," said Kingsley, swatting away a bothersome insect. "There's one just down the hall to the left."

"Thank you," said Simon, dimming the lights ever so slightly as he left. It couldn't hurt.

He forced himself to walk at a normal pace, but once the music started and the pair began harmonizing (painfully), Simon broke straight into a sprint.

The Kingsleys were rich beyond measure, collectors of rare and precious gemstones. Simon didn't usually go in for this sort of thing, but he'd recently met a man who wanted nothing more than to lay claim to one particular gemstone, an emerald that went by the most atrocious name of Greener Pastures. This man was willing to pay quite a sum for Greener Pastures—half a million dollars, in fact. Though Simon didn't care to deal with famous rocks that could be traced, he did care a great deal about money, especially when it came in such large sums. This is because Simon Helmer was not a young gentleman enjoying a night of New York City society. He was a thief.

As he tore through the residence, gripping doorframes so that he might make sharper turns, Simon was grateful the tour had been so exhaustive, as it had given him the chance to achieve one of his primary objectives: locating the best point of entry for when he returned to steal the gem. All he had to do now was locate the Kingsleys' safe, for that's where Greener Pastures was sure to be housed.

Simon eliminated the guest rooms; no one would keep his safe where a guest might find it. Where to start, then? The wine cellar? Were polished gems meant to be stored in cool places? Regardless, the wine cellar was three floors down, and Simon didn't want to waste that much time for half of a hunch. Where then? The billiard room? He checked behind all the paintings and knocked on the game table to see if it was hollow or had a false door of sorts. No luck.

Panting, red-faced, and exhausted, Simon searched what felt like dozens of rooms without the slightest hint of victory. Triple damnation!

Defeated, he limped back to the music room, hoping he hadn't been missing for too long. He had to force himself to look chipper upon entering.

"So sorry," he said with a sheepish grin. "Afraid I got a bit lost."

"No worries, my good man," said Kingsley, jumping off the piano bench as if it had bit him. "We were just coming to look for you."

It was clear by Miss Cardew's blush and Mr. Kingsley's awkward half-lean, meant to conceal his erection, that they were about to do nothing of the sort.

"Do you play any other instruments, Mr. Kingsley?" Miss Cardew asked to fill the silence, for Simon, depressed and silent as a stone, hadn't the heart to play the game of polite chatter any longer.

"Not well, not well," Kingsley replied.

"What about the guitar?" she asked, losing her embarrassment and returning to her prior nymphlike state of fluttering, oblivious bliss. "I do so love the guitar."

For some odd reason, a wicked smile painted Mr. Kingsley's face. "Actually," he said, "I do fancy the guitar myself."

Must we? Simon thought as Kingsley plucked a rather ornate guitar off the wall; he didn't think he could bear another concert. Mr. Kingsley strummed the instrument, sounding a chord so horridly out of tune that even Miss Cardew winced. Still Mr. Kingsley smiled.

"Let me see here," he said, fiddling with the knobs at the top of the guitar's neck. "Something's not quite right."

And then suddenly the guitar face sprang open like a door, revealing a mess of important-looking papers inside, along with Greener Pastures, nestled safely atop a velvet pillow.

Miss Cardew was in hysterics. "Again!" she cried, clapping. "Again! Again!"

Mr. Kingsley was about to oblige when Mrs. Kingsley entered, followed by the rest of the party. She shot a biting look at Mr. Kingsley, who quickly snapped the guitar closed.

"Here you are," said Mrs. Kingsley. "Are we to be treated to a concert?"

"Oh, do play them a song, Mr. Kingsley. He has the most marvelous voice!"

Perhaps she was cleverer than Simon had given her credit for; he was absolutely sure she was about to blurt out that the guitar was really a safe. More likely than not, however, she had instantly forgotten about the safe, living entirely in the present, like a dog or a rock. No matter; Simon had found the safe after all. And the more people that knew its location, the better, for when Greener Pastures went missing, as it was soon to do, there would be more suspects. And more suspects meant less suspicion on Simon.

He smiled throughout the entirety of the recital, though it was painful, long, and dull.

* * *

Simon practically skipped uptown, completely forgetting to pass judgment on the Village's desperately colorful denizens. He even greeted a few as he walked.

"Wonderful night, isn't it?"

"That it is," replied the youth. "Say, brother, do you want to hear a poem about Cuba?"

"Nothing would please me less, in fact. Have a marvelous evening!"

Truly a joyous stroll.

Simon finally reached his destination, a quaint brownstone on East Twenty-Third Street. After unlocking the door, he hung his jacket with care, humming merrily all the while, and fixed himself a whiskey and soda, heavy on the whiskey. Still humming a melody most blithesome, he took his tumbler into the bathroom and appraised his reflection.

"Good night, Mr. Helmer," he eventually said.

Taking a long, bracing gulp of his drink, Simon ripped off his prosperous mustache with a mighty tug. Next to go were the tops of his overlarge ears. These he removed with more delicacy, for they were fragile and custom-fitted at great expense. The rest was easy; off with the wig, and then, to clear away the darkening makeup on his eyebrows, the gentle application of a washcloth wetted with warm water and, finally, a quick, painless extraction of the plug that flared out his nostrils.

Hello, August March.

* * *

The summer after August graduated from the Willington West Academy for Gifted Boys, the free-spirited and drooping fashions of the 1960s still nearly a decade away, Sir Reginald Percyfoot took a few months off from work to get the boy back on his feet. Ever since August's production of *Lear*, the awkwardness between the pair had abated, and their frequent exchange of letters had patched up any remaining holes in the rickety lifeboat of their relationship. But now that both were unemployed and unencumbered, the comforting expanse of the Atlantic Ocean no longer separating them, would their newfound peace hold?

It did better than hold; it thrived. August and Sir Reginald shared a summer of theatre, of ideology, of long convoluted arguments in crowded cafés. Reacquainting was a smooth and painless process, possibly due to their shared past or maybe because they both consumed scads of liquor at every opportunity. At first Percyfoot tried to put up a mild protest to August's habit; after all, it was illegal. But August made it clear that he planned to drink, and Percyfoot reasoned that if they'd been in London, the boy would be of age (or at least approximately of age, since no one on earth knew how old August actually was), so what was all the fuss about?

Eventually their sepia-tinted summer faded, and Sir Reginald had to get back to work. A new play in London had been written especially for him, and it would be criminal not to appear in it. The role was irresistible, truly a once-in-a-lifetime chance. August gave his blessing, but once the bags were packed and a cab waited on the street, the old actor felt a strong tug of guilt.

"You're sure you don't mind me skipping off like this?" he asked.

"It's fine," August replied, leaning against the doorframe in a slouchy cardigan that did little to combat the approaching chill of fall. "I can take care of myself."

Percyfoot knew truer words had never been spoken, but after all the effort he'd expended through the years finding August March, it felt condemnable to voluntarily leave him. And they'd had such a splendid summer. Percyfoot found he quite enjoyed August's company now that he was no longer a detestable little shit. Rekindled relationship aside, he still hadn't forgiven himself for the haphazard way he'd abandoned the boy all throughout the tender years of his youth. Wasn't he doing it all over again? Putting his career above August?

As if reading the older man's mind, August said, "Go. I could use the privacy. Send me clippings of your reviews."

This put a smile on Sir Reginald's face. The notices were sure to be raves, every last one of them. Not that he cared about those sorts of things. But magnanimous creature that he was, he promised he'd send over whatever nonsense the critics had to say, for August's sake.

"Stay out of trouble," Percyfoot boomed from the open window of the cab. "And whatever you do, never purchase a television. Wretched things are more deplorable than the cinema, and that's saying something."

August waved until the cab was out of sight, and then, closing the door behind him, prepared to have a lengthy rumination about what in the hell he should make of his life.

August couldn't really imagine himself in an office. In all honesty, he didn't understand what people in offices actually did. Had he known that even people in offices didn't understand what people in offices did, it might've encouraged him to take the plunge into the world of suit and tie, but this knowledge was hidden from him, so his fate took a different course.

Should he work in a shop? August wasn't sure he had the constitution for that way of life. He didn't suffer fools very well, and it seemed that even the most sensible of people become fools when they enter shops, just as some of the wisest on this earth apparently lose their minds entirely once seated at a restaurant.

What then? He certainly didn't want to become a pickpocket again. He'd entered that life out of reluctant necessity, and having consistent meals became addicting, as did the assurance that he could sleep through the night without being stabbed.

August decided not to rush into anything. Along with her brownstone, Miss Butler had left him all her money as well. It wasn't much, but he wouldn't be in dire straits any time soon. He concluded that he would take life as it came to him. Relax for a bit. Enjoy himself.

August napped and drank and cavorted his way through the next couple of months, enjoying every moment of his newfound freedom. Being an adult was marvelous, he thought when he awoke shirtless on his couch one Wednesday at three in the afternoon. Scratching himself, he grabbed the post and smiled when he saw a letter from London. He and Sir Reginald had been enjoying a bombastic correspondence, and he was eager to hear news from fair Britannia.

The typeface on the letter gave August pause; Sir Reginald always wrote in longhand. He read on.

Dear Mr. March,

It is with deepest sympathies that I inform you that Sir Reginald Percyfoot has passed away due to complications with his heart.

He has named you as his sole heir. Please secure passage to London as soon as possible, so we might square away any outstanding details.

Sincerely,
Martin Brown
Brown &
Baker &
Burton &
Bunderfink

Everyone is simply walking on a frozen lake. Sometimes we're lulled into a false sense of security; the ice feels so solid, it might as well be bedrock. But there are always dark patches, and August had just misplaced his step. When he did, his world cracked, and the cruel, glacial waters dragged him under, filling his lungs, laughing as he drowned.

* * *

August hated London. He found it a dreary, dismal, depressing sort of place. That he was visiting for a funeral might have colored his opinion of the city, but he was in no mood for the knotty rationalizations of introspection. He was not in the mood for much of anything, in fact.

He sat through the ceremony in a daze, and once the songs were sung and the eulogies uttered, the mourners, of whom there were hundreds, left the church to bury Sir Reginald Percyfoot under a gray London sky, black umbrellas popping like maudlin champagne corks as the rain that had threatened all morning finally began to piss down. As August uncomprehendingly took in the scene, he was shaken out of his stupor by the profuse weeping of one particular man, standing hunchbacked at the gravesite. Much to his surprise, August realized that the one shaking with sobs was none other than the headmaster of Willington, Archibald Richmond. August had known that Richmond was Sir Reginald's friend, but this histrionic display of emotion, especially in the presence of so many typically stoic English mourners, was shocking. August watched his former headmaster's sloppy spectacle with envious bafflement, for August couldn't seem to muster a single tear, and surely he had more of a claim to Sir Reginald than a stuffy old boarding-school headmaster.

As Percyfoot had no immediate family, August was named his sole heir, and he headed back to New York a wealthier young man than the one who had left, though not by much. During the era of Reginald Percyfoot's fame, the Hollywood studio system wasn't exactly renowned for its generosity toward actors. Additionally, Percyfoot had squandered many years of his career when August was missing, taking on any part, no matter how small, so that he might stay in New York and search for the boy. So while there was some money to hand down, it wasn't as if August had suddenly become flush.

Along with his meager inheritance, however, Percyfoot had also left August a letter.

To the indomitable August March,

Rotten luck if you're reading this, but I suppose everyone has to go at some point. I'm not much good at this sort of thing, so I'll keep it brief.

Hopefully you're perusing my penmanship as someone very old and gray, or at the very least you're well settled and all that, but if, god forbid, you're still brimming with youth, pardon me while I dole out some unwarranted advice.

You are a child of the theatre, August, and in some capacity, there you must stay. The plays you staged at Willington were truly stupendous for someone so young. You were born in a theater. You were raised in a theater. You belong to it as much as it belongs to you. I hope you find happiness in whatever it is you choose to do, but I know you'd find happiness near the stage.

I'm afraid I've been rather a disastrous friend to you, and god knows I've made a wretched parent, but please know this: you are the most spectacular person I have ever met, and it's been bloody fun knowing you all these years.

Typically, his signature filled the rest of the document.

It was too much, this contact from beyond the grave, and August's grief swelled like a great cresting wave, threatening to engulf him. He needed to escape this sadness, this stark loneliness that always seemed to find him and ransack his heart. August shoved the letter into a rarely used desk that stood tucked away in the sitting room, where it might be forgotten.

As to the letter's contents, August couldn't have disagreed more heartily. The thought of having anything to do with the theatre, the art form that so reminded him of Sir Reginald and the beloved Miss Butler, made August sick with mourning.

But what would he do? August remembered his declaration that he'd take some time to enjoy himself. Had that really only been a few weeks ago?

To console himself he drank. Frequently. Always. Months and months of liquor-induced stupor blurrily passed, and the alcohol was so successful in numbing his pain that August became a career drunk. He was quite committed to this new course until one night at a party, the host of the event lost his patience and socked August in the face. After being tossed onto Madison with a black eye, August decided to lay off the sauce for a bit.

Without the constant haze of drunkenness to distract him, August was forced to take a look at his life. Just what on earth was he supposed to do? He wouldn't survive past the age of twenty-two if he kept up this besotted lifestyle. But though August had no prospects, family, or friends, he did possess a certain animal instinct that urged him to keep living, even if just to stubbornly prove that he could.

Sitting in the squishiest and most favored of armchairs in his brownstone on East Twenty-Third Street, August, with the help of a restorative Sazerac (though he was cutting back, he still allowed himself a drink or nine a day), finally succumbed to the inevitable: he would revert to a life of crime.

Not that he would become a no-account pickpocket again. He'd be something classier. A great art thief, perhaps, looting New York's finest museums of their most valued treasures. Or maybe he'd work his way up to stealing government secrets from foreign nations and become America's most celebrated spy.

Until then, he'd shatter windows and steal people's money. He could still scale any building with ease, and though his lock-picking muscles had grown slack as of late, it wouldn't take too much practice to relearn the skill.

True, August didn't *need* money. The inheritances bestowed on him by both of his surrogate parents would carry him through a few more years at least; if he lived prudently, he could possibly remain unemployed until he was thirty. But August had come to realize that when he remained idle, he took to drinking. And when he took to drinking, he turned rash. And when he turned rash, he got punched in the face.

So he'd be a cat burglar. And why not? After Willington, the myth that the upper class had somehow earned their wealth or status had been disproved. Surely some had worked hard to get their money, and others born to fortunes did much good with their inheritances, but the majority of the wealthy resembled the majority of the poor: greedy and stupid. So why not skim off the top?

* * *

Though August had never been that popular among the Willington set, there were a few boys he'd struck up a convenient camaraderie with during his years at school. A tainted few were as disillusioned with their lifestyle as August was, or at least claimed to be in the name of teenage ennui, and after August had elevated himself out of the category of social leper, it was to this type he gravitated.

Though it hadn't been long since graduation, he'd fallen out of touch with his school chums, but due to Willington's exhaustive alumni association, it wasn't difficult to regain contact. After dashing off a few letters, August was given the telephone number of Gregory Ashford, a boy who had appeared in nearly all of August's productions. Though August was sure Gregory was either entrenched in an Ivy League school or enjoying a cushy, nepotistic position at his father's law firm, the two had shared a few good laughs throughout August's school-age perdition, and therefore Gregory was August's best bet to becoming reacquainted with the cabal of high society.

"August!" Gregory shouted over the phone. "What the hell have you been up to?"

They exchanged some brief pleasantries before August finally got around to mentioning that he'd like to see some of the old crowd again.

"Of course," beamed Gregory. "You should come to the club on Friday. There's going to be loads from our class there."

"The club?"

"Yes. Willy's. Don't play dumb."

"I'm afraid I don't know what you're talking about."

Gregory laughed. "Willy's! That's what we call Willington's clubhouse in New York. All the old schools have one."

Of course a place as self-important as the Willington West Academy for Gifted Boys would have a clubhouse in Manhattan. After many assurances that he'd attend on Friday, August hung up.

He smiled. For the first time since Percyfoot had passed, he had a sense of purpose. The club promised to reintroduce him to some old acquaintances, who would in turn introduce him to new acquaintances, who August would in turn rob. He felt no guilt whatsoever about any of this. It wasn't as though he would be stealing enough to ruin these aristocratic morons. Besides, he planned to steal only from the wealthiest and most wretched of the lot—a modern-day Robin Hood who, instead of giving his earnings to the poor, would keep them for himself. Morally ambiguous, perhaps, but nothing compared to some of the more unethical scams he'd pulled with Sycamore all those years ago.

Friday arrived, and he met Gregory, who ushered him into Willy's impressive bar, where they traded reminiscences while August scoped out the rest of the men assembled. The place was a gold mine. Literally. Aside from the young set whose fathers hadn't done them the favor of dying off so that they might enjoy their inheritances, the poorest person present probably owned at least three residences. August had hit the jackpot.

Whistling all the way home, he was already planning his next trip to Willy's, a trip he intended to make in disguise.

* * *

Sir Reginald had left August his money and the blasted letter, but he'd also left August all his possessions. In those gray mawkish days August had spent in London, settling his benefactor's estate, he'd ordered almost everything to be donated to charity or thrown out, but even in his sorrow, he had managed to hold on to a few of the more interesting effects Percyfoot had accumulated during his lifetime. Among the salvaged was a chest that contained what seemed to be hundreds of costumes. Smoking jackets, breastplates, ascots, breeches, kilts, kimonos, and wig after wig burst from the opened chest. The sight of it had made August laugh, and for that reason he'd ordered the chest to be sent to New York, a jolly reminder of his departed friend. Now he was thanking his lucky stars for his grief-stricken sentimentality.

Though he couldn't very well walk into Willy's draped in a kimono, Percyfoot's chest was full of other treasures: makeup, prosthetics, and spirit gum, to name a few. To make any real money, August needed to ingratiate himself with a more established crowd. The boys his age were either still in university or living off allowances allotted by their parents; he wouldn't make much off them. To meet the older set, however, he needed to appear older, and he would do so using all the tricks of transformation inside Reginald's chest.

For the next few weeks, August practically lived in front of a mirror. His first efforts were amateurish to say the least. In an attempt to add convincing wrinkles and crow's-feet with an eyebrow pencil, he made his face look nearly identical to a basketball. The wigs and prosthetics did little to aid him either. It was all so tacky, so very Halloween.

He needed authenticity; he needed truth. Onstage, the actors had to play to the very last row of the mezzanine and make every gesture and expression read; reality was heightened. But August would have to pass in close quarters.

After much trial and error, he learned the fine art of subtlety. No one would ever believe he was a man of fifty, no matter how good his makeup. He'd need to stick close to his actual age. A dab of clay here to add a droop to his earlobes, a light application of pencil to darken in his eyebrows and make them slope upward ever so slightly, a plug in the nose to flare out the nostrils. These minor touches did wonders when collectively composed. A fine wig slicked with hair gel, and August looked just different enough to be an entirely new man.

Then there were all the added modifications of performance. August normally walked with a slight slouch, having just exited his apathetic teenage years. But the character he played had the ramrod posture of entitlement and led with a puffed-out chest. He also painstakingly practiced modifying his voice, so he now spoke with a slight dialect, that affected New England drawl that belonged somewhere between Katharine Hepburn and the Kennedys.

With all his alterations, August didn't look fifty, but he certainly didn't appear to be twentyish. He could pass for a very young thirty, which suited him just fine. His peers might not be fooled up close, but he planned on keeping his distance; he wasn't going to Willy's to make friends.

* * *

Soon he settled into a comfortable pattern of befriending rich men in gentleman's clubs and then robbing their homes. True, August could've simply picked their pockets at the clubs and made an easier living, but the rich prided themselves on stealing from one another only under the guise of business. To rob them forthright in their midst would've eventually been noticed, and August didn't want to bite the hand that fed. Besides, being a cat burglar was fun. It gave August a chance to use the skill set he'd accumulated through his unorthodox upbringing.

Willy's had taught him the ropes, but he quickly discovered that there were clubs that made Willy's look like a soup kitchen. It wasn't long before he was hitting every club in the city, alternating between them so as not to arouse suspicion.

All in all, August was enjoying the new shape of his life. True, he didn't have any friends. Or rather, he had hundreds of friends, but none that he actually liked. But when August got too lonely, he consoled himself with some of the haunts of his past; the oldest profession showed no signs of going anywhere, and now that his income was far steadier than it had been all those years ago, August could afford some of the classier bordellos the city had to offer. The women who worked these establishments were witty and captivating, the perfect charms to ward off the curse of isolation.

* * *

And so passed August March's twenties. But now that he'd entered both his thirties and the 1960s, August yearned to make a bigger score. He was a genuine adult now. He'd grown tired of swiping whatever spare cash was sitting on top of desks; he wanted to make a splash, join the big leagues. Poking around through all his networks, both legal and otherwise, August learned of one Charles Kingsley, a stupidly rich man in possession of a stupidly large emerald named (rather stupidly) Greener Pastures.

Simon Helmer, a character August had retired some time ago, was brought back into circulation, with a few minor adjustments to age him slightly, namely a large mustache. One last look in the mirror, and August (Simon) was off to the club in search of the fabled Charles Kingsley.

August was an old hat at this sort of thing now, but he decided to be cautious in the name of Greener Pastures. This was by far the biggest theft he'd ever attempted, and he didn't want to spoil it with haste. The first night, he settled simply for an introduction to Kingsley. The next time they met, Kingsley initiated the conversation.

"There you are, good fellow," said Kingsley, sidling up next to August, dressed as Simon Helmer, at the bar. "Rum swizzle, was it?"

Two drinks later, August, also known as Simon, blushingly accepted an invitation to Kingsley's home, where he would endure a dreadful party and learn that a gigantic emerald sat nestled inside a terribly out-of-tune guitar.

* * *

The wretched evening at the Kingsleys', full of limp conversation, uninspiring redheads, dissonant harmonies, and thinly veiled marital strife, was now situated blessedly in the past tense. With the newfound knowledge of the emerald's hiding place, August took to tailing the Kingsleys, waiting for them to go off and summer somewhere. He knew they had houses in the Hamptons, Newport, Provence. The trouble was, they never seemed to travel. As June surrendered to July and the heavy, oppressive heat of the New York summer drove all sensible people out, the Kingsleys went about their daily lives, flitting from event to event, seemingly oblivious to the humidity that was causing even the most tropical of vegetation to droop with etiolated despair.

Though he despised Kingsley's dull conversation, August (Simon) eventually forced himself to meet the man for drinks so that he might milk him for information. They chatted about nothing for a bit until August, an annoying flutter in his heart, gently steered the conversation toward the particular brutality of this summer and how he longed to escape the confines of the city.

"Well, then, you must come out to Newport with us this weekend," Kingsley offered. "We're leaving early Friday morning. I won't take no for an answer."

August concealed his jubilation with staid regret, claiming he had family in from out of town who were positively itching to see the city's sights.

Kingsley rolled his eyes. "Nothing as dreadful as family, is there? Well, next time I'll make sure you get an invitation."

Good fortune! August ripped his cursed mustache off and danced his way home, swinging on lampposts and doing strange imitations of a bell kick, a talentless Gene Kelly.

Saturday seemed the best night for emerald snatching. Regardless of how late they left for Newport, or even if they decided to return a day early, the Kingsleys would most assuredly be out of their apartment Saturday. And August had gleaned from his careful conversation with Kingsley at the club that the staff would be out of town or dismissed for the weekend as well. Saturday would give him free rein, so Saturday it was to be.

The night arrived, and August, dressed all in black, walked downtown. As he was going to the Village, his crepuscular attire wasn't in the least conspicuous. A person wearing a sheer robe who called herself Twilight had just put a hand to his cheek and told him she would be married to him in their next life, so an all-black ensemble hardly merited comment.

It had been unbearably hot earlier that day, but now the sky turned an ominous purple, thunderclouds threatening. This was of no concern. If it rained, people were even less attentive than usual, blinded by umbrellas and too concerned with ducking under awnings or hailing cabs to notice a jewel thief in their midst. Also, a good old-fashioned thunderstorm might cool the air a bit, which would be such a goddamned relief.

A quick survey of the brownstone proved the Kingsleys weren't at home. No cars, no lights. Nothing. August smiled and headed a few blocks south.

The encyclopedic tour August had been given over a month ago had been agony at the time, but because of its thoroughness, he knew of a window in one of the lesser guest rooms that stood a few feet above a neighboring rooftop. With a boost from a well-placed dumpster, he was slipping his fingers into mortar cracks, slowly working his way up the side of a building five blocks down from the Kingsleys. His fingers were wider than they'd been as a malnourished teenager, so the task was no longer as simple as climbing a rope, but he had kept in good practice, and it wasn't long before he gripped the iron security of a fire escape. After hoisting himself up, August climbed the staircases up to the rooftop and leapt across the small gaps between the buildings until he was standing beneath the window of a fourth-floor guest room at the Kingsley residence.

The window was locked, of course, but it was old. With the careful application of a small crowbar, August was able to implement enough pressure to break the weakened lock and get a grip on the bottom of the frame with his free hand. The window creaked loudly as he shoved the sticky frame upward, but eventually he was able to slide inside. He wanted to release a triumphant laugh, but he was a professional. Caution prevailed, and he settled for a smug Cheshire grin.

Standing still and silent for a moment, he got a feel for the house while regaining control of his breath. Not a sound. He made his way to the music room and Greener Pastures.

The guitar that housed the emerald was still hanging where Kingsley had first plucked it from the wall. August lifted it off its mount and took it to a hideous divan so that he might fiddle with it in relative comfort.

A grumble of thunder complained outside.

August had known cracking the safe would be the trickiest part of his operation, and he'd decided in advance not to get frustrated with the mechanism. He had plenty of time, and if worse came to worst, he could just smash the damn thing open and make a run for it. Ideally, however, he would pick the lock, steal the emerald, and place the guitar back on the wall in pristine condition so that it might be weeks or even months before Greener Pastures was reported missing. Then it might still take a great deal of time for the Kingsleys to put it together that Simon Helmer had known of the jewel's location. By that time Simon Helmer would have disappeared off the face of the earth, his particular combination of wig, mustache, and ear extensions never to be seen again.

August sat on the couch, messing about with the guitar. He'd thought from watching Kingsley that the secret to opening the thing was in the tuning pegs on the guitar's neck, but he'd rotated each of the things with painful attention to detail and hadn't felt even the slightest catch.

Without letting discouragement overtake him, he tried to remember what exactly had happened that night of the dinner party. The trouble was he hadn't been paying Kingsley any heed when his host started strumming the guitar; he'd been depressed about his failure to locate the safe. And then Kingsley played a chord that had made the most awful racket.

Maybe that was the answer! Maybe the right chord had to be struck before the tuning knobs would operate. But what chord? August had about as much musical talent as a fountain pen. And even if he were some sort of savant, how would he remember a random chord that he'd heard over a month before?

Another crack of thunder sounded, this time accompanied by a flash of lightning.

Perhaps Kingsley had simply strummed the strings, not played an actual chord. August tried, as quietly as he could manage, and then turned the knobs every which way. No luck. He tried again, trying to mimic guitarists he'd seen by placing his fingers randomly on the neck of the guitar. Another strum, another go at the tuning knobs. Nothing.

"Damn it," he whispered.

August was at the knobs again when a voice from behind interrupted his efforts.

"What are you doing here?"

August nearly threw the guitar into the air as he jumped up with fright. He turned to see who had caught him in the act and was surprised to find the silly redheaded girl from the dinner party staring at him.

"You?" said August. Then, remembering he'd been in disguise when they'd met, he amended his statement. "I mean . . . who are you?" A bit weak, but to be fair, he was under duress.

"Don't be an idiot," she hissed, and August was again thrown for a loop. The redhead of the party, whatever her name had been, was not the sort of person inclined to hissing. She was more the sort who favored making wishes on flower petals and whispering secrets to acorns.

He tried to recover. "There seems to be some sort of misunderstanding, miss. I've never seen you before in my life."

"Well, that's interesting, because I've seen you," she whispered, throwing a harried look over her shoulder and out the door, which she moved to shut. "Though last time we were introduced, you were dressed for a costume ball."

August tried to reply but only managed, "What . . . how . . . why?"

"Please," she said, raising her voice slightly after she shut the door. "I've never seen a cheaper-looking wig in my life. And when you turned in profile, I could see the light through your prosthetic ears. Pathetic."

August slumped back onto the divan in shock. That this woman, whom he'd thought to be as vacant as Christ's tomb on Easter, should have recognized him so easily was possibly the greatest surprise he'd ever received in his life.

"I knew you were after Greener Pastures that night," she said, taking the guitar out of August's hands. He put up no resistance. What was the point? "Honestly, all that talk of a tour? You couldn't have been more transparent if you tried. Luckily, Kingsley's an even bigger idiot than you are and just showed us the damn thing, no questions asked." She'd put the guitar back on its mount and was now standing back a few paces, studying the instrument, getting perspective. "It's no use opening the safe. I've been trying for weeks. And I'm sure as hell not letting you have the emerald after all the work I've sunk into this operation."

August was coming to and desperately needed some clarity. Unfortunately, the only thing he could think to say was a reprise of his earlier convoluted question. "What . . . how . . . why?"

The thunder was really rolling now, the drunkest person at the party.

"Eva?" came a voice from the hall. "Eva, are you in here?"

"Shit," she swore. "Behind the couch. Now!"

"The couch or the divan?" he asked, for they were distinctly different pieces of furniture.

"I don't care if you crawl under the fucking ottoman, just hide!"

He didn't waste any time arguing. Discovery would be terrible, of course. The authorities would become entangled in his business; he might be sent to prison. But what he honestly feared more than incarceration was upsetting this Eva woman, a person he'd come to greatly admire in the past few moments. August dove behind the couch, hitting the ground with a thud just as Mr. Kingsley entered the room wearing a ridiculous silk bathrobe.

"Darling," he said, mercifully tying the robe shut, "what are you doing in here?"

Instantly the sharp spark of intelligence abandoned Eva. Dewy as a May morning, she replied, "The thunder woke me. I was frightened." Then, sobbing real saltwater tears, she collapsed onto Kingsley's breast.

Sensational.

"There, there," Kingsley soothed, "there's nothing to be afraid of."

"Charles!" came a monstrous voice from downstairs. "I know you're here!"

Kingsley, who seconds before had assured Eva that there was nothing to fear, screamed like a child and threw the young woman onto the couch as if she were a hot iron.

"Good god," he whispered, pale as a ghost, "she's here!"

"There's no use in hiding, Charles!" came the banshee call of the rampaging termagant, her malice underscored most effectively by the bellowing thunder. "I'll find you and the little slut!"

"Quick," Kingsley said to Eva, "hide behind the couch."

Eva hastened to obey and, with a sprightly leap, landed squarely on August's rib cage. August, quite naturally, cried out in anguish, thus alerting Kingsley to his presence.

"What the devil is going on?" Kingsley asked, astonished.

It was Eva's turn to mutter the now popular refrain, "What . . . how . . . why?"

Kingsley soldiered on. "And just who are you, sir?"

"A burglar," August replied, eschewing good sense in the face of such barefaced madness.

"A burglar?" Kingsley cried.

But there was no time for further questioning; the alarming screams of the executioner were drawing ever closer. "I'll cut off your cock and feed it to you, you adulterous bastard!"

Petrified for the future of his genitals, Mr. Kingsley dashed to the balcony doors and threw them open. "Leave! Both of you! At once!"

"But Charles," Eva wept, "I'm scared of the rain!"

"And I'm scared of my wife! Now get the hell out of here before I throw you off the balcony."

Eva dropped the ingenue act and slapped Charles Kingsley hard across the face. "Goddamn you! You're a silly, silly man and a horrible lover."

Mr. Kingsley was more than shocked at Eva's sudden shift in personality, but August had grabbed her by the waist and was carrying her out the balcony doors.

"Don't mind her," he said. "Hysterical and all that. Lovely to meet you, sir."

"Likewise," mumbled Kingsley, at a loss.

Climbing down the face of a building wasn't easy, especially when a thunderstorm was in full scream and a feisty person was applying several feisty kicks to his shins. Still, August kept his head and his footing, and descended the brownstone safely. The following altercation was overheard from upstairs before he was out of earshot.

"Where is she?"

"Darling, a burglar! Just scared him off! You wouldn't believe the fright I've had!"

"A burglar, is it? Well then, I'll just go to the bedroom and make sure he hasn't taken any of my brooches."

"Er . . . avoid the bedroom, dear. He's ransacked the place something awful. Especially the bedsheets. He's even strewn some women's clothing about. An absolute madman!"

Gripping Eva's wrist, August charged uptown, leaving the Kingsleys, their marital strife, and their emerald behind him.

* * *

Eva pulled her wrist, slick with rain, from August's grip and marched west, away from him.

"What're you doing?" August chided, chasing after her.

She whipped around, mad as the thunder, tendrils of her hair clinging to her face. The rain had changed her hair's coloring so that it was now blood-dark, and the pieces plastered across her cheeks looked like deep angry gashes.

"What am I doing?" she shouted. "I'm leaving! Do you have any idea how much work I put into that job? How much time that cost me?"

August shuffled in the rain.

"Months," she answered. "Months of planning. Months of preparation. And then finally, over a month of fucking that son of a bitch just so I might get a *chance* at opening his safe. Then you come along with your latex ears and mustache that wouldn't even fool a child, sit through one dinner party, and ruin everything!"

August didn't think she was being quite fair. He had, after all, endured drinks with Kingsley at a very pretentious gentleman's club. When he mentioned this to Eva, she turned redder than her hair.

"I fucked him!" she screamed. "I let him have sex with me! Did you fuck him at your club while you were playing checkers?"

"We never played checkers, just cards."

Eva slapped him, and August didn't protest. He deserved it, he felt.

"God!" she screamed, heading west again.

August caught up to her and put an arm on her shoulder. "Wait."

"Don't touch me! Who are you? Why are you still talking to me?"

"I live nearby. If the Kingsleys do end up phoning the police, you're probably the only person who'd match the description they'd put out."

Eva took stock of herself, saw that she was wearing nothing but a sopping dressing gown, and balled her fists in fury.

"Fine," she said, obviously restraining a number of violent impulses, "take me to your place. But if this is some kind of trick, I swear to god—" But her threat remained unfinished; she seemed to be literally choking on her anger.

"Fair enough."

They couldn't catch a cab, and the rain never let up the whole walk home.

* * *

August unlocked his brownstone on East Twenty-Third Street, ushered Eva inside, and immediately went in pursuit of a towel. When he returned to Eva, even the water pooling about her feet seethed in resentment.

"Would you care for some tea?" he asked, handing the towel over.

Her only answer was a skeptically raised eyebrow; Eva was making no effort to hide how ill at ease she was at being alone, nearly naked, with an admitted criminal in his apartment.

Taking her bitter silence as consent, August dashed off and threw the kettle on, then fussed over which tea he might serve. Living with Sir Reginald had made him somewhat of a snob when it came to tea, and he now maintained an extensive collection of leaves and such from all over the globe. Eventually he settled on a mild monk's blend—not the most robust of brews, but it couldn't be beat for comfort.

While the kettle worked up the mood to whistle, August bounded up the stairs to Miss Butler's old room. He hadn't changed a thing, not having a need for space, so the closets were still full of Eugenia's garments.

Though she'd been old, Miss Butler had been a gifted seamstress, and had an eye for clean lines and flattering cuts. And though Eugenia Butler had been taller and thinner than Eva, the simple cotton frock he picked out would certainly be preferable to the dripping robe the young woman was currently donning. And she'd look lovely in this shade of green. At least he thought so. Or hoped so.

The kettle sang as August ran down the stairs, skipping every other step. He poured the tea, and while it was steeping, offered Eva the fresh garment.

"Thanks," she said, distracted. The towel had restored her somewhat and, no longer sopping, she was surveying the brownstone with a furrowed brow, her tongue worrying the inside of her mouth like she was digging in her cheeks or individually counting each tooth.

"Bathroom's just down the hall," he said.

"Uh-huh," Eva replied, leery.

As soon as she was gone, August ran back to the kitchen and set the tea on one of Miss Butler's cozier serving trays, artfully fanning some of the sweet biscuits Sir Reginald so adored across a china plate. Carefully carrying the whole display to the living area, August laid out the tray on the table where it would receive the most advantageous lighting, then seated himself nearby and crossed his legs. Then uncrossed them. Then crossed them again. And what to do with his arm?

Good lord, but he was atwitter! And whatever for? Perhaps it was because he rarely had guests. Well, that wasn't entirely true. August often had guests of the feminine variety, but not this sort. They were dalliances, candy. But currently changing into one of his adoptive mother's dresses was a full-course meal. Steak, potatoes, and dessert.

God, what an awful thing! To compare a woman to a dinner. Just what was he thinking of?

He uncrossed his legs as Eva entered, still toweling herself off. But what was this? Her hair had changed color completely, and was now a dark mess of chocolate tangles.

Eva saw the confusion on his face. "What? You think you're the only person who uses wigs? It's drying in your sink right now. I swear to god if the rain ruins it, I'm charging you. That thing cost a fortune."

August mumbled some inane response, too concerned with studying Eva to make simple conversation. He'd been right, she looked radiant in the green dress he'd picked, even with her new hair color. But there was something else. Now that she was no longer bewigged, Eva had an entirely different air about her. The mass of springy red curls had made her seem daffy and silly, an impact she no doubt intended. But the brown? Though it was currently matted and frizzed, it grounded her somehow. Gave her an earthy quality that was most becoming. And her jawline—how had he not noted it sooner? Striking, yet familiar in a way. Where had he seen its like before?

"Is this whole place yours?" Eva asked. She'd helped herself to the tea tray while August was lost in analysis, and her mouth was presently filled with biscuit.

"It is," he replied, joining her in the tea.

"All four floors?"

"Five, actually." August was generally of the opinion that size didn't matter, but if you've got it, flaunt it. Was he mixing adages? No matter.

"Hmm," was Eva's only remark. They sat in an uncomfortable silence that Eva eventually broke by asking, "Aren't you going to change?"

Ah. Of course. In his haste to ease her troubles, August had forgotten to remove his equally drenched garments, and was now soaking the chair and puddling the rugs. How embarrassing.

August sprang up. "Won't be a minute," he cried. "Make yourself at home."

What to wear, what to wear? It all seemed either too formal or like the tattered rags of a beggar. He didn't want to look as though he was trying to impress her, but he couldn't very well limp toward her shaking a tin mug, imploring for alms.

He settled on a cardigan layered over a button-down and some unassuming trousers. He might've been a humble poetry professor excited for an evening alone with his scotch or an easygoing millionaire slumming it at his beachfront property. A perfect look.

When he returned downstairs, Eva was browsing the bookshelves while blowing on a fresh cup of tea. Catching sight of August, she let out a sigh, clearly relieved to see he wasn't wearing tiger-skin loungewear or some ensemble of equal suggestiveness.

"What's your name?" she immediately asked.

"August March," he answered, not even thinking to lie. "And yours?"

She stopped at this. Obviously she thought him quite daft. True, he may have been acting slightly touched, what with the wet clothes, and not clocking her as a fellow con artist had been a true debacle, but August wasn't moony enough to believe that she'd given the Kingsleys her real name. Perhaps this first bit of good sense in their brief history of acquaintance impressed her, for she replied, "Penny York."

Penny York. He liked it. Of course, she was probably lying, but at least it was a good lie.

"Do you live here alone?" she asked.

"I do."

"And you own this entire building with money you've earned? From stealing?"

It has often been said that relationships are built on trust and that honesty is the best policy, but come to think of it, August wasn't sure he'd ever actually heard those crumbly old sayings spoken aloud. They were more the sort of thing one read, and you can't believe everything you read, now, can you?

"Oh yes," August said. "I could've gotten something flashier, of course, but I didn't want to attract too much attention. She's a simple little place, but I'm fond of her." Here he patted a wall as if it were a prized spaniel.

Penny blew on the tea. "So you're not a complete idiot."

"Jury's still out," August joked.

"Why do you have out-of-style women's clothing in your home? Are you a serial killer?"

August snorted tea up his nose, which was beyond painful and not an experience he would ever recommend even to those he thoroughly disliked. Attempting to recover, he managed, "What?"

"A serial killer. Like the Boston Strangler, or Norman Bates."

Besides a detestation of anything French, Sir Reginald had imprinted a cinematic prejudice on August's malleable young mind, so while Penny's latter reference went over his head, he got the gist of her question.

"I can assure you that I'm not a serial killer. Pry up any floorboard you wish."

"Then why does a man who lives alone keep out-of-date women's clothing in his apartment?"

Never had August encountered a person who could so frequently make his mouth dry.

"I . . . like . . . things?"

Well done, old boy! The human race had yet to utter such a clever turn of phrase!

"What a unique response, August March," Penny said. "I'm a very good judge of character, but the longer I know you, the less I understand."

August was a skilled flirt, and more than most things, good flirting depended on timing. Up until this point, their conversation had gone from combative to delicately neutral, but with her last comment, Penny had deliberately given him an opening. "Would you like to understand me better?" he asked, innocent but for a faint impish lilt.

"Frankly, I'm not sure," Penny replied. "You're just such a weirdo."

And as that small bit of slang escaped her lips, just like that, the floor dropped out from underneath August, his world reinvented. He sat on the couch, winded with the shock of sudden comprehension.

"Oh my god," he said.

"What?" asked Penny.

"I'm the weirdo," August told her.

"I know, that's what I said—"

"No. Not *a* weirdo. *The* weirdo."

She wasn't following, so August explained. Or tried to. Here again, over a decade later, was the girl with the dark curly hair, though it currently looked quite ratty, as it had been pinned up underneath her wig for several hours. The girl he'd spied upon through a large window, the girl he'd shared a flask with in a Catholic-school stable, the girl he'd met at an ostentatious dinner party, thinking her to be someone else entirely.

If the realization had blown the breath out of August, it made Penny restless and fidgety. She set down her tea and started wringing her hands, looking more uncomfortable than she had a half hour ago when she was drenched and shivering. "Have you been following me all these years?" she asked him. "What do you want?"

"Nothing," he answered. "I swear I'm just as amazed as you are."

She glared at him, hard, as if trying to see his very skeleton. August withstood her scrutiny, for he was staring back with matching zeal. Finally she broke the silence. "Do you have any shoes I might borrow?"

"I beg your pardon?" This evening had, without a doubt, contained more surprises than any other in his entire life. The loaning of shoes was definitely the last direction he'd suspected this conversation to take.

"I asked if you had any shoes. The rain's stopped, and I should be getting home."

August couldn't help but feel crestfallen. He'd hoped she'd stay the night. Not in a sexual way. August wouldn't have dreamed of making a pass at her. Not that he didn't want to sleep with her. He'd never wanted to sleep with anyone more, in fact. But they'd found each other! Again, after all these years! Surely that merited something? A champagne toast? A steak dinner? At the very least a cute quip about how small the world could be. But instead, August was back in Miss Butler's closet, choosing several options of footwear for the girl with the dark curly hair, who, as it turned out, was named Penny York, and coincidentally enough, was also a thief, and good god, why was she leaving?

Penny picked out a pair of flats, looked like she was about to say something, but then thought better of it.

August walked her to the door.

"Good night," she said with terse finality.

"Good night," August dribbled as she stalked off, never once looking back.

He was tidying up the tea things, still too astonished for his low spirits to overtake him, when he found her sopping red wig in the bathroom. He clutched it to his breast, laughing, while it soiled his shirt with its dampness. But he didn't care. It seemed they were fated to remain intertwined! And here, dripping against chest, was a reason to call on her!

But as he was dancing about with the wet curls, he realized he hadn't gotten her telephone number. Or her address. Hell, he probably didn't even have her real name. Now the despair consumed him with ease, for he'd lost her. He'd lost her again.

August forced himself to bed after downing an unhealthy quantity of rum, the most depressed he'd been in recent memory.

* * *

August didn't spend too long wading through the rivers of regret, for three days later, a package arrived at his door. Inside was a green dress neatly folded, a sensible pair of outdated flats, and a note.

Thanks for the getaway.

No return address, no signature. But what rapture! What bliss! It was as if the walls of Jericho had come tumbling down, releasing Noah's flood on the unsuspecting hordes, yet the burning bush of August's heart stayed miraculously lit. But honestly, who had time for the Bible at a moment like this?

August knew he would see her again. A woman like Penny kept to herself in order to survive. He understood; didn't he share her profession? That she'd made contact, however nil, spoke volumes in August's favor.

At first, the fact that he could do nothing to reach her irritated him. After a week, irritation had evolved; now he was a bloodshot insomniac who jumped into the air at the sound of the telephone's ring. Another week gone, and August's mind was more than unhinged. He would've done anything for a simple courtesy call, even toss Samson, Esther, and Solomon's halved infant into the furnace with Shadrach and company. When he wasn't fretting over Penny, August worried about his sudden obsession with the good book. Perhaps he was going mad, like King Nebuchadnezzar. Dammit!

Another intolerable week gone, and August had decided to put Penny York out of his mind, or at least pretend to. With no clear destination in mind, he stepped out of his apartment into the heat of the month that was his namesake. Movement of any kind was preferable to all this sulking and stewing.

Upon opening the door, he was nearly struck dead by the sight of Penny York seated on his stoop, finishing a cigarette.

"I have an idea," she said.

August fumbled for words until he eventually settled on "Tell me everything," which sounded slightly debonair. At the very least, it was better than what he wanted to say, which was *Praise the gods, she lives! She lives, and now so can I!*

"Let's grab a bite."

They found a sad little diner and both had wilted salads and weak iced teas. It was a terrible lunch, but they were too hot to be hungry, so there was no harm done. The plates cleared, Penny got down to business.

"I'd like to run a job with you."

August's heart fell prey to all the clichés a heart can succumb to, stopping and leaping and skipping beats. It was all rather embarrassing, actually, but he maintained a sangfroid facade and asked, "What kind of a job?"

"Before we get into particulars, I need to know a little more about you. Do you really own that apartment?"

"Yes, but I inherited it." He saw no point in deceiving her. She was cleverer than him by half, and he'd only get snared in his lies.

Penny looked upset by his admission. It was plain she'd hoped August had been an accomplished thief, and by working with him she'd become rich beyond her wildest dreams. An idiot with a fake mustache and a trust fund, however, does not a master criminal make.

"I suppose an inheritance is better than being a call boy for some rich old hag."

"What about you?" August asked, his curiosity burning. "How does one go from being a Sainted Sister of the Slaughtered Lamb to a redheaded thief?"

Penny assessed him over her watered-down tea. "A few years ago my father died and left his new wife and children everything. Guess he conveniently forgot about his firstborn."

It was strange; when he'd been a boy, August often stood outside Penny's home, gazing in, thinking her family to be the very archetype of domestic bliss. But it had been an illusion. Perhaps all the seemingly perfect families August had bitterly envied throughout the years were the same, little farces brimming with their own private feuds and discord. It certainly painted his peculiar upbringing at the hands of Miss Butler and Sir Reginald in a better light.

"Your father sounds like a proper bastard," August said, forgetting for a moment that he himself was born nowhere near wedlock.

Penny shrugged. "It is what it is. At any rate, I wasn't about to marry some rich asshole the way all my schoolmates did. I've seen how that works out."

August smiled. "No. Uxorial duties wouldn't suit you at all."

"What?" Penny asked.

Damn his vocabulary! It would bring their catechumenal relationship to a premature necrosis if he didn't subjugate it forthwith.

"I said nothing," August lied.

"In any case, I sort of just fell into a life of crime. But I like it. I'm good at it. And you have to be good when it's paying your rent," she added, clearly a dig at August's inherited brownstone.

"I am a good burglar, too," August insisted, on the defense. "It's how I've made my living the past ten years. And I worked with a con man when I was a kid. Mostly two-bit stuff, but we did make a few big scores over the years. I can pick any window or lock, simple safes, too. And there isn't a building in New York I can't climb, even without a rope. Honest!"

August hadn't meant to sound like a bad Mickey Rooney picture, but Penny disconcerted him. Where was his sardonic aplomb, usually so readily accessible? Oh well. At least it was all true.

Penny sucked the last of her iced tea through her straw. "You're really a good cat burglar?"

"I swear it on Ibsen," August replied.

"Ibsen? Who's Ibsen?"

The urge to educate was strong, but he brushed it off. "Never mind Ibsen. Remember how I carried you down the side of the Kingsleys' building in the rain?"

"If you're trying to impress me, you might want to avoid mentioning that night," Penny said.

"I'm good," August said, and feeling a bit of his former self returning, he added, "Are you?"

Though she didn't like her competence challenged, Penny seemed to respect his confidence, for she started explaining her newest plot.

Penny's cons were always the same. She'd meet a rich man and play the beautiful fool. Inevitably he'd fall for her, invite her back to his home, and make love to her. After the mark fell into the deep euphoria of postcoital slumber, Penny would plunder him of his treasures and slip out into the night. Trouble was, Penny was getting tired of sleeping with scads of lecherous old men. Go figure.

She aimed to keep the first half of her cons the same.

"But while I'm out wining and dining the mark, you break into the empty apartment. We split the take, and I don't have to fuck any more men who remember the Jefferson administration. Sound good?"

Anything Penny said would've sounded good to August, but this plan actually *was* good. The worst part of robbery was the uncertainty of whether or not the owner would walk in while the misdeed was being done. But if Penny could guarantee August's security while he worked?

"It sounds perfect."

* * *

And for a time it was. Penny's presence opened up a whole new world of possibilities. When working alone, August was forced to hunt for marks within his peer group. After all, what cause would someone of August's age have to approach a millionaire of seventy or eighty? The moneyed gentleman would instantly think that August was a no-account gold digger, which of course he was, but that wasn't the point.

When sex was added into the equation, however, all bets were off. Penny could saunter up to any man, regardless of his age, and start laying on the charm. It was a wonder to watch her work. On rare occasions, a mark would see her for what she was and brush her off with a cold shoulder or a light threat. But usually, one look into Penny's carefully painted eyes would thaw any good sense any man ever had. Willingly they'd divulge their secrets, including but not limited to their telephone numbers, addresses, what nights their staff had off, whether or not they owned a dog, whether or not that dog was of the biting variety, their social security numbers; the usual sort of things people talked about on a first date.

Penny, with open-faced cherubic innocence, would remember every last word. After bashfully accepting an invitation to a second date, she'd make her exit and then relate everything she'd learned to August. When the patsy next met Penny for another evening of dreamy blessedness, August would head straight for his home and leisurely rob him blind.

Theft had never been so simple, so antiseptic. After the Kingsley incident, August and Penny decided that whenever possible, the men they targeted should be romantically unattached. This way, neither felt any guilt at the possibility of breaking up a marriage, and more important, August was less likely to be interrupted when he was working.

It was an ideal partnership, two professionals benefiting from years of combined experience. The phone would ring, and Penny's greeting was always the same. "I have an idea." It was her shorthand; she'd found another man, another mark. These calls came so frequently that August rarely responded when he answered the telephone; it was easier to wait for Penny to start the conversation. Generally speaking, the pair and their now thriving business were getting on famously.

At least, that's what August kept telling himself. Though he was no longer reduced to blathered infantile stutterings when in Penny's company, he was still infatuated with her, and that was putting it mildly. But they'd been working together for some time now, and Penny hadn't given August the slightest hint of mutual interest. The chemistry between the two was undeniable. They were like a pair of mated falcons, each performing a highly specialized task that couldn't be achieved without the other; they were positively symbiotic. So why was Penny so goddamned oblivious?

One evening Penny was curled on August's couch, counting the proceeds of their latest venture, a fat smile on her face.

"Well done, Mr. March," she said, placing his share on an end table and tucking her own cut into her purse.

The accounting finished, August poured out two celebratory tumblers of Irish whiskey, a custom they'd developed.

"To a financially advantageous partnership," Penny toasted.

"Indeed," he replied, clinking his glass against hers with a distinct lack of gusto. He drained its contents in one go, then poured himself another.

"What's wrong?" Penny asked.

"Nothing," August answered, sounding petulant even to his own ears.

"You're upset. Tell me what's bothering you."

August swished whiskey about in his mouth, a tempest of booze he longed to spit straight into her face. How to say he wanted her? Wanted her more than anything?

"It's nothing," he repeated. God, was he a teenager again? His angst was practically visible, a third party in the room.

Penny laughed, careless and indifferent. She was on a luxury yacht while August was packed elbow to asshole in the third-class cabin of an immigrant ship doomed to capsize.

"Now you have to tell me," she said, her eyes wide with delight. "I'm dying. Do you think I'm cheating you out of money?"

Without meaning to, August chucked his glass across the room. "Goddammit, Penny, is it always about money? Can't you see that I'm crazy about you? No. You just sit there twiddling your hair with all the insouciance of the ficklest calico. Well, I can't take it anymore! You're driving me to madness! Madness, I say! Soon I'll be seeing specters, a neighborhood institution, muttering banalities on street corners. Or I'll fling myself from a skyscraper, loudly singing the William Tell Overture as I plummet to my death."

"There are no words in the William Tell Overture."

"Whistling it then!"

Penny shook her head. "Why haven't you said anything before?"

"As if you'd listen, you wicked quickhatch!" spat August, who was now deep into one of his rather exasperating loquacious monologues, the type that even Shaw might have found too prolix. "Doesn't it strike you that our destinies seem intertwined? That ever since we were children, fate determines to bring us together time and time again? No. You care for me no more than the crocodile does the wildebeest. Than the jackal cares for the carrion carcass it teethes in the desert moonlight. If I were to lie down on the train tracks and be disemboweled by a runaway subway car, you'd shrug, take another bite of your croissant, and say, 'Good while it lasted. Guess it's back to fucking the marks.'"

Penny stood up and slapped him. August slapped her back. Penny threw her whiskey in his face. August cursed and tried to wipe the stinging liquid out of his eyes with his shirtsleeve. Penny came too close, as if to slap him again, but instead she dragged her tongue across his face, licking the whiskey off him. Burning eyes forgotten, August kissed her and drew blood.

* * *

Both agreed that their business partnership couldn't be jeopardized. Their affair would be a casual one, a comfortable sweater to slip into. In no way would it interfere with the work.

"I don't want to end up riddled full of bullet holes on some dusty road in Louisiana," Penny said.

"It must be bad luck to bring up the grisly demise of other criminal couplings, even so celebrated a pair as Bonnie and

Clyde," said August, splitting up the money he'd stolen earlier into two even piles.

"Is it bad luck to mix business and pleasure?" she asked, slipping her share of the earnings down the front of her shirt.

"Let's find out," he answered, removing the money and the garment that had held it in place.

Though each found the other thoroughly distracting, they did manage to keep the enterprise thriving; apparently there was an inexhaustible supply of rich, stupid, single men in New York City. August's phone hardly stopped ringing.

"I have an idea."

It was a wonderful time for August, the summer of his life. Never had he thought this sort of thing could happen. Penny was different from other women he'd been with. August actually cared for her. Most mornings he would wake next to a girl and just wish she would leave. But when Penny was gone in the mornings, even if it was just to pop out and buy them both bagels, he felt a sharp pang of sadness, a regret, a death.

What the hell was this?

And now that he cared, he found the act of sex altered. There was still carnal lust, of course, and sometimes their lovemaking was silly or wild or carefree, the bedsheets tangled with laughter. But at other times, it could be serious. Their eyes would lock, and great secrets could be wordlessly exchanged. Promises. Oaths. It could be frightening, the depth of his feelings. August, generally unflappable, hadn't known that sex could be so portentous, that he could taste fear, could hear it, could touch it, yet still be simultaneously overcome by the pleasures of his body.

"I love you," he dared to utter one night, buried in Penny's perfection.

"How do you know?" she whispered back.

For some reason, this response was the most erotic thing August had ever heard, and he came instantly, forever and ever, until he was dead.

Penny, calm and unruffled, allowed August a brief respite before arching her back, liquid and lithe.

"Finish me," she commanded.

And August obeyed, still drowning in the dark fearsome waters of himself that had hitherto remained uncharted, undiscovered.

What the hell was this?

* * *

"I have an idea," said the voice on the other end of the line.

"Tell me everything," August answered, unable to keep the smile out of his voice.

"It's a big one," Penny said.

Was it healthy for a somewhere-around-thirty-year-old man to get an erection while talking on the phone? August found he didn't give a damn one way or the other.

"Go on."

"Have you heard of the Barreth Hotel? That big beastly thing in Times Square?"

This August had not been expecting. Neither had his erection, which aggressively wilted. For the Barreth Hotel was the very same building that stood on the bones of August's childhood home, the Scarsenguard Theater.

"The name does ring a bell," August said.

"I met the owner."

Another shock, for the Barreth Hotel was owned by none other than Mr. Barreth, the mustachioed villain of August's youth. August hadn't thought about him in years, or he had, but in the way that one thinks of embarrassing mistakes made in adolescence; best to shuffle the mental deck of playing cards and quickly deal out a new hand.

"Was he nice?" August asked, for he could think of nothing else to say.

"What kind of question is that? No, he wasn't nice. He was horrid. He's who we're going to hit next."

August then did something he'd never considered himself capable of: he hung up on Penny. Then, calm as a sainted martyr, he crossed to the liquor cabinet, poured a healthy dose of the first bottle he grabbed, and took a deep swallow.

This was going to be interesting.

* * *

"I don't understand," Penny said, picking at the pickle that was served alongside her tuna melt. "You grew up in a theater?"

Trying to relate his cryptic past was proving to be harder than August had imagined it would be, and he had imagined it to be impossible.

"Yes," he repeated.

"And you were brought up by a costume lady?"

"She was a laundress, but close enough. She raised me alongside celebrated English actor Sir Reginald Percyfoot."

"And they were married?"

August nearly spit out his coffee. "Lord, no. She could've been his mother."

"But she was your mother."

"Precisely."

Penny chomped into her pickle and spoke with her mouth open, a habit August normally only tolerated in the mentally handicapped, but given that most of her acumen was currently devoted to sorting out his rather labyrinthine history, he let the matter slide. "And Barreth was what, your uncle?"

August snorted, which was rather uncomfortable, as it forced scalding coffee up his nasal passage. He seemed to always be inhaling broiling liquids in Penny's presence. He soldiered on. "He was most certainly not my uncle! The man was a scumlord whose twisted soul was bent solely on the acquisition of profit. Ebenezer Scrooge incarnated, he stalked the halls of the Scarsenguard, a vulture searching for orphans to displace or widows to rape."

"August, talk like a person."

"Sorry. He was an asshole."

"All the more reason to rob him, then!" Penny exclaimed, brandishing her pickle. Always brandishing, Penny. A brandisher if there ever was one. "I met him at the bar last night in the lobby of the hotel. He's crazy about me. We could make a fortune!"

Revenge would indeed be sweet, but throwing Penny into Barreth's path didn't sit well with August. The last thing that August had seen in the man's path had been the Scarsenguard, and Barreth had pulled it to the ground with a team of wrecking balls.

"I have reservations," was all he said.

Penny threw her head back and laughed. "I knew you'd come around! We'll go to the Barreth tonight. It'll be fun."

Somehow, August doubted it.

* * *

"That statue's imported," Penny pointed out as they crossed the lobby of the Barreth, heading to the bar. She looked resplendent in a light blue dress, her heels clicking gaily against the tiles. "Genuine marble," she said, when she noticed him studying the floor.

But August hadn't been pondering the merits of the marble. He'd been trying to imagine which part of the Scarsenguard they'd have been standing in. Probably the orchestra section of the theater, somewhere around row J. Below his feet, where staff currently bustled about the kitchens, had been the site of the world-famous Backstage Bistro. Royalty had danced in the very same spot that now housed a deep fryer. And over where the check-in desks stood would've been one of the cramped staircases that led up to the green room where Miss Butler had held court. There August had foraged for food and learned to read and had his childhood. Now a sunburned European was being handed the keys to her room while the terrier she cradled yapped incessantly.

Was nothing sacred?

They settled at the bar and ordered drinks, August a martini, Penny champagne. He crinkled his forehead at Penny's choice of beverage; she was generally a proponent of hard liquor.

"Have to play the part," she said.

They sat sipping their drinks, making stilted conversation, August sticky with guilt the whole time. This wasn't right. They were in the Scarsenguard, dammit! He felt like he was having an affair or peddling tacky plastic key chains shaped like totem poles on an Iroquois burial ground.

He was well into his third old-fashioned, Penny still taking dainty sips from her first glass of champagne, when Barreth finally appeared. Penny gripped August's arm tight as a vise, a ghastly habit she had when excited.

"That's him," she hissed.

She didn't need to say anything; August had already recognized him. He was older, heavier, and balder, but some things hadn't changed. For one, he was still trailed by a horde of twitchy young scribes, who penned his words as hurriedly as the Israelites might have gathered manna on those early desert mornings. And he still had a preposterous mustache, a boneless badger hanging from his face.

After her initial excitement abated, Penny went immediately to work.

"My name's Elizabeth," she mumbled under her breath. "I just met you tonight. We hardly know each other. You'll leave in a couple minutes."

"What?" August replied.

But Penny was off to the races. "Yoo-hoo!" she cried, waving an arm emphatically to catch Barreth's eye.

August had never heard "yoo-hoo" used outside of the most saccharine movies, usually ones starring little girls who wore their hair in tight curls and spoke with a faint lisp. To hear the colloquialism uttered in actual life was off-putting, to say the least. Barreth, however, turned and smiled, which was a far more off-putting sight than Penny's childish greeting had been. Truly disturbing stuff.

"Miss Elizabeth," Barreth said with what August supposed was intended to be a jovial tone. "How lovely to see you again."

"Oh, Mr. Barreth, I was hoping you'd be here tonight!"

Though it gave him a distinct case of the willies, watching Penny work was astounding. Just moments ago she'd been surveying the Barreth with shrewd eyes and tossing off quick and biting quips. Within an instant of her spotting Barreth, however, her eyes were wide and dewy as a cartoon doe, her voice two distinct octaves higher, and though she'd done nothing to alter her wardrobe, her breasts were undeniably more prominent. And, dear Christ, was she dumb.

"Mr. Barreth," she started, "may I introduce to you my friend Mr. Andrew . . . oh dear, I seem to have forgotten your last name. This champagne is going right to my head."

August was so taken with Penny's sudden transformation that it wasn't until she bestowed a swift kick to his shin that he realized he was supposed to speak.

"Mr. Andrew Burke," August supplied quickly. "Pleasure to make your acquaintance. Absolutely splendid hotel you've got here, sir. A real wowzer."

Penny gave August the briefest of looks that translated to *Why the hell did you just say* wowzer*?* before plowing forward.

"I met Mr. Burke tonight, you see, and I was just going on and on about your hotel."

"She sounded like a first-rate cuckoo bird, if you want to know the truth of it."

Another clandestine kick was granted to August's shin, but he was undeterred. If Penny was going to pretend to be a moron, then by god, he would help her.

"I was trying to tell him about some of the hotel's more fabulous features, but I thought it would be better just to show him."

"Poor girl couldn't remember the word for 'elevator.' Kept calling them 'lifty-boxes.' But that's women." August shrugged, throwing a wink at Barreth.

"Quite," said the old bastard. "You said you met tonight?"

"Yes," answered Penny, jumping in. "We were at a concert—"

"And after the thing was finished, sweet Elizabeth here was trying to hail a taxicab by chucking nickels at it. She was getting mighty popular with a gin-soaked hobo, but she would've been carted away to the loony bin if yours truly hadn't stepped in. That's when she started clucking about your hotel, and I said, Well hell, let's go take a gander. And she was right! This place is real fine. Big though. Sort of spooky." August paused for less than a breath. "Feels haunted."

Barreth's eyes bulged, and even his lips went pale. "This hotel is most assuredly not haunted. That I can guarantee."

"You sure? Not even one little spirit?"

August was making Barreth (who had just slyly performed the sign of the cross) extremely uncomfortable and Penny extremely agitated, but he couldn't have cared less. He hated everything about this scheme. Just talking to Barreth felt like blasphemy, like he'd dug up the bones of Miss Butler and was pissing on them.

His feelings hardly mattered, however. Penny was an absolute pro and had already spun August's bit of fun to work in her favor.

"Mr. Barreth," she whispered, all eyelashes, "might we go somewhere a little more private?"

Barreth, visibly relieved at any change in subject, flexed his chivalry.

"Of course," he bellowed. "Would you care to join me for dinner at my private table?"

Penny squealed and clapped like a wind-up monkey.

"I'm afraid there won't be room for you, Mr. Burke," Barreth sneered.

"No worries there, friend. I've got an appointment with a couple of ladies who'll serve me more than dinner, if you know what I mean."

Barreth reddened and escorted Penny off at once.

"What *did* he mean?" August heard Penny ask as they walked away, Barreth's lackeys trailing them like flies on shit.

"Nothing, dear, don't give him another thought."

"What are those called?" Penny asked.

"Chandeliers, my dear. Do you like them?"

"They're so twinkly."

"Aren't they? It's very clever how the lightbulbs are hidden from view, don't you think?"

"Lightbulbs? What's those?"

They rounded a corner and August heard no more. He paid the tab and left. He supposed he should've taken the opportunity to scope out the hotel, find the best place to make a score, but the truth of the matter was that the very thought depressed him, and the ghosts of his childhood were haunting the place with far too much vigor.

As he walked, he grew angrier at Penny with each passing step. They had a good thing going—why did she have to drag Barreth into it? He couldn't believe she was sitting down to dinner with him right this very minute, laughing at his jokes, pretending to be impressed. August knew it was all for show, that men like Barreth disgusted Penny, but that did nothing to salve his wounds. He tried to drink away his resentment at a few seedy bars before deciding he would take a page from Andrew Burke's book and visit a strip club after all. His thoughts were too tangled, though, and he couldn't surrender to the artifice, so after two drinks and some half-hearted flirting with a young woman named Cherry, he left.

His sleep that night was fitful and full of tugging, restless dreams.

* * *

Though August tried to convince her to drop the whole plan, Penny was determined to make the most off Barreth. However, the old tycoon was proving harder to woo than the usual rube. After weeks of meticulously constructed serendipitous encounters that inevitably led to drinks and dinner, Barreth had offered Penny a chorus-girl contract in one of the bawdy reviews he still produced.

"Can you imagine? Me covered in sequins and feathers, shaking my legs?"

August found that he could imagine, very easily and with relish, but for the sake of harmony, he acted as offended as Penny seemed to feel.

"All this time he thought I'd been chasing after him so I could be a chorus girl. I told him I'd rather die than be in some stupid music review."

August hoped that this misunderstanding would've put an end to the Barreth affair, but alas, hope proved to be as dead as Dickens.

Still, August tried to persuade Penny it was a lost cause.

"Look at this," he told her on one of the rare evenings they shared together, as she now spent most of her nights with Barreth. "In New York he owns the Barreth, two restaurants, and countless apartment buildings. But there's more. He owns a new hotel in Aspen and has shares of a casino in Las Vegas."

"What's your point?"

"My point is he's out of our league. Our last job was stealing diamond cufflinks off a man so old you could count all six of his teeth."

"We're ready to move up in the world. Make a name for ourselves."

"No, Penny. We're small-time crooks. We're not mysterious international thieves that live on yachts in exotic locales where the women serving the drinks all speak broken English and smell vaguely of sweet roasting pork."

"Such a specific fantasy."

"It's too big. He'll catch us. We'll go to prison."

"We need to make him jealous," Penny decided.

August sighed. "How do we do that?"

"You'll have to play my young lover."

It was said with such finality that August didn't even bother to object. "Fine, but we need to practice the lover part if I'm to play the role with any shred of competency."

Penny tossed away the magazine she'd been brainlessly thumbing through. "For the sake of competency, then."

* * *

It had been some time since August had opened up Percyfoot's chest of wonders. Penny was far superior at luring in marks, and not just because of her feminine attributes. The character she played, though dumb as a soap bubble, really was believable. August was very clever with makeup and wigs, but the young men he portrayed always tasted ever so slightly of gimmick and made the con a bit too sweet to swallow. Perhaps it was from growing up in a theater or from receiving much of his tutelage at the hands of the less than subtle Sergeant Sycamore, but when in costume, he was undoubtedly contrived. His talents were far more suited to breaking and entering, and August was too much of a big-picture man to make a stink at not being included in the more delicate first half of their cons.

Still, he missed it. He loved picking a lock or scaling a building's facade with spectral ease, but there was something about hiding in another person's skin, about making someone believe you were another, that was truly intoxicating.

"Perhaps I'll be a banished Indian prince," August suggested, carried away by a teal scarf he'd just unearthed from the trunk. "Raised in Britain by a cruel and severe governess, I eventually fled to America, with nothing but my title and unshakable sense of duty to my homeland."

"I don't think you could pass as Italian, let alone Indian," said Penny. "Let's try something far more Caucasian and far less colonialist."

August continued, undeterred. "A Russian spy keen to discover the secret of America's space program!"

"Why would a Russian spy be dating some idiot girl in New York City?"

"Ah, but perhaps your young idiot girl is *also* a spy. German? Or maybe French? The point being, our partnership, carnal to begin with, soon descended into the shadowy, unlit caverns of love, and though we both know in our hearts that the affair is doomed, that we will most likely be executed for our crimes, our passion for each other cannot be quenched."

Penny rapped August atop the head with a cane she'd found in the chest. "You're going to be a trust-fund kid. From California."

"Perish the thought!" cried August, who thanks to Sir Reginald, had a prejudice against California deeper than the most ancient subterranean metropolis.

"Fine. You can be from Nebraska."

The thought still rankled, but it was better than the alternative.

After they'd settled on his disguise and worked out a few details, Penny felt they were ready to snare Barreth. She had an uncanny knack for knowing exactly where and when the tycoon would be. August, bedecked in light prosthetics, brought this fact up to her as they walked to their destination.

"There's nothing uncanny about it," she replied. "I bribed one of his assistants."

"You did? How much did you pay him?"

"Not all bribes are financial," was Penny's maddening reply.

August was flabbergasted. "You didn't? Did you really? Which one? How far did it go? And for how long?"

"For god's sakes, August, stop asking so many questions! You sound like a toddler."

"I'll kill him! Unless it's that strong-looking one. Is it that strong-looking one?"

All his queries went unanswered, for Penny had been tipped off that Mr. Barreth had reservations at a restaurant called Birdsong, and they'd just arrived at the very pretentious entrance to said establishment.

The host or maître d' or High Lord of the Door greeted them with a low, sycophantic bow, as if they were volcanic gods that would soon require a blood libation.

"Welcome to Birdsong," the man whispered reverently. "Do you have a reservation for this evening?"

"We do not," Penny replied flatly.

The change in his manner was sharp as a tack. "Our next available table is sometime in April."

Penny was unfazed. "Alistair Linton is my father."

The host was once again all supplicating unctuousness; he might as well have been a crippled gazelle willingly surrendering itself to the cheetah's jaws. "Right this way, my lady fair. Your table awaits."

"Who is Alistair Linton?" August murmured as they were being seated.

"One of my old marks. Richest guy I ever knew. Lives in Europe now."

The first of their servers came, and Penny ordered the most expensive bottle of champagne on the menu. August, by no means poor, but then again, by no means rich, blanched.

"We have to make him see that his money isn't the only reason I'm going after him," Penny explained as she casually ordered eleven appetizers.

"That's all very well," he said, trying to keep his calm while doing some silent mental addition to see whether he'd have to put his brownstone up for sale to pay for the meal, "but I don't quite understand how we're meant to pay for all this."

"Lighten up, August."

He tried to take her advice, sipping his champagne, but it was for naught; he found he was calculating the net worth of every swallow, and the results were staggering and bleak.

Barreth finally arrived after Penny had ordered them two entrées each.

"Don't get his attention," Penny whispered. "Let him come to us."

But it seemed Barreth was fully ensconced in conversation with the two besuited men he'd come in with, for he hadn't even flicked an eyebrow in their direction, and they were already halfway through the first of the entrées, a spoonful of caviar served atop what looked to be thinly sliced zebra haunch.

"This is ridiculous," Penny whispered, not even enjoying the zebra.

August agreed but didn't have time to say so, because Penny suddenly let out an aria of a laugh, high and loud and gorgeous. The entire restaurant fell silent under the spell of the laugh; when it had concluded, August thought he even heard some applause from a distant table.

Barreth was hovering seconds later.

"Miss Elizabeth?"

"Mr. Barreth!" she trilled, hand on her chest, still recovering from the rapture of her private joke. "If I didn't know any better, I'd think you were my shadow."

Barreth smiled, but was instantly perturbed by the presence of August.

"Who is this?" he asked.

Penny and August both felt they'd done a good job with August's camouflage, and as Barreth didn't recognize him, it appeared they were right. August was lean by nature, but under his suit they'd padded him ever so slightly so he appeared more muscular, or corn-fed, as Penny kept saying. His hair had been dyed a sun-touched blond, his nose had the slightest upturned piggish quality thanks to a clip in the nostrils, and a pair of shaggy sideburns did their part to mask his distinctive cheekbones.

"You look quite handsome," Penny had told him as he slipped on a pair of shoes that added two inches to his height.

"Thank you, ma'am," he said bashfully in his best aw-shucks voice.

"Do people really go in for that sort of thing?" Penny had asked, appalled.

"Some must," he replied, thickening his eyebrows with a pencil. "Thank god we don't know them."

At the restaurant, Penny feigned shock and embarrassment. "Please forgive my manners. This is Mr. Andrew Linton," she said, borrowing the surname of her former mark.

Barreth's eyes widened. "Any relation to the Lintons on Park Avenue?"

"A distant cousin," August answered with a faint midwestern twang he'd picked up from a production of *The Man Who Came to Dinner*.

"Andrew is . . . well . . . I guess you could say he's my . . . boyfriend."

Now Barreth's eyes were wide as a midsummer moon.

"I didn't realize you were seeing anyone seriously, Miss Elizabeth. And just where is your chaperone?"

Chaperone? Were they in New York City or at Ashley Wilkes's barbecue?

"Oh, but Mr. Barreth, we don't need a chaperone." The following question she directed at August. "May I tell him?"

August gave her a patronizing nod.

"Andrew and I are engaged!" she whispered.

Barreth looked as though he'd been shot. It seemed Penny had gotten her hooks into him after all.

"Mr. Barreth, you're white as a ghost. Please, take a seat."

The old man sank into a chair and was instantly given a glass of champagne by the waiter who circled their table like a buzzard.

"How . . . how?" was all Barreth could manage.

"We met last week." Penny tittered. "I'm afraid it was a whirlpool romance."

"I think you mean whirlwind, dear," corrected August.

"No, whirlpool. We met at a fountain."

Incredible.

"Money?" Barreth interjected, still unable to form complete sentences, but desperate for facts.

"Mama's daddy owned the biggest corn farm in all America," August replied, dumb as a hay bale, "and my daddy found fortune down in Texas. Oil," he added with a wink.

Though he was more familiar with the northern types of wealth—inheritance, industry, and entertainment—the words *corn* and *oil* still held power. After all, they were the cornerstones of America, along with big cars and the subtle, almost gentle genocide of the country's indigenous people.

Barreth was devastated, and August delighted in watching him shrivel.

"Soon as we hitch up," August said, "I'm taking this little lady back home to Nebraska with me. We'll settle down on

Daddy's ranch. Four thousand acres, all full of corn and cattle."

"Can you imagine?" breathed Penny. "Andrew tells me Nebraska is flat as a pancake."

"Flatter," said August. "And we got bugs the size of Utah. But there's a certain beauty to it. The land gets to you. Shucks, I can't explain it, especially to a fancy New York City type. You ever been to Nebraska?"

"God, no," Barreth moaned.

"Well, you'll have to come sometime. You can stay in the guest room. My grandmammy died in there. Said she couldn't stand the smell of cow shit for one more day and took her own life with a revolver—but she always was on a different level than the rest of us. Genius type. And our maid got the blood out of everything. It's a good room. You'll like it."

"Miss Elizabeth," Barreth whispered, "may I have a private word with you?"

"Anything you need to say to me, you can say in front of Andrew," Penny said, batting her eyelashes.

"No worries, Lizzy, my love," said August. "My rattlesnake has to shed a few tears. You two old friends talk freely."

August excused himself and went to the bathroom, which was large enough to house a midsize orphanage. When he got back to the table, Penny and Barreth were gone, though a wad of cash sat on the table, presumably Barreth's apology to Andrew Linton for stealing his fiancée.

It was all artifice, but August couldn't help feeling jealous that he'd been bested by Barreth. He knew he was winning in the long run, that Penny was just buttering Barreth up, but it irked him to know that she was off gallivanting with the man he most despised. Though it was easier to enjoy the second entrée, knowing it was on Barreth's dime.

* * *

August slept late the following morning; after Penny and Barreth's departure, he'd finished his meal, left a lavish tip, then spent the rest of the night getting stinking drunk on the remainder of Barreth's money. Buying drinks left and right, August made hundreds of friends. He toasted each of his newfound comrades with an identical salutation, "To Mr. Barreth, the biggest bastard in New York City!"

So it was well past noon when August, deeply hungover, stumbled into a diner and feasted upon eggs over easy, bacon, hash browns, and cup after cup of terrible coffee. After the meal, his hangover wasn't gone, but it was behaving itself. He went back home and awaited the inevitable phone call from Penny, detailing her half of the evening and what their next step was.

But the call never came. August didn't worry; Penny generally slept later than he did. She was probably exhausted after a tedious night spent with Mr. Barreth. On days like this, she usually called in the late afternoon, wanting to grab a spot of lunch, though humans operating on a normal schedule would've called the meal dinner. August napped off the rest of his hangover and woke just after five. No calls, and no messages on his service either.

With a spine-cracking stretch and just a tug of worry, August decided to walk over to Penny's apartment. He could use some exercise after a day spent lounging, and Penny was probably still asleep. He'd wake her, they'd have dinner and spend the rest of the night in bed. What a charming notion.

He rang her buzzer with aplomb. Knowing full well that Penny could sleep through a bombing, August alternated between short staccato bursts of buzz and long, drawn-out wails. Finally a tinny voice answered through the intercom.

"Who the hell is it?"

The voice belonged not to Penny but to her detestable roommate Carol, a woman with the soul of an asp.

"Carol, it's August. Is Penny in?"

"Why should I tell you?"

All conversations with Carol, even the simplest, were transformed into a battle of wills.

"Carol, please buzz me up. Penny and I have a dinner engagement."

"How do I know you're not in some terrible fight, and this is a ploy to get upstairs so you can kill us both?"

"For god's sakes, Carol, just ask Penny if we're in an argument, if you're so concerned."

"Can't," was the reply.

"Can't what?"

"Can't ask her."

"And why not?"

"She's not here."

August slowly but forcefully pounded his fist against the brick wall of the building.

"Penny isn't home?"

"Nope."

"Was she home earlier today?"

"Not sure. Last time I saw her was last night. She rushed in and packed a suitcase."

"A suitcase?" Why the hell would she pack a suitcase?

"I gotta go, my show's on."

"Wait, Carol! Did she say where she was going? Carol?"

But the intercom was silent. He buzzed the buzzer with scathing conviction, but to no avail; she'd probably disconnected the damn thing, the heartless snake.

As he was preparing to pick the lock of the front door in broad daylight, a practice he tended to avoid, a man who lived in the building came out, and August was able to slip inside before dashing up the four flights of stairs to Penny and Carol's apartment, where he promptly started pounding on the door.

"Who is it?" came the trumpet blare of Carol's voice.

"It's August March, you wretched villain! Now open the door before I break it down!"

"My show's on!" Carol screamed.

August had no patience. He didn't break the door down because he was an elegant man, and also not strong enough. He did, however, make smart work of the lock, and was in the apartment within twelve seconds.

"Help!" Carol screamed as he stepped inside. "Murder!"

August shut the door. "Silence, you inhuman gorgon! You piceous witch! Where is Penny?"

"I don't know," Carol said, stunned into answering. "She burst in last night, going on and on about how everything was working out, and packed up her suitcase."

"Did she say where she was going?" August demanded.

"No. I figured she was moving in with you, the way you two have been carrying on. Not that I judge," she added, though in his experience, people who said they weren't holding judgment had already tried and sentenced the defendant.

August was baffled. He ran a hand through his hair and paced Carol's apartment absentmindedly.

"A suitcase? Why a suitcase?"

Carol, though deplorable, did have a strange man stalking about in her apartment in a state of duress, and was well within her rights to say, "I think I'm going to call the police."

Frustrated, August threw the telephone out the open window and shouted, an exact facsimile of a madman, "Never! Never shall you call the police again, oh wretched shrew!"

Carol screamed, in genuine terror this time, and he was hauled back to reality. "I'm sorry, Carol. Afraid I lost my head a bit. Do you remember anything else, anything at all, that Penny said?"

"No, you crazy bastard! Get the hell out of here!"

The walk home was an angry streak of confusion, as was the rest of the night, though he tried to dull it with whiskey. But no matter what he drank, the questions kept haunting him, viscous specters that fed on his unrest.

Why a suitcase? Where had she gone? What was the plan? When would she return?

And why a suitcase?

Where was Penny?

* * *

During the first few days of Penny's absence, August had imagined all sorts of sensational fates for his beloved. The classics, of course: murder, kidnapping. But the longer she stayed away, the more elaborate his dark fantasies became. Maybe Barreth had her chained up in some abandoned hotel room and was torturing her. Or she had packed her suitcase and gotten on a plane, but the plane had crashed and she was now clinging to a piece of wreckage somewhere in the Atlantic, dying of dehydration and exposure. Or maybe Carol had killed Penny. Fuck Carol!

Days passed, each more terrible than the last. This state of unknowing was insufferable. Why did people always leave? Was it so hard to stay in one place, to put some roots down and be solid? Dependable? Why had Penny left him?

August toyed with going to the police, but what could he possibly say?

"Excuse me, Officer. I'd like to report a missing person. She was last seen with a dastardly millionaire whom she was attempting to swindle for a large sum of money. Me? I'm her partner. While she woos the men, I break into their homes and steal their belongings. We're also sort of dating. I guess you could say I'm madly in love with her, but I'm unsure of her feelings toward me. I know she enjoys the sex, but it might just be that. She's a hard person to read, and I'm terrified of letting her know my true feelings because if they're not reciprocated, I fear she'll leave me, and I'm not sure my constitution could withstand such a revelation. I had an eccentric upbringing, you see, often left alone for long stretches. Didn't seem odd at the time, children being so malleable, but as I age, I've come to understand that the insecurity of my youth may have had an adverse effect on me. I can't trust authority, for one. Even talking to you, Officer, is a trial. But I also assume people will abandon me. The only people that ever cared for me are dead, you see. I'm not fishing for sympathy, just presenting the facts. Penny York, that's the name of the missing person, is the only person who cares whether I live or die, and I'm honestly not even sure she does care, at that. At any rate, let me know if you find the poor girl. I'll be at home, drinking far too heavily and waiting by the telephone, praying it will ring."

It wouldn't do.

It wasn't until a week later, *a week later*, that he received a postcard from Penny, though it did nothing to lift his spirits.

Sorry I had to run off. Will explain everything later!
—P

The postmark was from Paris.

August felt some minor relief (at least she was alive), but his already tangled thoughts grew even more knotty and gray.

Paris? She was in Paris? That explained the suitcase, at least. But why? After some thought, August decided that Barreth had spirited Penny off to France to escape the influence of her fictional fiancé. That made sense.

Still, August was surprised Penny had gone. Why not keep Barreth in New York, hook some information out of him, let August make a robbery, and be done with the whole affair? An off-the-cuff sojourn to Paris seemed extreme.

Without Penny around to distract him, August spiraled. What was he doing with his life? He was somewhere around thirty and had nothing to show for himself. August envied his Willington classmates their predetermined destinies. The second those boys had gasped their first taste of oxygen, they'd had their entire lives mapped out. Career, family, legacy, all decided, a tree-lined path they could follow; someone else had already cut back the brush and planted the oaks. They even had the choice of rebellion!

Stray from the path, break the mold, and mow down a dynasty. What fun!

August had none of that. He was a bastard born in a dressing room. There was but one soul on this earth who even knew he was alive, and she was inexplicably in Paris. He didn't exist.

Why had he let himself fall for her? Hope is dangerous; August had learned that lesson countless times. But instead of growing from his past and bettering himself, he'd chosen to reside in a gossamer ice castle of fantasy. What had he expected? That he and Penny would get married? They were business partners. She was amused by August, certainly, but that was all. He was her dawdling affair to while away the hours.

But didn't fate want them together? Penny was the girl with dark curly hair! At this point, she was the longest constant in his life. She was gone now, obviously, but he'd lost her before. Twice! And he'd found her again. Who's to say he couldn't do it again, that the third time wouldn't be the charm? Maybe this next time she would stay.

No. No more of this. He was through with the fickleness of those he gave his heart to. August would never again allow this to happen; never again would he rely so heavily on someone. People leave. They die. So why bother? Everyone's alone. Fight. Cheat. Steal. Survive.

When the phone rang about a week after the postcard had come, August hardly felt anything as he answered.

"Hello?"

"Oh good, you're home," Penny prattled, as if nothing had happened, as if she hadn't left. "I'm at the Barreth. The penthouse. Come over straightaway, I've got so much to tell you."

And then she hung up.

The thing August hated the most about himself was that as soon as he set down the receiver, he realized he was going to go. He'd promised himself to forget Penny; his feelings for her had been a breach in good sense. No matter. Dust her off and be done with it. From this point onward, he'd operate alone.

But her voice . . .

Damn it! One phone call, and his resolve was shattered? How pathetic was he?

He'd go. But it would end tonight.

August was able to slip past the front desk and into the elevator, his stomach stone. The lift climbed up to the penthouse until, either finally or suddenly, it opened. He walked toward the door at the end of the hall, his feet sinking slightly into the plush carpet with each step.

Quicksand, he thought, quick and errant.

Was the door getting farther away? God, his arms were heavy; his throat was dry.

Any last words?

Why would he think that? His palms were clammy, his socks too tight.

Could one quit Penny? Willingly quit her?

The carpets were red, with a drop of nauseous pink mixed in. Why, tell me why, God, would anyone choose such a color for anything?

And there was the door, solid and imminent and inarguable. August knocked, and the knock was dread.

Quickened footsteps, the knob turning.

Penny.

Upon seeing her August felt every one of his feelings, equally and in unison, and it nearly tore him open.

"August!" Penny cried and threw her arms around him. "God, I've so much to tell you!" She dragged him inside and closed the door behind them.

The penthouse, as to be expected, was extraordinary. Penny pulled August straight to the master bedroom, but even in his brief, madcap tour, he could see that a family of six could comfortably live here with room to spare, though a family of ten could make do.

The master, with its own private sitting room and fireplace and probably bowling alley, was lovely, and Penny finally released August and perched herself on the edge of the bed, the open doors that led out to the balcony framing her like a woman in a Leighton painting. August was still in shock; here was Penny York, alive and in the flesh and so goddamned beautiful it made him sick. He stood, awkward and impotent, waiting.

"Where to start?" Penny giggled, oblivious to August's groundlessness. Her eyes were full of a mischievous guilt as she thrust her arm forward, presenting her hand. August noted the large diamond ring on her finger.

"What is that?" he asked.

"I married him, August."

He paled, shrank, dried up like the husk of a deserted chrysalis.

"You what?" he managed.

"I married Barreth."

A hand to his chest, August sat on the edge of the bed. The end had come. The sun had finally abandoned its post, and now all would wither and die and rot.

Penny, finally aware of the pain her words were causing, tried to explain. "It won't be for long. After a few months, I'll divorce him and take half his income. It's perfect! We'd never have gotten through the safes in here at any rate. They're far beyond your skill level."

"You're a fool, Penny."

"Call me Elizabeth when we're here," Penny said, looking over her shoulder as if someone might overhear them. "Elizabeth Barreth, actually."

"Do you really think Barreth hasn't taken precautions against a plan like yours? There'll have been a prenuptial arrangement, or he'll get the thing annulled. You won't get a cent."

Penny rolled her eyes. "I'll take care of all that, August. I have a meeting with the lawyers next week, and I've been reading up on divorce law. Did you know that there's several loopholes in most—"

But for the first time since meeting her, August wasn't taken with her enthusiasm. "You're a goddamned fool, Penny."

She reddened. "What the hell is wrong with you?"

"I told you this was too big a job. From the very start I said it was too big!"

"Then why did you go along with it for so long, if it was such a terrible idea?"

August was seething, but his anger hadn't boiled hot enough to let him expose himself fully. He changed the subject.

"How was Paris?"

Penny, not to be tossed by August's twisting conversational tactics, answered, "It was lovely."

"And the wedding? An intimate gathering or social event of the season?"

"Intimate. Just the two of us and some witnesses in a little cathedral."

"And I'm sure once the deed was done, Quasimodo himself rang the goddamned bells!"

"Please, August, don't be dramatic," snapped Penny, ending the game in exasperation.

"Dramatic? I'm not the one who disappeared, leaving only a mysterious note like she's a spy from a radio serial in—"

"August, please, we need money! This was the only way to get it!"

"Why? Why do we need money? We have enough! We don't need all this," August yelled, gesticulating wildly to the penthouse.

"So are we supposed to keep pinching wallets and cufflinks for the rest of our lives?"

"I don't know! Maybe we stop stealing?"

"And do what? Open up a bookstore? A little café?"

"Better that than—" But August was drowning. Nothing to cling to in this argument. Change the subject. "Is he a good screw?"

"Jesus Christ. So I had sex with him. Who cares? I've done worse for less."

"But you're not going to get anything, Penny!"

"I've already got all this!" she exclaimed, borrowing August's wild gesticulations from a few moments prior.

"But at what cost? God, you're such an idiot! I can't believe you did this!"

"Then why are you still here, if I'm so stupid?"

"Because I love you, which proves what a fool I am, I suppose."

"I love you, too, you fucking idiot!"

"You what?"

"I love you!" Penny screamed.

"What's going on here?" asked a third party, a voice at the door.

Mr. Barreth stood at the entrance to the bedroom. He didn't look angry, just confused. Penny's mouth opened and closed like a fish, her casual cleverness stripped away in her surprise.

August supposed he should've been frightened. His police record was far from clean, and Barreth had the wealth and power to throw him into prison for a very long time. But he felt no fear. Perhaps the revelation that Penny loved him buoyed him with courage, but the more likely truth is that August was still drunk with rage. The hot hush of anger he'd been aiming at Penny was now redirected at Barreth. Here was the man who'd stolen his home. Here was the man who robbed him of the adolescence he might've shared with Sir Reginald. Here was the man who was married to the woman he loved.

Inspiration kissed August, and, lowering his voice to its deepest, most resonant baritone, he began to bellow, "Barreth, you feckless waste! It is I, the Scarsenguard Spirit, here for vengeance!"

To say Barreth turned white as a sheet wouldn't be a particularly apt simile, as the linens at the Barreth were a pleasant shade of mocha, but there was a considerable amount of paling, to be sure. August continued.

"I claim your soul, fetid chaff though it is. Now I take my due, Barreth, to the darkest caves of hell, where I'll dance upon your bones and spit inside your memories!" For effect, August added some cobbled-together Latin he'd picked up at Willington. The closest possible translation follows: "Books are water, and there is a Jesus in your hair."

Penny, master of reading a room, shrieked shrieks that could have shattered glass. In an unexpected display of gallantry, Barreth ran to her and held her tightly.

"Take the girl," Barreth whimpered, using Penny as a human shield.

Already furious, August went blind with rage. He picked up a silver ashtray, heavy as a brick, and heaved it at Barreth's head. Violent madness spoiled his aim, and truthfully, he'd never been very sporty to begin with. The ashtray missed its target and instead crashed into a lamp, shattering the bulb. The room was plunged into darkness.

Penny released some more screams, and Barreth let out a wavering moan of his own. August, still raving, joined in.

"Perish, Barreth! Asphyxiate upon your own mustache!"

The millionaire didn't intend to die, however; he was on the run. August heard him bump into a desk across the room and bark out a swear word.

August screamed and charged through the dark.

Barreth yelped, then backed through the open balcony doors.

Outside, August lunged at Barreth, who feinted left and avoided the attack. The dodge proved to be a mistake, however, for the shift in weight caused Barreth to trip, stumble, and then plunge off the balcony into the open sky of New York City, his mouth a perfect rounded O of shock. Forty-eight famous floors later, Barreth ended his life atop a Chevrolet or a Chrysler or whatever the hell it was called.

Penny joined August on the balcony, both hands clutched over her mouth in horror. August stared at her in shocked silence. Finally she whispered, "What just happened?"

How to explain? After brief contemplation, August deduced it was impossible, but he hurriedly breathed out an abbreviated history of the Scarenguard Spirit. When it concluded, Penny said, "That makes no sense!"

"I know!" August replied.

"He thought you were a ghost?"

"Yes."

"But how did you know he'd react like that?"

"I didn't!"

"Then why did you pretend to be a ghost?"

"I don't know! I thought it might buy me some time to clear the room."

"But that makes no sense!"

"I know!"

They were desperately close to the cusp of hysteria. Had they committed murder? No. Had they intended to commit murder? Of course not. But Barreth was dead, and it was due to August's bit of artistry, and they had intended to rob the man of half his fortune, so regardless of intent, they *felt* like they'd committed murder, and even though they hadn't, they'd both just watched a man die, something neither was familiar with, so a brief dip into delirium was not at all an unorthodox reaction given the circumstances.

"You need to leave," Penny said.

August took stock of the situation, and to an outsider's eye, it did seem very likely that a jealous young lover had stormed into the penthouse of his beloved and thrown his competition out the window. And how could he honestly explain to the authorities that Barreth had accidentally died because he'd thought August to be a vengeful ghost of yesteryear?

August grabbed hold of her arms. "Penny, I—"

She interrupted him with a kiss. "Not now," she said after they broke apart. "Go."

Out of breath but on the streets, August ducked away as ambulance sirens pierced the air.

* * *

Penny hadn't called for a week, but August wasn't worried this time. To call would have been to arouse suspicion, and Penny, being the new wife of a recently deceased millionaire, was under enough suspicion already without throwing an attractive young lover into the mix.

He was nervous about whether or not they'd be implicated in the death, but August checked the papers every day and found no cause for concern. Other than the story covering Barreth's death, nothing had been reported about suspicion of foul play.

So, though the week passed in tedium and a consistent nagging anxiety, August was feeling good. Excited, even. Penny had finally said she loved him! They could be together, and not just in the strange half-life they'd been sharing, but fully together. The fantasies he painted in his mind were rich and elaborate. They'd buy a home somewhere in the mountains. Vermont? No, Colorado. A humble, simple place, nine or ten bedrooms. They'd live there for years, just the two of them and their dog, an impish but lovable St. Bernard named Toby. Every other month or so, August and Toby would have to rescue Penny from a bear she'd encountered while she was out picking wild berries. The sex after these rescues would be earth-shattering. Eventually they'd have enough children to populate their cabin, and the two lovers, after a rich and glorious life together, would perish at the very same instant, holding each other's hands as they sat in their rocking chairs, watching the sun dip behind the mountains, a perfect punctuation to their beautiful union.

Or they'd live on a boat. Something fun.

When a knock came at his door, August leapt to answer, fully expecting to embrace Penny and start their new adventure together. When the knocker turned out to be a private messenger, August was disappointed but unalarmed. Penny was surely busy arranging funerals and meeting executors and whatnot. The letter would reveal all. He tipped the man handsomely and then snuggled up on his couch for a cozy read, detailing all Penny's developments.

The postmark was from Paris.

August hated Paris.

He opened the letter.

A,

Firstly, everything's fine. The police had hardly any questions. You were never mentioned. All is well.

B left me everything. Every cent. Your P is a millionaire. His mother is furious. I've already gifted her a great heap of money, tax-free, just to shut her up, but she can't stand it. Luckily he had no children. Can you imagine?

Now to the difficult part. I don't even know what to say, but I need to be away. What we did feels wrong. I know neither of us intended for it to end the way it did, but still, it feels too . . . too big, maybe? You were right, this wasn't our kind of job. I see that now. But going about the way we were before would be impossible for me, and I think for you, too. It would feel disingenuous. Am I making sense?

Don't think I'm trying to swindle you. You'll get your cut. I can't give it to you right off or there'll be questions, but it will come to you.

I'm so sorry. I really do love you and wish you well. Perhaps one day, god, this all sounds so ridiculous, but perhaps one day we can be together again, or friends at the very least. I'll be in contact soon, or if not me, then a lawyer. Again, I'm so sorry.

Love,
P

August read the letter once, then twice more. Afterward he built a fire, burned the letter, and crawled into bed, forever.

PART FIVE

Over four months had passed since Mr. Barreth died, and those four months had not been kind to August March. He'd hardly bathed, let an unbecoming beard take his face hostage, and sunk into a deep and slothful depression. Food, when it was consumed, was either excessively greasy or miserably stale, but more often than not it was skipped entirely, replaced instead with whatever nourishment can be gleaned from alcohol. August's social life consisted of the few bartenders that hadn't yet banned him from their establishments. Needless to say, this eclectic and modestly limited group of individuals was composed of characters who were not the sort of people one would introduce to one's family.

August was frequenting an establishment run by one of the more revolting members of his acquaintance, a man called simply the Donkey. Most of August's other friends had nicknames of this sort, but the source of the moniker was generally self-explanatory. One-Eyed Sue, for example, had one eye. The Mouth was a man who talked incessantly and loudly. August didn't know how the Donkey came by his pseudonym, and for whatever reason, was terrified to ask.

It was just past two in the afternoon, and August and the Donkey were in the midst of a furious game of darts. Both were so drunk, however, that the game had devolved into a form of hide-and-seek, both parties searching for their lost darts, thrown violently into nowhere. Still, the players were treating the game with the utmost seriousness and were in a heated argument about who currently held the lead.

"It was a bull's-eye, you bastard!" the Donkey slurred, though in his heart of hearts he must have known he was exaggerating, for the red center circle was empty, as was the entire dartboard.

"It may be a bull's-eye," August agreed, for reasons we will never know, "but you, my fine fuck, are a cheater! A cheater most foul!"

The Donkey swung a punch at August's face that connected instead with a jukebox that stood fifteen feet from the intended victim. The Donkey howled while August doubled over with laughter. He was eventually shaken out of his convulsions by a stranger in uniform.

"Are you August March?" the shaker asked.

"Depends," August answered, which was quite a clever retort, considering he was clutching a barstool as the freefaller might a parachute.

The man extended a letter. "I've been searching for you all morning, sir. I'm to deliver this letter to you and you alone."

August took the letter, yet the young stranger remained. August stared at him blankly for half a minute. The young man coughed. August belched.

"A tip, sir," the letter bearer eventually said.

"Of course, of course. Donkey! Can you tip this young man out of your till? Put it on my tab."

Instead of lending August money, however, the Donkey delivered the punch he'd intended to land earlier, directly to August's face.

The scene devolved. The messenger tried to help August up from the ground, but August was drunker than a dead fish and refused to be lifted. The Donkey, thinking the messenger was propping August up for another blow, pulled back his arm and delivered a second drunken punch. However, August's dead weight was finally too much for the young man to bear, and he dropped August, so the Donkey's swing hit the messenger instead of August. The messenger, now infected with the foolishness that comes from being young and virile, rolled up his sleeves and tackled the Donkey. Though the older man was hopelessly outmatched by his young opponent, he had the stupid strength of the drunk, and attacked back with quite a gusty show of force. Both men were drawing blood and losing teeth in equal measure, though the messenger would surely come out on top in the end, that is, if the Donkey didn't use any of his concealed weapons, of which he had three.

Meanwhile, August was coming to on the bar's grimy floor. He took one look at the messenger and the Donkey tussling like inexperienced but eager lovers and decided it was time he took his leave.

Limping back home, he fell onto his couch and into sleep, the letter clutched lightly in his hand, unread.

* * *

August awoke to stale darkness and set about his evening, which would be a continuation of his afternoon, meaning he was going to attempt to drink himself to death.

He didn't notice the letter for hours, and when he finally did, he was almost too drunk to read it.

Through hazy vision, August saw that the postmark was from Paris.

Fucking Paris!

Had he been sober, he would've thrown the letter away instantly, or burned it and pissed on the ashes. But, drunk and rash, he ripped the envelope open, ready to curse and wail and add new fuel to the fires of his misery.

August read:

Dear Mr. March,

You are cordially invited to the demolition of the Barreth Hotel. The festivities shall begin on September 5 at promptly seven in the A.M. *Your hostess regrets to inform you that she can't attend but that she will most certainly be there in spirit.*

Yours,
P.Y.

But what could this mean? August reread the letter once over, and his muddled brain finally derived its significance. Penny, sole heiress to the Barreth fortune, had ordered the pride of his empire to be torn down. August tried to stand but his legs were rubbery due to the contents of the letter, and he crashed into an end table instead.

On the floor, he read the letter again. September 5? But that was tomorrow!

August looked at the clock and saw that it was four in the morning.

Not tomorrow, but today! Sweet felicity! Praise every god dead and living!

August took a celebratory shot of tequila, packed a quick bag of provisions (booze), and then was out the door and on his way uptown; he wanted to make sure he got a good seat.

It took August over an hour to reach his destination, not because of distance but due to the fact that he got lost on his way there and had to stop more than once to pee and more than twice to vomit. By the time his feet were planted firmly in front of the hotel, August was far less drunk than he had been when he set out, though he smelled far worse.

The wait was positively Mesozoic, but at last the wrecking balls arrived. Immediately August introduced himself to the demolition crew, who were confused as to who he was, but put their bewilderment behind them when it became clear that he was handing out free drinks, a practice he kept up all morning. Eventually, August had become so friendly with the crew that by the time they were ready to start the actual demolition, he was allowed to make a short speech.

He awkwardly shimmied up the side of a crane and settled atop the operator's cab, holding the base of the crane's lattice for support. Surveying the gathered team below, all gazing up at him with tipsy eyes, August knew the moment was a special one, and forced himself to take a deep breath and savor the weighty feeling of profundity before starting his speech.

"Friends," he began, "today we witness the end of an era. An era of greed. An era of tyranny. An era when the senseless jaws of Commerce were allowed to rape and swallow the provocative goddess we call Art."

The construction crew's perplexity was nearly audible, but August was so solemn that they remained silent. A few even removed their hard hats and placed them against their breasts.

August continued. "Today, we make amends. Today, when the brick and mortar fall, we can celebrate as the Hebrews did when the sea crashed closed behind them, swallowing the Egyptians. As the citizens of Gondor and Rohan must have done when Barad-dûr collapsed. For today, justice prevails, and an unholy boil that festers on the face of our fair city will be lanced and expunged.

"Go to your deed, my good men, and do it well. Do it with pride. For today, you aren't but mere workmen. Today you are heroes! Legends! Gods! Destroy what evil has built and become forever immortalized in the pages of history!"

Most of the men present enjoyed their jobs, but never before had they thought it particularly significant or righteous work. August's speech changed all that. The men cheered and cried and pounded their beating hearts and felt hot blood move through their veins. They ran to their equipment as men mounting warhorses and charged into their great and glorious cause.

The foreman, as alight with August's speech as the rest, bellowed out the order to commence without the aid of a megaphone, and his voice was glorious; Gabriel's trumpet.

When the first wrecking ball smashed into the side of the Barreth, August wept. Each boom was a Beethoven. Every crash a Tchaikovsky. The sounds of the smashes were finer than any Shakespearean soliloquy, and August was all delight and life. In his euphoria, he even allowed himself to forgive the sins of Penny York, for it was she who had orchestrated this blessed event.

Well, mostly forgive, anyway.

* * *

The Barreth's demise pulled August out of his own. Such a massive building was not obliterated in a single morning, and visiting the site every day gave him something to do, a reason to get out of bed. He also enjoyed the companionship of the men working the job, bringing them snacks and sandwiches and bits of gossip and booze by the gallon. They were far better company than men like the Donkey, whom August hadn't seen since their last encounter, the one that left him with a black eye. For their part, the demolition crew liked August, assuming he was an eccentric who owned the property on which the Barreth formerly stood. Not all rich people were bad, they decided as they drank his liquor and listened to his long unintelligible rants concerning people they'd never heard of and words they were sure he'd invented on the spot.

Delighted as he was to be kept busy, what August found truly satisfying was the experience of closure, a feeling that up to this point had remained most foreign. All the major events of his life had happened *to* him; he'd never had any control. Miss Butler died and was carted away; August hadn't even attended the funeral. Sir Reginald had passed suddenly as well, and right when they were getting to know each other as adults. Though August had been present for Percyfoot's service, the whole affair had been odd and disconnected, hardly a fitting finale to the most influential man in his life.

The loss of the Scarsenguard, being plucked from his life as a pickpocket, Penny flying off to Paris just when they might've gotten started; August had never had anything to grab. Life was smoke, a fog he kept trying desperately to clutch. The death of the Barreth, however, was something he could stick a flag into. Here was an ending, a fulfilling and definitive outcome.

Weeks passed, and the demolition site was no longer an exciting place to visit. All the pomp and circumstance was over. Now it was on to the quieter, more thankless tasks such as removing rubble and serious conversations about copper wiring and whatnot. August drifted away but wasn't tempted back into his former life of the previous months. He hadn't given up drinking, but he had cut back considerably, and he was consuming at least one square meal a day.

After receiving the tingly glow of contentment from the Barreth's demise, August decided to rifle through his brownstone and sort through other aspects of his life, attempting to re-create the high brought on by closure. At the very least, he would throw out some of this old shit.

As it turned out, however, cleansing an apartment was not as exciting as watching a skyscraper crumble to the ground, so when his buzzer rang, August gleefully tossed aside the papers he'd been sifting through and fairly sprinted to the door. A messenger delivering yet another letter bearing a blasted postmark from Paris. My god, but these things were popping up with a frightening frequency. Signature given, August braced himself for the latest from France.

All that was inside, however, was the deed to a plot of land on West Forty-Third Street with a note attached:

Take it off my hands?

So the Barreth was his. But it wasn't the Barreth anymore. It was nothing. So nothing was his. Leave it to Penny.

August went on cleaning out the brownstone, not bothering to make any decision about what to do with his strange gift from Penny. He really didn't care what happened to the land now that the Barreth had been destroyed. A little diner might be nice, but he had no desire to work in a restaurant. Truth be told, he had little desire to work at all. He wasn't good at much except scaling buildings, and he was beginning to think that talent might be fading with age. He'd proved time and again he was no great master criminal, just someone who could pick a lock and pass as somebody else if there was enough makeup involved. Now that Penny was gone, he hadn't really thought about what he was going to do with his life. She was everything; all his plans were wrapped up in her. What to do now that he was simply August March?

Upstairs one afternoon later that week, he was combing through a sitting room he hardly entered. He was practically upending a desk, throwing nearly all its contents into the trash, when he came across a letter from Sir Reginald, locked away in the bottommost drawer.

It wasn't long, and though there was more to it, one particular paragraph struck August fierce as lightning:

You are a child of the theatre, August, and in some capacity there you must stay. The plays you staged at Willington were truly stupendous for someone so young. You were born in a theater. You were raised in a theater. You belong to it as much as it belongs to you. I hope you find happiness in whatever it is you choose to do, but I know you'd find happiness near a stage.

Damn these letters! They always caused one such trouble. How could paper and ink hold so many landmines?

When the door buzzer bleated, August was weeping, holding the letter to his chest for fear of smearing the writing with his tears. Whoever it was would have to wait while he got ahold of himself. Hadn't he waited long enough for a life of his own?

For that was why August was crying. There were many reasons, of course. But the principal contributor to August's unexpected outburst was that he was suddenly certain of his future. He knew now what he would do. He supposed he'd always known, but it took the splashy, overwrought penmanship of Sir Reginald to remind him.

August was going to build a theater.

* * *

As it turns out, building a theater, or any structure in New York City, was difficult. Or, to put it a bit more eloquently, a goddamned pain in the ass. Never in his life had August imagined that every day, people sat at long tables and traded mind-numbing monotonies concerning codes and regulations and standards and compliances and god knew what else. Whenever possible, August avoided these meetings, but at times he was forced to attend so he might scrawl his signature across some dreaded document that gorged with humdrum. Really the whole thing was wretched, the stuff of nightmares.

Then, once every single person in New York City was satisfied that a theater should be built, there was the drama of finding an architect worthy of the job. Most wanted to cut corners and use cheap substitutes instead of the genuine authentic materials. Linoleum for tile, that sort of thing. No matter how often August assured them that money was no issue (Penny was funding the operation through her team of high-powered, soulless lawyers), they insisted on shortcuts, until August was sure that every building constructed after 1960 was made solely out of cardboard, held together by chewing gum and prayer.

When August finally found a man excited by the prospect of building a glorious, honest-to-god theater, there was no small amount of horror when he discovered the architect to be a Frenchman. His famously prejudiced upbringing aside, Penny running off to Paris without explanation not once but twice hadn't raised the country's flag any higher in August's heart. Still, the man was a genius, no doubt about it, and August supposed he might set aside old national animosities for the sake of creation and beauty.

Alas, the collaboration was not an easy one.

"I will not arrange the stage in such a manner," complained the architect in a thick French accent. He might as well have been slurping down escargot. "It is hideous."

"It is not hideous," snapped August as the pair pored over what must have been the thirty-seventh draft of blueprints. "This way plays can be performed standardly on a proscenium or, if the director chooses, on a thrust stage, an arrangement I personally find far preferable."

The point was conceded, at least momentarily, but new complaints were instantly lodged.

"Why do you insist on all these, how do you say, nooks and crannies everywhere? They do not make sense!"

"In case a young boy needs a place to hide! My god, man, don't be daft!"

"It is impossible. I will not attach my name to it."

"I'll double your pay."

"Perhaps something can be arranged."

A blueprint satisfactory to both parties was eventually settled on, and construction on the theater began in earnest. August visited the site daily and tried to become as close with the construction crew as he had been with the team who tore down the Barreth, but it was not to be. A perfectionist, August couldn't resist giving what he thought to be helpful tips and advice, like how the men should hold their hammers or the best method for sawing wood. Needless to say, his presence was barely tolerated. August couldn't help it; he needed his theater to be a masterpiece. To combat his rather overbearing personality, August lavished gifts upon the crew so that even though they could hardly stand the sight of him, they still wanted the job done right. August wasn't completely out of touch; he knew that people are better employees if treated fairly and equitably, and he was never skimpy when handing out compliments or bonuses for men going above and beyond. Now if they would only put a little more thought into how they laid the floorboards.

The process was painstaking and glacial.

Finally, after what seemed like decades, the theater was finished. It was a glorious building; an homage to the Scarsenguard, yet improving upon many of the old theater's faults. August spent entire days wandering down the narrow hallways, sitting in all the seats, carving out an hour to simply experience each dressing room. He adored the place.

But it needed a name.

Throughout the construction process, August thought he'd simply call it the Scarsenguard, but once the theater was finished, that didn't feel right. This wasn't the Scarsenguard; it was someplace new. It had its own distinct personality, and it felt like an insult both to the original theater and to this virgin venue to simply recycle an old name. August would install a plaque chronicling the history of the Scarsenguard, but its name was officially retired. So what to call his new mecca?

It was fashionable to coin a theater after a famous playwright or actor, so of course, Sir Reginald Percyfoot sprang to mind. The Percyfoot did indeed have a fine ring to it, and would have undoubtedly been a wonderful name, but after a few rereleases of his films over in London, Sir Reginald was having a bit of a comeback in his homeland. There was already some sort of new acting award called the Percyfoot, an honor, August thought, Sir Reginald would've despised. How could anyone possibly give away an award for something so subjective as acting? A scholarship in his name had been instituted, another dagger in the side of the late Percyfoot, as he'd hated universities and most sorts of formal education. There was a garden in one of London's larger parks that held his name, along with a sandwich in one of Percyfoot's favorite pubs, the latter being the only recognition Sir Reginald would've cared for. Still, one man can't have everything, so the Percyfoot wouldn't do for the new theater.

And then it came to him. A play was not simply the person who wrote it or directed it or the cast who brought it to life every night. Hundreds of people made a production run smoothly. Stage managers, of course, but so many others.

Lighting designers, makeup artists, technicians, stagehands, costume designers, electricians, dressers, conductors, wig makers, sound designers, dialect coaches.

And laundresses.

August's theater was christened the Butler, taking its name from the employee who'd put more hours into the Scarsenguard than any other: Miss Eugenia Butler. The sign that spelled out her name in lights was installed, and one abysmally cold December evening, switched on for all West Forty-Third to see. The Butler, bright as Broadway itself. August was covered in goose bumps. He thought Miss Butler would've liked it. He even thought she might've been proud. August was proud of himself, at least. And that was enough.

* * *

It was April, and the Butler's inaugural production was up and running. *King Lear.* It had to be *Lear.* For one, August wanted to honor Sir Reginald in some way, and his portrayal of Lear, the one that had enchanted August so as a boy of six, was still the finest interpretation of the character he'd ever seen, so it was only fitting that the first play running at the Butler would tip its hat to Sir Reginald. Second, it was August's favorite, and since he was the one who would direct, he got to choose whatever damn play he wanted.

If the producers of the production were wary at having an untested first-time director at the helm, they needn't have been. The reviews were in and positively glowing. All the principal actors came away with fine notices, something they swore they cared nothing about, but every critic unanimously agreed that August's direction was the true star.

A few months into the run, while the simulated storm raged below onstage, August sat in the small office tucked away on the topmost floor of the Butler, poring over some new scripts. *Lear* wouldn't run forever, and he wanted the Butler's next play to be an original piece. If the theatre was to survive, it would need to cultivate new talent, and August, being in a position of financial security, intended to be on the forefront of fresh artistic development. The problem was, most everything was terrible. Currently he was reading a play penned by none other than Vivian Fair, the actress who had kissed August once at the Backstage Bistro. Now that she could no longer conceivably play ingenues or sexpots, Miss Fair, desperate to cling to her fading celebrity, had taken up writing. As with most people who suddenly decide to take up writing, the results were disastrous. August tossed the script aside. Had he known that Vivian Fair was his birth mother, he might've given the script a second glance, but probably not; it was complete and utter shit. Leaning back in his chair, drained, August massaged his tired eyes.

Who would've ever thought that this would be his life? A precocious orphan. A homeless criminal. A recalcitrant schoolboy. A petty thief. How had this jumbled equation produced a shrewd and reserved theater owner?

Did he yearn for the adventures of his past, for the carefree conduct of the wanderer? Sometimes. But life was confusing. August had always tottered on the edge of disaster, flirted with the fringes of society. True, Willington with its ivy and stone had been the very picture of elitist conformity, but it had wanted him gone, had accepted him only obligatorily, and was happy to see the back of him. And even now, the most stable he'd ever been, with a job and a home and a team of employees, August was finding that he was a hard man to know. Opinionated, stubborn, verbose, critical, distrustful. He'd go out with the cast after the show and feel disconnected. They'd talk of their hometowns or their colleges or their husbands or wives or sisters or cousins. Everyone was associated with someone else, threads stretching across time and space, a tangled web of connectivity. Yet August was so singular, a solitary pin on a map.

Would he change it if he could? Be raised under the watchful eye of a doting family, carefully cultivated for a safe and respectable existence? Of course not. August's experience had made him who he was. He didn't yearn for an easy life. There was no easy life. Of course there were pleasures along the way, enormous joys and great stretches of genuine happiness, but survival was a struggle, and he was grateful he'd learned that young. August liked the man he'd become. The path he'd walked wasn't straight by any stretch of the imagination, but it had been his path, goddammit. His own. His life.

At times, however, it could be lonely. How to associate? How to relate? To fasten? To join?

August tried to read another play, but found he was too exhausted. He was packing up his bag, thinking he'd catch a second wind at home and peruse at least the first act of something, when his office phone rang.

An operator chattered, "Mr. August March, you have a long-distance call. Will you accept the charges?"

"Yes," August replied, confused.

The call was connected.

"I have an idea," said the voice on the other end of the line, a voice he hadn't heard for far too long.

Life swelled into August, barbed and sweet, and he gulped it down, thirsty for more.

"Tell me everything."

ACKNOWLEDGMENTS

This is surreal.

Thank you to my entire family, especially the readers. Mom (Nancy Jackson), the teacher; Dad (John Jackson), the collector; Mammam (Lou James), the librarian; Grandpa (Jim James), the editor; Sissy (Celia Brewer), the witty scribe; and, most important, my sister, Amy Jo Jackson, who was my first reader and is the world's greatest living actress—no hyperbole, full stop. You all instilled in me a zealous passion for the written word and I am forever grateful and indebted.

To my agent, Byrd Leavell, for being a champion of this book and for holding my hand throughout the process. I couldn't have asked for a better guide. Also, you have an incredible name.

To my editor, Sara Nelson. I grovel. You're obviously a literary icon, but you're also a gay icon, and that's the highest praise I can give. Having a drink with you in a little SoHo restaurant on a rainy November evening made me feel like Truman Capote. Thank you for your brilliant work, insight, and support. I am truly so humbled.

To Mary Pender, Meredith Miller, Dan Milaschewski, and everyone else at UTA for all their hard work.

To Mary Gaule, Nikki Baldauf, Miranda Ottewell, and the entire HarperCollins team.

To Fred Hashagen and Kirsten Ames for your doggedness, encouragement, and for picking up the bills at restaurants I could never afford.

To my husband, Michael Sullivan. I can't think of adequate words to describe you, so these will have to do: You are my favorite part of life.

To Isaac Oliver and Sophie Santos for the "writer-business-talks" at Julius'.

To the many friends who read a draft or offered encouragement along the way: Josh Sharp, Jeff Ronan, Jo Firestone, Bowen Yang, Peter Kelley, Grace Leeson, Nate Dern, Caitlin Burke, Ashley Kielian Shinick, Ryan Jones, Blake Daniel, Betsy Cowie, Jeff Jablonksi. There are hundreds more, but I thank you all for your lovely minds, your kind words, and for making the world a more entertaining place to inhabit.

And a gigantic, red-carpet, billion-dollar thank-you to Langan Kingsley, who not only gave her perceptive thoughts, but also line-edited a disastrous early draft for *free*? Truly, the queen stays queen.

To the New York City comedy community, particularly the LGBTQ+ branch, thank you for being the funniest, most persevering, inspiring group of artists I have ever had the pleasure of working with. Even though most of you have insufferable online presences, I am so honored to be counted among your number. I love you all, you're creative behemoths that have made me both a better artist and person.

And finally, to Mrs. Sandy Thompson, my fifth-grade teacher who let a precocious child read his paraphrased Goosebumps novel aloud in class. I won't say you created a monster, but you certainly opened the cage and let one loose. Thank you so very much.

ABOUT THE AUTHOR

AARON JACKSON is a writer and comedian. With Josh Sharp, he optioned and adapted a screenplay of their stage musical *F*cking Identical Twins*, which is currently in development with Chernin Entertainment. He was recently a cast member on Comedy Central's *The Opposition with Jordan Klepper*, and has also appeared on *Broad City*, *The Detour*, *Crashing*, *The National Lampoon Radio Hour*, and Funny or Die's *Jared and Ivanka*, a series he also co-wrote. He lives in New York City.